THE BESOTTED BARON

THE BAD HEIR DAY TALES

BOOK FOUR

GRACE BURROWES

GRACE BURROWES PUBLISHING

Copyright © 2025 by Grace Burrowes

All rights reserved.

No part of this book may be reproduced in any form or by any electronic or mechanical means, including information storage and retrieval systems, without written permission from the author, except for the use of brief quotations in a book review.

If you uploaded this book to, or downloaded it from, any free file sharing, internet "archive" library, or other piracy site, you did so in violation of the law and against the author's wishes. This book may not be used to train, prompt, or otherwise interact with any generative artificial intelligence program WHATSOEVER.

Please don't be a pirate.

DEDICATION

Dedicated to anybody who has had to deal with, endure, or navigate around the Lady Josephines of the world

CHAPTER ONE

In the opinion of Camden Huxley, twenty-eighth Baron Lorne, attending the burial had been safe. Women did not usually participate in graveside services, and to his unseemly relief, Aunt Josephine had been absent.

Leopold St. Didier *had* been on hand for the late baron's final obsequies, though, and thus Cam had been put on notice. A minor delay would be tolerated, but outright shirking of inherited responsibilities would bring unpleasant consequences.

Not that Camden Huxley had ever in his entire earthly sojourn *shirked*, despite all temptation to the contrary.

"You've waited three months," St. Didier said, pouring two exactly equal servings of cognac. "If you don't see to the place now, soon it will be three years." Camden's host held out a drink, the firelight giving mere potation flaming depths. "To your health, my lord, and to the prosperity of Lorne Hall."

"The two haven't been related for some time." Camden nosed his drink. Apples, a whiff of damask roses, a hint of nutmeg, all trailing into citrus and cinnamon.

How did St. Didier afford such an indulgence, and where did he procure it?

Camden drank sparingly. One wanted his wits about him in any encounter with St. Didier. To look at, the fellow was unremarkable. Tallish—not as tall as Cam's six feet, three inches— dark-haired, neat about his habiliments, soft-spoken. Wore his hair long in the old-fashioned style and wore his family's downfall with an understated indifference Camden envied.

"Your *reputation* and the health of the barony are related now." St. Didier settled into the opposite wing chair, both seats designed for sizable, sturdy occupants. "Will you sell the business?"

No, Cam would not. "That seems to be the general assumption." The business Cam had spent ten years building up from nothing. The business that was thriving more robustly than ever now that the Continent was once again open to English trade. The business that Cam had gambled on extending to the former colonies and with notable success.

The self same business that could in no wise be excused by polite society as a mere investment. Camden was *in trade*, and in that fraught and occasionally lucrative location, he intended to remain.

"When have you ever behaved in accordance with general assumptions?" St. Didier sipped with a sybarite's focus. "I'll accompany you to Yorkshire if you like."

St. Didier was regarded as shrewd, intelligent, frighteningly well connected, and honorable. The conscience of reluctant peers, the silent minion of the College of Arms, and unnervingly self-contained.

Cam respected him as one respected the patronesses at Almack's. To cross them was to court ruin, because they wielded immense power despite lacking any legal authority. Even a lowly tradesman understood that much.

Something about St. Didier's casual offer smacked of a threat. "Why would you escort me to the Hall? I know the way there well enough if I choose to go."

"I might accompany your lordship, firstly, because you are

overdue for a repairing lease and cannot be depended upon to take one. You look closer to forty than thirty, you're a good stone underweight, if not two. You aren't getting enough sleep and haven't for some time. I would attribute the insomnia to grief, except that it predates the late baron's passing by years."

"I sleep quite well." Camden did not sleep *enough*, though. Drifting off into an exhausted slumber while poring over the ledgers was a nightly ritual.

"You work to the point of daily collapse, a very different proposition. My second reason for offering to travel with you to your family seat is that your cousin Bernard has asked me to see that you look in on your inheritance."

"Bernard never used to be a busybody."

"He and his mother are worried about you."

Well, of course. Aunt Josephine had turned selfless concern for others into a high and bothersome art.

"They are worried about his living at St. Wilfrid's," Cam said, "which is secure. I can write him to that effect." Another sip of heaven. Mention of sleep was having a soporific effect. Cam sat up and set the cognac aside. "I'll pay a call at Lorne Hall later in the year."

"Later in the year, you will conjure up some superficially compelling excuse," St. Didier said gently. "This being high summer, you are shipping goods in quantity all over creation before the autumn storms start. As autumn progresses, you will be planning for next year's markets, dunning those who are slow to pay, and looking for new merchandise to add to your inventory. In winter, travel is difficult. In spring, the ships go out again."

A perfect sketch of the commercial year, but without mention of the risks, rewards, and excitement that came with every single day spent piloting the enterprise.

"Lorne Hall can manage harvest quite well without me," Camden said. "They've been doing so for generations." *I would just be in the way.* Indisputably true, also close to whining.

"They've not had to manage harvest without any lord of the manor at all. Besides, your family seat is one of the most beautiful estates in all of Yorkshire. I'm in need of a respite myself, and Lorne Hall suits my plans."

"Then go and enjoy yourself with my blessing."

The Hall was breathtaking, and its appeal as autumn approached was unparalleled. Golden sun, peaceful bucolic vistas, sheep and cattle fat on summer grazing, the Hall itself glowing with contented splendor. "The twentieth baron designed the place, set it up so it aligns perfectly with the equinoxes. I was named for him."

St. Didier's eyes took on a gleam that in another man might have presaged a smile. He said nothing, merely sipped his drink and gazed at the fire crackling in the hearth.

Why not go? Why not get it over with? Let them all gawk at the prodigal returned. Let Bernard pontificate a bit and Aunt Josephine advise and admonish. Look in on the tenants as Papa used to, greet the neighbors in the churchyard. Do the expected, just once, and be done with it.

"You should make the journey for another reason," St. Didier said, peering into his drink. "Now is the logical time to retire the old guard, promote from within the ranks, or bring in new talent. Your brother's will made provisions for a few pensions and minor bequests, but the likes of Mrs. Shorer, Beaglemore, and Singleton won't step down until they have your blessing to do so."

"Mrs. Shorer won't step down until God Almighty gives her leave, and then she'll take her own good time doing it. I can send Beaglemore a glowing letter commending his decades of service, and Singleton is hardly of an age to retire."

Housekeeper, butler, and land steward. They were the triumvirate that presided over the Hall's workings, and they each excelled at the job assigned.

"Surely Mrs. Shorer has a replacement in mind?" Camden went on. "An underhousekeeper trained up for the past twenty years in the ways of cleanliness and domestic industry?"

Mrs. Shorer had been a force of nature in Cam's youth. Never still unless addressing her employer and then only for as long as necessary to report news or receive orders. She was the sworn enemy of dust and sloth, but she had a soft heart when it came to restless little boys and moody adolescents.

"Mrs. Shorer's preferred understudy ran off with the first footman last year. Both parties doubtless reasoned that waiting for the end times to earn a promotion was beyond them. They are employed in the same household down in Shropshire, last I heard. Secretly married, if my sources are to be believed."

"How do you know these things?"

"I correspond with my friendly acquaintances. You should try it sometime. One learns the oddest, most useful things simply by putting pen to paper for social rather than commercial purposes."

"And then, St. Didier, one is condemned to spend the livelong day burdening the king's mail with platitudes and gossip because one's social letters result in replies, and the replies must result in same, until half the realm is wasting its days in tittle-tattle." What exactly was a friendly acquaintance anyway? More than an acquaintance, less than a friend?

St. Didier rose, tossed a square of peat on the fire, and resumed his seat. "There speaks a man short of sleep."

Oh, probably. "How is Beaglemore getting on?"

"Slowly. Poor old thing has the rheumatism. Not so bad in the warmer weather, but cold, rainy days try him sorely."

Merry Olde had a surfeit of those in any season. Beaglemore had been an institution for as long as Camden could remember. Almost as a complement to Mrs. Shorer's incessant bustling, Beaglemore never moved faster than a dignified strut, like a rooster patrolling his yard. The old fellow ruled over the footmen and porters with an iron hand, but he had a wry sense of humor too.

"Has Beagle suggested which puppy ought to replace him?"

"Lately, he's had his nephew in mind for that honor, but the man was offered a post as underbutler in a ducal household. In all good conscience, Beaglemore had to support the change of employment."

Our title is older. The familiar retort, heard since infancy, served no purpose. British dukedoms had first been created by Edward III in the 1300s, while the oldest British royal baronies—Lorne among them—dated from the 1200s.

"Well, surely Singleton will be tending to the land for some time to come."

"Singleton has seen his seventieth year," St. Didier replied, "and his granddaughter claims he's losing both sight and hearing. A steward must be out in all weather, all year long. The job is better suited to a younger man."

Singleton could not be seventy. Not possibly. The image of a tall, fit, white-haired man came to mind. Cravat always spotless and neatly tied, despite mud and worse on his boots. Sat his horse with more dignity than Wellington on the eve of battle and had a way with animals that defied science.

To think of Singleton's powers withering... Dover's cliffs should fall into the sea first.

Cam tried for a casual sip of his brandy. "Miss Singleton is still in the area?"

"She is."

Damn St. Didier's reticence. "I don't suppose her husband could take over as steward?"

"She hasn't one of those, that I know of."

Why on God's green and gorgeous earth would Alice Singleton remain unmarried? Had Yorkshire's bachelors lost their wits? She was smart, confident, robust, and she also...

Cam's business instincts tapped him on the figurative shoulder. Alice likely had *no dowry*. Her grandfather was in his dotage and would leave her little save a collection of pipes, and she, while kind, had no patience with fools.

Cam had always respected that about Alice. "Stewards are two a penny these days," he said. "Singleton will have left the estate in good trim, and I'm sure he'll be on hand long enough to acquaint a successor with the basics."

St. Didier finished his drink and took his empty glass to the sideboard. "An estate is not like a shipping business, my lord. In your countinghouse, you can hire and sack clerks by the week, and the new fellow will add up his sums as competently as the tippler he replaced. A steward, butler, or housekeeper is more like... *you*. They stand at the helm of an enterprise that produces measurable results. Prosperous acreage or a comfortable abode for family, guests, and staff. If you treat replacing these senior retainers casually, the whole estate will suffer for it."

That came close to an accusation of shirking. "I cannot leave my business, St. Didier. It does not run itself, and while I have good managers, they are managers only. If a ship is two weeks late, then the decisions to be made belong to me alone. If one of the managers expires of food poisoning, I alone can step in and take over his responsibilities."

"One of your managers died of food poisoning?"

"Another ran afoul of a rusty nail. Another came down with a serious case of religious zeal and decided he must impose his gospel on the otherwise perfectly contented denizens of some far-flung wilderness. I was sorry to lose him. He was honest to a fault and always smiling."

Cam stopped himself from recounting other dramas, of which there were many. Affairs of the heart, embezzling, rivals attempting to plant spies, spying *on* rivals... The simple business of exporting goods in demand made Drury Lane look staid by comparison.

"Then," St. Didier countered, "you understand what your people at Lorne Hall are facing. Their managers are all mustering out, and the rank and file have no lord of the manor to keep order while the guard changes. They will be grateful to see you and will take direction from you willingly. Leave them to flounder and bicker and argue for another three months, and you will not receive half so genial a welcome."

"You should have been a barrister."

"You *are* a baron, whether you like it or not."

The St. Didier title had fallen into escheat—no legitimate male heir, assets reverted to the crown—and thus St. Didier's observation landed like the reproach it was meant to be.

"I am in trade." *I am in trouble* would have been the more accurate admission. "I have no use for Lorne Hall or its acreage." Other than to sell it. "And the Hall isn't the family seat, technically speaking. Lorne Hall was originally a dower property, though the dower house was built on a far grander scale than the original baronial abode. Wealthy brides will insist on these measures. The historical family seat is Loarnoch, a small manor ten miles north of the Hall."

St. Didier's brows drew down. "I was not aware of this."

Cam glanced out the window to the twilight that passed for a summer evening in London. "The sky remains in its assigned location, despite troubling evidence that you have limitations. Loarnoch is pleasant enough for a mere manor with a couple thousand acres fit mostly for sheep. It's also still entailed. The twentieth baron and his son broke the entail on the Hall and a few other properties, some of which have been sold."

A spare was brought up to know this arcana, but not to have a use for it.

"What has been done with the older property?" St. Didier asked. "Rented out? I don't recall the solicitors mentioning it."

"When did you have occasion to speak with my late brother's pet weasels?" Cam had dealt with them by correspondence. Always better to have a written record when lawyers were involved. More of the wisdom of the shop.

"You really do need to have a look at your inheritance," St. Didier replied, which was, for him, an awkward prevarication. "Your brother might well have sold this other place, and one wants to know where the proceeds went."

"He could not sell Loarnoch. The entail hasn't been broken. My consent would have been necessary, and I was never asked for it."

St. Didier scowled at the fire. "Signatures can be forged, meaning no disrespect to the late baron."

Who had been unwell for some time prior to his death.

You should go. Something might be amiss. You have the authority to put it right. The voice belonged to Alice Singleton. Practical, forthright, *unmarried* Alice. Why hadn't she found a husband?

Cam finished his drink. "I'll need a week's preparation at least, and I can't be gone for more than a fortnight. You are welcome to join me." *Welcome* being an overstatement. One wanted St. Didier where one could keep an eye on him.

"You shall have three days to prepare for the journey, and considering that Yorkshire is nigh two hundred miles distant, you should plan to be gone a month."

"Three weeks, including travel."

"We leave in three days. When you return—if you return—is up to you. Send your pigeons with the baggage coach and be prepared to move fast."

Cam rose and bid St. Didier a cordial good night, though he had the sense he'd just struck a bad bargain with familial duty. In Cam's experience, family duty was unparalleled at creating drama and misery, the only greater sources of same being Atlantic hurricanes and—in the young and callow—unrequited love.

"Did you plan this?" Cam put the question softly, lest the footman waiting at the bottom of the traveling coach's steps overhear.

"Certainly not." St. Didier tapped a top hat onto his head and passed Cam a high-crowned beaver. "But who am I to quibble at a traditional display of affection and respect that dates back centuries?" He pulled on his gloves and eyed the scene in the courtyard through the coach window. "Seems like rather a lot of them."

The retainers of the House of Lorne had lined up in rank order, old Beaglemore holding pride of place at the head of the queue. Mrs.

Shorer stood beside him, a good foot shorter, but every inch as dignified.

"Forty-six inside servants, twenty-five outside, not counting the dailies and seasonals." Cam had studied the ledgers on the journey north, when he hadn't been napping. St. Didier's coach was a marvel of modern comfort, and St. Didier was such quiet company Cam might have had the coach to himself.

The respite had done him a power of good, not that he'd admit as much to St. Didier for anything less than a bottle of that most excellent cognac. With each mile more distant from London, the air had become more breathable, the sky clearer, the countryside more open and inviting. Cam's mind had quieted, and his body had rested—or begun to.

"How did they know when we'd arrive?" Cam asked, yanking on his gloves and regarding the silent line of footmen, maids, kitchen staff, gardeners, groundsmen, and assorted others. A fickle breeze caught the occasional hem or coattail, but all was otherwise motionless.

Somewhere in the line were two seamstresses and an apprentice to them, an alewife who also served as the chandler. A potboy, bootboy, goosegirl, two dairymaids, a head shepherd, two gamekeepers…

A host of employees, each of whom had to be supervised and regularly paid.

"I did not send word ahead," St. Didier said, "if that's what you're asking."

"They posted a lookout in the sentinel oak, then." Gave some shepherd boy a mirror and sent him up the ancient tree. Posted the junior-most footman in the schoolroom and gave him a mirror too. The best strategies were often the simplest. The porter would wait on the drive for the signal, then sound the alarm. That system had already been in place when Grandpapa had been in dresses.

"You'd best get on with it," St. Didier said. "These people have work to do."

Cam wanted to argue. These people were probably enjoying a

chance to tarry for a moment in the mellow late-afternoon sunshine while the gentlest of breezes blew off the Dales. Lorne Hall sat in a natural bowl, sheltered from the worst of the wind, surrounded by green hills. The view down the drive was magnificent, but not as impressive as the spectacle of the Hall itself.

Cam stepped from the vehicle and nodded to the footman who was maintaining a militarily correct stance by the coach steps.

"You'd be Chapman?"

"Aye. I mean, yes, sir. My lord, rather." The fellow blushed, despite being at least ten years Cam's senior. One did not earn the first footman's post without spending time in the ranks.

"Don't tell anybody," Cam said, "but that 'my lording' part is taking some getting used to for me as well."

St. Didier descended and hung back when he might have smoothed the way. He'd been corresponding with someone near the head of the line, hadn't he? Mrs. Shorer would be Cam's guess. Consulting her on recipes for furniture polish and managing to do so with every appearance of earnest sincerity.

"Beaglemore, good day." The butler, even in his sober black suit, wore a black armband, as did the rest of the male staff. The females wore black ribbons affixed to their lapels. The baron was dead, long live the baron. All very respectful.

And tedious as hell. Alexander, may he rest in peace, would have agreed.

"My lord, welcome to Lorne Hall." Beaglemore creaked into a bow and remained in that posture long enough that Cam feared he might be stuck. As a boy, Cam had thought Beaglemore ancient, but now the butler was truly venerable. His face was a map of sagging-parchment wrinkles, his blue eyes had faded, and his white hair was thinning. He was shorter than Cam recalled too.

Mrs. Shorer was positively elfin. "My lord." She curtseyed crisply. "Welcome home."

My homes are in Mayfair and Surrey. "Mrs. Shorer, a pleasure to see you and Beaglemore again. If the outside is any indication,

Lorne Hall has continued to thrive in the care of its senior retainers."

Mrs. Shorer beamed, Beaglemore allowed one, "Very good, sir," and Cam moved on.

He ran out of names once he got past the second under-parlormaid. From there on down, he resorted to, "And you'd be...?"

He stepped up the pace when a small boy shifting from foot to foot caught his eye. "And who are you, young man?"

"Parkin, milord. I'm the potboy, and I'm ever so good at my job. Cook says the best potboy in Yorkshire, though I talk too much."

"You also forgot to heed nature's call before you assembled for parade inspection, didn't you?" *Makes two of us.*

"Forgot to pee, y'mean? Aye."

Somebody snickered. Cam raised an eyebrow at the surrounding kitchen staff. The snickering stopped.

"Be patient another few minutes, young Parkin, and we'll have you back at your post."

Cam increased his pace, nodding cordially to each retainer, thanking them for greeting him, manufacturing pleasantries the same as he would have if passing among his clerks, who could also be prodigious snickerers.

Five minutes later, Beaglemore was escorting him into the house, while the rest of the line stood at attention like soldiers anticipating an advancing enemy.

"If I might speak just a bit out of turn, my lord, please do forgive the boy. He is new to his responsibilities and really ought to have remained in the kitchen."

"He's a pleasant little fellow and clearly proud of his post. Including him did no harm."

Beaglemore blinked several times before the open front door. "Very good, my lord."

If I hear one more 'my lord...'

"Please excuse me, Beaglemore, I'll have a look around the house on my own. Where will you put my trunks?"

More blinking. "In the baron's suite, sir."

Why would he...? Right. "Of course. One did not want to presume. I'm sure I'll be quite comfortable." *Eventually, maybe.* Alexander, strumming his harp on some celestial cloud, was doubtless laughing his halo off.

"You'd not like a tray in the library, sir?"

Cam would *like* to leap into the coach and depart immediately for London. The whole rigmarole on the drive had been pointless and tiresome. New faces or faces gone elderly on him, nothing in the way of a familiar visage or a genuinely warm welcome.

"Give me an hour to stretch my legs, and then a tray in the library would be most appreciated. If you can locate St. Didier, please invite him to join me."

"Yes, my lord. Mr. St. Didier will be in the Rose Suite, and we will inform him of your plans."

Another bow far too solemn for the occasion, and Beaglemore decamped, putting Cam in mind of the last coach in a funeral procession.

Cam ducked into the music room and risked a peek at the line on the drive, still seventy-one souls strong. Beaglemore descended the front steps, resumed his place beside Mrs. Shorer, and nodded regally. She stepped away from him, and the female staff fell in behind her, like a sloop coming about through the eye of the wind, in what was clearly a choreographed exit.

The male staff waited in turn, then collected themselves in rank order as Beaglemore led them back into the house.

The lot of them had doubtless rehearsed that maneuver, and thirty years on, Parkin would be teaching it to the junior footmen when the next baron had the great misfortune to inherit his title—if there was a next baron.

That thought topped the growing heap of Cam's already towering pile of misgivings and sent him from the music room down the corridor, past the library, and headlong toward the conservatory, the one place in the entire Hall that always felt welcoming, informal, and *safe*.

Such was his desperation to reach the sanctuary of greenery and quiet that he did not check his speed as he flung open the door and strode into the shadowed, humid interior…

Only to collide with a substantial mass of curves, muslin, temper, and fragrance. The fragrance got through to Cam's panicking mind first, and something about the nature of the temper closely followed.

Attar of roses and female asperity, sweetness and spice in equal measures that could only and always be *Alice*.

CHAPTER TWO

In Miss Alice Singleton's estimation, quiet was the first requirement for any space that aspired to be pleasant. The conservatory boasted an agreeable silence and also bore the delightful aromas of healthy plants, rich soil, and blooming flowers. Best of all, Alice's favorite part of the Hall was usually deserted by noon. The gardeners worked their indoor magic in the early morning, while the dew was still on the grass, and then the conservatory became a haven for a lady seeking solitude, repose, or a fresh bouquet.

When the new baron troubled himself to look in on the Hall, Alice's flower-poaching would be suspended, but so far, his lordship had remained far to the south. He was expected at the Hall in the general sense, but Alice hadn't heard any particulars.

Not yet. If the celestial powers were merciful, his lordship would remain in London, and there he would bide until—

One moment, Alice was deciding whether to risk a few sprigs of lavender among her carefully chosen red roses, and the next, she and her posies were knocked top over tail to the bricks of the walkway.

The following instant, a substantial weight came down atop her, knocking the breath from her lungs.

"Jumping Jerusalem!" She thrashed and kicked and shoved, but the human boulder above her refused to move. "Please take your infernally heavy self—"

"For pity's sake, stop..." The weight was male and, in predictable fashion, giving orders.

Alice retaliated with a mighty heave. "Get off me," she panted. "Get *up*, you oaf. Get up now." She was tempted to clout him on the side of the head for good measure, but wanted him gone more than she wanted to pummel him, which was saying a great deal.

"Hold still, you blasted creature. We're caught."

He'd levered up on all fours a few inches above her, a horribly intimate posture, but at least Alice could breathe.

"Well, uncatch yourself this instant." As she took a very shallow breath, she realized what prevented an immediate disentanglement. The chain of her locket had become snagged on the pin buried in the folds of his cravat.

"Please don't break it," she said, even as the thought flitted through her head that footmen did not wear gold cravat pins. "The locket belonged to my mother."

"I know. If you hold still, I can try to undo the fastening on the chain."

His words made no... A memory tickled the back of Alice's mind, of Cam Huxley home from university, his voice deeper, his shoulders broader, his restlessness more palpable. The man above Alice was motionless, and yet, he'd come thundering into the conservatory with the momentum of a charging bull.

Of all the mortifications. "I shall be immobile," Alice said, "if you can be quick."

"Lift your head a bit."

Alice did not move.

"Please, would you mind lifting your head, Miss Singleton, so that I can extricate us from this awkward situation?"

She'd never been *Miss Singleton* to him before, but beneath his exasperation, she heard humor. And he'd said *please*. She raised her head and felt warm, blunt fingers brushing against her nape.

"The catch is delicate," Alice said. "Go carefully."

"I am the soul of patience when it comes to delicate negotiations."

Camden Huxley had also become the soul of distracting fragrances, despite the roses scattered about. This close, Alice caught notes of orange blossoms and ginger, a perfect blend of heady sweetness and exotic spice, and doubtless created exclusively for him.

They'd heard he'd done well. Of course he had. Such a head for numbers and a determination beyond all bounds.

His touch was careful, brushing her hair away from the chain, using two hands to ply the clasp.

Alice studied the ceiling of the conservatory above his shoulders —which were broader still than she recalled—and tried not to think or feel.

"Got it." He angled up until he was kneeling over her, her locket and chain dangling from his cravat pin.

His dismount was swift and careful. Alice bolted to sitting and flipped her skirts over her ankles. She still felt unaccountably out of breath, also bruised in a location a lady did not mention.

"My apologies." Cam rose to an impressive height and offered Alice his ungloved hand.

She allowed him to assist her to her feet, which was rather like allowing a horse to bolt. One moment, she was on her backside, legs inelegantly extended before her as she considered strategies for regaining an upright posture that would offer minimal further insult to her dignity. The next, she was on her feet, two large male hands steadying her by the biceps.

He'd boosted her up as if she weighed no more than a bouquet of dried lavender.

"You're home." She brushed one rose petal from his hair and another from his shoulder.

"I am back," he countered, "for a short stay only. You'll want your locket." He considered the entangled jewelry.

"Allow me." Alice slipped her fingers beneath the folds of his cravat. The linen was pristine, though he had to have been traveling all day. The warmth from his person was just as palpable to her fingers as it had been to the rest of her.

She unpinned the golden dragon rampant and took possession of both items. "The links are so small. I really ought not to wear such a delicate piece, but today would have been Mama's birthday." She moved closer to the glass wall in search of better light. The temptation to bat at the back of her skirt was nigh overwhelming.

Cam—his lordship, rather—swatted at his knees and brushed at his elbows, then set about collecting roses and sprigs of lavender.

"You still miss her?"

"I still feel her absence." Not quite the same thing. The little gold links were hopelessly knotted around the neck of the dragon. Alice resorted to a tactic Grandpapa had shown her years ago and gently rolled the chain between her fingertips. "You can leave the flowers. I'll tidy up later. What had you in such a hurry?"

His lordship took out a knife and began trimming stems. "I tend to move quickly, and I wasn't expecting anybody to be in here. Wellington's entire army was assembled on the drive to inspect me, though I didn't see your grandfather."

The purpose of the all-hands muster had doubtless been to give him a chance to inspect his staff. The reality of Cam Huxley's situation made Alice a bit sad. He'd never wanted to be the baron. Whatever had been true about him as a younger fellow, he'd not coveted his brother's birthright.

The chain loosened, which was a start. Alice unfastened her watch from her sleeve and used the point of the pin to coax the chain out of its knots. Slow going, which suited her.

"Harvest has started," she said. "Grandpapa decided to stay on the job rather than spend an afternoon idling about at the Hall. The wheat must be brought in when it's ready—what wheat we grow."

"You should be growing more barley and hops." His lordship gathered up the trimmed blooms into a bouquet, the lavender sticking out higgledy-piggledy, and wrapped the stems in a plain white handkerchief. "I hope this will do?"

The roses were somewhat the worse for their ordeal, but salvageable. The combined bouquet was an interesting combination.

"Your dragon, my lord."

He accepted his cravat pin, she her locket, all without so much as brushing fingers. Alice set the locket on a potting table and put the flowers in a watering can by the door to the side garden. The last piece of business before making some sort of exit was to fold up his handkerchief and return it to him.

A spot of blood marred one corner. "My lord has been bitten by a thorn, methinks."

"I will survive. My knees are likely to protest their abrupt acquaintance with the cobbles, though. You?"

His voice had always had a slight rasp, but at some point, that rasp had deepened, such that every utterance had the quality of a confidence, an admission wrested from silence.

"I am prepared to forget this unfortunate little contretemps ever happened." She smiled serenely over the dull throbbing of her right *hip*.

"You have a bargain, Miss Singleton, provided you and your grandfather will accept my invitation to supper tomorrow night."

He smiled with equal self-possession, though Alice did not recall him having such an abundance of straight, white teeth.

Questions sprang to Alice's mind. Why invite the steward and his spinster granddaughter to supper when so many neighbors of higher standing would doubtless covet such an invitation? Why so soon? Why not recover from a long and taxing journey up from London? What was the rush?

Common sense set the questions aside. Grandpapa would work himself to death if she permitted it. An invitation to dine with the new baron at the Hall could not be ignored, and Grandpapa would delight in bending his lordship's ear *at length* on all matters agrarian.

"What time, my lord?"

His smile slipped. "I don't know. Whatever dinnertime the household usually observes at this season."

"Don't do that. Don't let the past dictate how you go on. If you are accustomed to Town hours, then the household can accommodate your schedule. That's what you pay them for, and if you give them a reason to grumble, they will be doubly delighted to have you in residence."

She'd spoken more sharply than she'd meant to, but he ought to know better.

"Very well, then, we'll dine at seven."

The perfect hour. Still plenty of light, but Grandpapa would have put in a long enough day to enjoy a respite at the end of it.

"Do we dress?"

"Alice... it's just me. We do not dress for supper."

A relief, that. She had only the one truly formal ensemble left. "Until tomorrow, then." Also a relief to be escaping the whole encounter.

He retrieved the bouquet from its watering can and held it to her, stems dripping. "Don't you want your flowers? Here." He produced the wrinkled handkerchief and wrapped the stems again. "I insist. I don't like to think you're taking only bruises away from our first encounter in ages."

His smile was the personification of masculine charm, and Alice resented it mightily—so mightily that she grasped the bouquet too firmly and got a jab in the palm for her efforts. She nonetheless bobbed an easy curtsey and wished his lordship a pleasant day.

She exited the conservatory through the side garden door and kept a resolute pace all the way across the park. Only when she'd reached the safety of the home wood did she examine her wound, which had turned her palm slightly bloody.

"Drat him and his smiles anyway." And yet, she couldn't quite sustain a real temper where Cam Huxley was concerned. He'd come home when Mrs. Shorer had been certain he wouldn't. He'd look after the Hall despite Mr. Beaglemore's dire predictions to the contrary, and he would commend Grandpapa to a happy and secure retirement.

Camden, Lord Lorne, was being responsible. That he had also become a magnificent male specimen, with both manners and muscles, well... that had nothing to do with anything.

Though the whole awkward quarter hour left Alice feeling bewildered, an all-too-familiar state of affairs where Cam was concerned. Not quite angry, not pleased, not even exactly flustered, but... bewildered.

Alice Singleton had grown dowdy.

This astonishing fact preoccupied Cam sufficiently that the first footman had to clear his throat twice after setting the tray on the library desk.

"Will there be a reply, my lord?" Chapman glanced portentously at the tray, which bore a towering epergne full of comestibles. A second footman, already departed, had brought a full tea service, despite supper being less than two hours away.

A reply. Cam extracted a folded epistle from the edge of the tray. Cousin Bernard's flourishy handwriting hadn't changed. An examination of the missive confirmed that Bernard's ability to blend presumption and flattery was in good form as well.

Cam located a pencil in the desk drawer, scrawled a few words onto the bottom of the note, and then as an afterthought added, *We shall dine at seven. Informal attire.*

"My reply, which is not urgent."

"We'll deliver it to the vicarage within the hour, my lord."

"You might also alert Cook to the fact that we'll have company tomorrow evening. Vicar and his mama have invited themselves for supper and taken the liberty of extending invitations to a few other neighbors. Lady Josephine suggests a buffet, the better to accommodate the numbers on short notice."

Chapman was hardly new to service, and yet, he made a moue of distaste. "Very good, my lord. I will inform Cook."

Very annoying, more like. "My thanks, Chapman. That will be all."

That Alice had become dowdy was also annoying, in addition to astonishing. A woman of her impressive dimensions ought not to be wearing ruffles, much less big, droopy ruffles that obscured her figure and put one in mind of governesses on annual seaside holidays.

St. Didier had at some point stepped into the room. He lurked by the door until Chapman withdrew and only then approached the desk.

"I will not eat at the desk," Cam said, rising and lifting the epergne. "You would scold me for it. Mind you, the food will taste the same regardless of where we consume it and will just as effectively spoil our suppers."

"You ate barely anything at luncheon. This looks delectable." St. Didier hefted the tea tray and set it on the reading table. "You survived the parade inspection?"

"No thanks to you. Where did you get off to?"

"The Rose Suite. A little communing with soap and water, a short nap, and I'm a new man. Please do compliment the housekeeper on the scented soaps. The lavender is heavenly."

Cam filled a plate with cheese tarts, rolled slices of ham, and two lemon tarts. The fare wanted some plain, cool, summer ale, rather than damned tea.

"You are scowling," St. Didier said, filling his own plate. "Has your review of the premises revealed creeping damp and evidence of mice?"

Were ruffles worse than mice? "The house appears in good trim, but I did not nose around the attics and cellars, where signs of neglect would most likely be found. Are you acquainted with my aunt Josephine?"

St. Didier poured out, taking his tea black.

Cam added sugar and milk—well, no, *cream*—and sipped cautiously. Hot, sweet, rich. He set his cup down after a single taste.

St. Didier selected a variety of fruit tarts. "Lady Josephine, relict of the late Reverend Ambrose Huxley, your uncle, and said—most notably by Lady Josephine—to have been in consideration for a suffragan bishop's post when he went to his celestial reward. Bad fish, though the lesser lights of the congregation might have been heard to whisper about bibacity as a contributing factor. Her ladyship presides over the vicarage at St. Wilfrid's, a post beneath the dignity of an earl's daughter, but within the ambit of a doting mother's dreams, to hear her tell it. This is good tea."

"Are you surprised?" Cam was surprised. Surprised at Alice Singleton all grown up and full of curves she tried to hide. Surprised she'd truss her gorgeous chestnut mane up in one of those crocheted black net thingums. An abomination against the natural order, to see her hair confined thus.

St. Didier sipped again. "If your property is well cared for, I am pleased, I suppose. The house has been without a lord of the manor for months, and your brother's decline was lengthy. One might expect standards to have slipped."

"The old guard has prevented that, though I'm certain Aunt Josephine will take the credit. She has invited half the shire to a buffet here tomorrow night. You can plead the fatigue of travel if you'd rather be spared."

"Bold of her."

"A formal meal would have been bold. She'll doubtless make the attempt if I'm ever here when the household is not in mourning. Is three months too soon to dispense with the black armbands and covered portraits and mirrors?"

"Not the armbands. One mourns a sibling for six months."

"Lorne's will—Alexander's will—specified no deep mourning."

"Armbands on livery are not deep mourning. Neither does mourning prevent you from hacking out early tomorrow to have a look at your acreage."

"I'm not much of one for hacking out." Every fashionable bachelor in London paraded himself through Hyde Park at an ungodly hour, and half the heiresses and diamonds did as well. Cam had no wish to be confused for an eligible on display. "I prefer to spend my mornings in productive pursuits."

St. Didier raked him with a pitying glance. "You fall asleep at your desk, you wake up at your desk, your cheek stained with ink. You eat barely enough to keep body and soul together, and you grow fretful if you're not in sight of an abacus. One would despair, except that you have, by the grace of the Deity and my own selfless efforts, landed in the middle of the most beautiful shire on earth in its most beautiful season. If you lie abed tomorrow morning, I shall disown you."

"Empty promises will never move me, St. Didier." By sheer self-discipline, Cam did not glance at the abacus gracing the windowsill nearest the corner. He instead started on his cheese tarts.

"Empty promises should move nobody, but the beauty of Yorkshire is irresistible. Your brother claimed you used to be out of doors more than in and spent most of your summers on the back of a horse. For all you know, the land has been neglected terribly, but here you sit, eating—or pretending to eat—in the library, because books and ledgers are the only landscape you now recognize."

For St. Didier, that was a tirade.

"Thaddeus Singleton will insist on taking me about. He'd probably rather I wait for his escort." The cheddar was perfectly aged to have flavor with a hint of bite. The crust was exquisitely light.

"Old Singleton will show you what he wants you to see in the light he wants you to see it. That's not how you find the truth of the place. When I visit my former family seat, I ride about at will, seeing what's before my eyes. I don't call upon the present owner and take tea overlooking the sunken garden."

That St. Didier visited his ancestral pile was a revelation. His *former* ancestral pile. "How is the place holding up?"

"It isn't. The English climate will take prisoner any structure left undefended, and the current inhabitants of The Gables haven't the first notion how to repel the elements. You are attempting to change the subject. We will ride tomorrow before breakfast."

The hell we will. "After breakfast. Even you have said I need more rest and sustenance."

St. Didier made an unconvincing effort to look abashed. "Very well. We ride out *after* breakfast, but no later than eight of the clock."

Cam was usually at his desk well before eight, and some sort of mounted inspection of the property was required sooner or later.

"What do you call those net things women wear over their hair when they bun it all up at the back of their head?"

St. Didier obliterated the last of his tarts. "A bun at the nape is a chignon."

"Not the bun itself. The little woven net for trussing it all tidily together. Widows wear them, and the yarn is often black."

"A snood. Old-fashioned, modest. Why?"

Cam finished his cheese tarts and started on the rolled slices of ham. "No reason. I don't care for them. Too antiquated. Could not think of the word. Will you attend tomorrow's supper buffet?" Even the word sounded dowdy. *Snood. Rhymes with prude, rectitude, platitude, brood...*

"I would not miss my lord's debut in local Society. You'll have to strike the right balance between sorrow at your brother's passing and joy to be home. Wants delicacy."

"Wants dishonesty, you mean. Lorne was more than ready to go, and I did not begrudge him an end to his suffering. Far from it. And lest you think I am unaware of your maneuvering, St. Didier, this visit to the Hall is an occasion of duty rather than joy."

St. Didier finished his tea, wrapped three raspberry tarts in linen, and rose. "Duty and joy can overlap, which you'd know if you ever lifted your gaze from your ledger books long enough to behold new parents with their infant offspring. I'll see you at supper, and we can plan tomorrow's outing over a good meal, though I do believe you've eaten almost everything on your plate."

"One is supposed to, lest good food go to waste. I've not touched the lemon tarts."

"Yet." On that telling shot, St. Didier took his leave, and not a moment too soon.

Cam finished his lemon tarts, finished the remaining ham, and had two cups of tea, but still, he did not quite feel satisfied.

Snood. Homely, frumpish word. Disappointing word. None of the ladies vying for Cam's attention in London would be caught wearing a *snood* while reading fashion magazines on a rainy morning at home.

CHAPTER THREE

"Lady Jo wasted no time, did she?" Grandpapa muttered. "Every biddable belle in the shire on display for his lordship." Grandpapa sipped his punch, hiding a smile behind his glass.

Alice was not amused. She'd flattered herself that Ca—Lord Lorne had issued an impromptu, informal invitation out of... what? Spontaneous graciousness? Fondness for a few old memories? Chagrin at having literally knocked a lady onto her tail?

Of course he'd simply included them in a scheduled gathering, a formality to be endured, and of course he would have left the guest list to Lady Josephine.

"The display of belles might be for Bernard's benefit."

"Bernard has had years to take a wife. As long as Lady Josephine rules the vicarage, no woman with common sense would give the vicar more than a passing wave of her fan."

She would give him that, though. Bernard was the handsome cousin, as opposed to the charming cousin (Alexander) or the serious cousin (Cam). Bernard was tall and fashionably slender. He wore his blond hair swept back a la Brutus, and his attire was always bang up to the understated mark. He was articulate in the pulpit, not given to lengthy oration, and not above a dash of humor.

Grandpapa was right that the primary impediment to marriage for Bernard Huxley was his own dear mama. Lady Josephine was an impediment to many things, chief among them sloth, idleness, impiety, personal privacy, and joy.

"I see the late baron has lost his mourning ribbon," Grandpapa remarked, lifting his glass in the direction of the portrait over the formal parlor's mantel. "What was Eunice Shorer thinking? The man insisted we not mourn him with any great displays, and what does that woman do? Drapes the whole house in black."

Grandpapa's feuds with Mrs. Shorer were legendary, numerous, and fought with equal vigor on both sides. The footmen laid wagers, the housemaids informed against their superior, and the gamekeepers kept the tallies.

Grandpapa nonetheless invited Mrs. Shorer to dance at least once at every quarterly assembly. On every occasion, he let it be known to Alice and anybody within earshot that he led the poor old dear onto the dance floor out of gentlemanly pity. Mrs. Shorer made similarly audible remarks, citing a charitable responsibility to save lonely old widowers from the exclusive company of the wallflowers.

Across the parlor, Lord Lorne was bowing over Lady Josephine's hand. She simpered prettily—she was a handsome woman, give her that—and beamed at him as if he were her long-lost son, not a nephew she had all but ignored.

"I believe I need another serving of this excellent punch," Grandpapa said. "Might I top up your glass as well, my dear?"

"No, thank you. I suspect the punch of having a nefarious ingredient or two, Grandpapa. Tread lightly."

"Quite tasty, isn't it?" He sauntered off, one of the taller men in the room, though not as tall as the current baron. That worthy was being led around the room by his doting aunt, who had likely told each hopeful young lady where to stand, such that an order of precedence was created.

"He's showing off." That comment was offered quietly by the Honorable Blessington Peabody, who made it a habit to stand too close to Alice at every opportunity. He smelled of parsley and camphor, which compared disagreeably with orange blossoms and ginger.

Alice Singleton, get hold of yourself. She plastered a vapid smile on her face and began to swing her hips gently from side to side so her hems brushed at Peabody's boots.

"I think his lordship looks quite well," she said. "A bit pale, but then, he did lose his only brother not three months past."

"Precisely, not three months past, and here he is, half the neighborhood making merry under his roof. If this is how one shows respect to a departed sibling in London, then spare me the sophistications of the metropolis."

Blessington Peabody was a high stickler without portfolio, though he did command some expectations. When his papa bid adieu to the earthly realm, Bless would inherit a tidy manor, considerable grazing acreage, and several tenancies—also two unmarried sisters whose greatest delights were shopping sprees in York.

Alice felt sorry for him, but not that sorry. "Everything in London is sophisticated," she said. "All the fashion magazines say so. Grandpapa reads *The Times*, and that's all the really important news there is." She tittered, like a schoolgirl who had just recalled a poetical quote correctly, much against all expectations.

"Miss Singleton, you must trust me that London is a cesspit of vice and venery, despite what the papers would have you think. I have been to Town and do not care to repeat the ordeal. A lady of your humble standing simply cannot grasp just how unhealthy a London existence can be."

He was calling her backward, also very possibly stupid, and long might he regard her as such.

Alice opened her eyes wide. "I do wish I could go sometime and see all the sights. The lions in the menagerie, the bloody Tower, maybe even the Regent himself!"

Peabody patted her arm. "Such innocence in a lady of mature years is refreshing. Might I bring you another glass of punch?"

Now she was elderly. "No, thank you. I believe I'll step out for a breath of fresh air."

"A beautiful time of year. A pity it also brings so much hard work for some of us." He aimed a fulminating glance at the baron and stalked off toward the punchbowl.

While the rest of us work hard year-round. Alice passed through the French doors onto the wide back terrace. Another footman presided over another punchbowl before the balustrade, and several of the young ladies who had already been introduced to the new baron were comparing notes by the steps.

"Not as handsome as Vicar," Miss Dorothea Considine observed, and hers was considered the weightiest opinion among the local young ladies. "A bit brutish, in fact. Charming, though. Has Town bronze, as they say."

"Not bad-looking," Miss Annabelle Dingle countered. "You must admit he is not bad-looking, Dotty."

"Dorothea, please, and I never said he's bad-looking, but he's not up to Vicar's polish."

"And he's a bit vigorous?" Miss Davina Halbertson ventured. She was always venturing, suggesting, or positing, but she never actually admitted to an opinion or observation. She was the prettiest of the trio, in a delicate, retiring way, but she'd never see herself as attractive.

The other two young ladies considered her.

"He's healthy," Miss Halbertson said. "You are right about that. Poor Lorne—the late Lord Lorne—was not healthy. A pity."

They observed a moment of silence for the late lord and his unsuitability as a spouse.

"Their chattering will drive a man mad." Harrington Bottle murmured on Alice's right. "Do they think of nothing more profound than who might be inveigled into marrying whom?"

Alice mentally swiveled her cannon, from brainless twit to bluestocking pedant. "Marriage is a serious matter, Mr. Bottle."

He blinked pale blue eyes. "I agree, but to hear that lot discussing a man's prospects, you'd think the issue no more momentous than the weekly livestock auction at Farnes Crossing. If those women aspired to any sort of adulthood, they'd be reading the great works of the day, acquainting themselves with advances in herbology, and preparing for the weighty responsibility of motherhood."

"And how is it, exactly, that men prepare themselves for the weighty responsibilities of fatherhood? Enlighten me, please, because I doubt that public school pugilism or a few years of shooting at the French has served as proper preparation for the job anticipated by our revered scions."

Poor Bottle actually shuddered. "Miss Singleton, the reply I could make to your question is so very lengthy and well reasoned that I fear I must fortify myself with a trip to the punchbowl before treating you to the benefit of my viewpoint."

"I shall await your diatribe, Mr. Bottle. I do fancy a lively debate, provided my opponent can offer accurate literary citations for his theories."

He marched off, shaking his head. Alice sidled the other direction, toward the westering sun, into the side garden, and from thence to the refuge of the conservatory.

To keep every bachelor in the shire at bay, all the while appearing gracious and appropriate, was hard work, and Alice was growing mighty weary of it.

"You've retired from the affray too?" Bernard Huxley stepped forth from beneath the potted lemons. "Mama is launching the baron's visit with full honors, isn't she?"

"One commends her familial loyalty." Meant sincerely, for the most part. One also had a healthy respect for Lady Josephine's ambitions as well. "Has she chosen a wife for you yet?"

Bernard gestured to a wooden bench that faced out over the side garden. "Let's sit, shall we? Mama knows that in three regards she must mind her step with me, lest I commend her to a prolonged visit to the York town house."

Alice sat, glad to get off her feet. "She is not to comment upon your sermons."

"Not to comment, suggest, criticize, editorialize, or emend. She is not to interfere in spiritual matters in any regard."

"What other prohibitions do you enforce?" Alice liked Bernard and regarded him as neither ally nor foe. They left each other in peace, but could share an occasional moment of commiseration.

"Mama is not to make designs upon my bachelorhood. If and when I marry, I will do so where I please and without regard to Mama's sensibilities on the matter."

"My grandfather opines that no sensible lady will consider your suit while your mother presides at the vicarage."

Bernard came down a proper twelve inches from Alice. "Plain speaking. Good to know I can still rely on you for plain speaking. The third domain in which Mama must abide by my wishes includes the household finances, and upon that subject, I can speak very directly when the occasion warrants. How does Cam seem to you?"

"A little pale." Tired, tall, shrewd. "He will make a credible baron." As Bernard would have, for that matter, and perhaps Bernard was the better candidate for never having sullied his hands in trade.

"Cam will make an adequate baron, if he leaves his London business in the hands of factors or, better still, sells the lot. Lorne Hall needs a real baron, not a jumped-up cit who sympathizes with the rabble."

Bernard was the vicar, and the vicar belonged to the church, and the church belonged to the crown. Holy writ took on a decidedly Tory bent when Bernard chose to wax political. God's will apparently ran parallel to the pecuniary interests of the peerage. This view was contradicted by nearly every word of Scripture that Alice had ever read, but then, that same Scripture had dictated that women were to keep silent in the church.

She was abruptly unwilling to share the conservatory with

Bernard, though she derived some consolation from the notion that even the vicar wasn't worried about being found alone with her in dimly lit surroundings.

Alice rose. "If you'll excuse me, I'd best see that Grandpapa doesn't do too much justice to the punch." She would also ensure that his plate was full and that he got home at a decent hour. He'd be up at first light regardless of how little sleep he'd had, and fatigue would make him snappish and difficult.

"Sorry." Bernard rose. "Did not mean to sermonize. The barony is no business of mine, but I do want to see Cam succeed. His was not an easy path."

"Perhaps your dear mama can find him a baroness who will ensure that he gives up his commercial enterprises and finds contentment in the blandishments of Yorkshire." Alice dipped a curtsey and departed.

As she made her way around to the terrace, she admitted to herself that she wanted to see Cam Huxley not merely successful, but also happy. From what little Alexander had said on the subject, Cam and commerce were a good fit.

Grandpapa was not on the terrace. He wasn't in the formal parlor or the music room. Alice smoothed the ruffles of her bodice, ignored the tantalizing scents coming from the buffet set up in the library, and made her way to the Huxley family portrait gallery.

She expected to find Grandpapa, glass in hand, gazing soulfully at the formal portrait of the current baron's grandmama. Instead, she found Cam Huxley, sans libation, scowling at a sketch of himself with his older brother and cousin.

∼

The door latch clicked, and Cam realized he'd set himself up to be *pursued*. The twits, gigglers, and slow-blinking misses had sized him up as Aunt Josephine had intended them to, and they had found him worthy of their interest. He got to his feet, determined to gain the corridor before the small talk even started.

"I was hoping to find Grandpapa here." Alice Singleton hovered in the doorway, peering about in the flickering shadows. "No need to get up. I shan't disturb you."

"You already have. Might as well join me."

Alice edged into the room, leaving the door open. The resulting draft caused the flames in the two lit sconces to flicker, which gave the denizens of the gallery walls an oddly animate quality.

"The buffet has been set out, my lord. You really ought to be among your guests."

The opening of the buffet had been Cam's opportunity to bolt. "They are Aunt Josephine's guests. I thought she'd round up a few of the local squires, the mayor, the magistrate. I underestimated her."

"The squires are well represented. Mr. Bottle's papa is the magistrate. Prone to gout, though, so Lady Josephine contented herself with the bachelor son. He's a decent fellow."

"Does he fancy any of the young ladies Aunt Josephine has assembled?"

Alice took another two steps into the room. "Davina Halbertson would make him a devoted and sensible helpmeet without annoying his mama, but he doesn't notice her because she is shy. Blessington Peabody is our mayor, and he does a conscientious job. Grandpapa wasn't in here when you arrived?"

"He was not. He's probably catching forty winks by the kitchen hearth."

Alice peered at the late dowager baroness's portrait across from the unlit hearth. "He comes here to pay his respects to her. Grandpapa says she was the finest lady he ever knew, save for the woman he married. I believe he and the baroness were friends when they were both bereaved. He's not supposed to presume belowstairs here at the Hall. Mrs. Shorer has importuned me no end to break him of the habit."

"If I importuned you to give up those awful ruffles, would you heed my request?" Cam's question was honest, also ungentlemanly. "My apologies. Too much of that excellent punch has loosened my tongue and hidden my manners. The dress is lovely."

The dress was *pink*. If ever there was a color Alice Singleton should not wear, it was that particularly violent shade of pink.

She continued to study the portrait, but the line of her jaw had changed. "You don't care for ruffles?"

In for a penny... "Not when they obscure what was meant to be appreciated. For Miss Halbertson, ruffles might help draw notice to what would otherwise be ignored. You have no need of such sartorial subterfuges."

Alice moved on to a portrait of Cam's grandpapa. "Do all London gentlemen comment so freely on a lady's attire?"

"Most men do, though not necessarily in the lady's hearing. I apologize if I've given offense." The ruffles offended Cam somehow. Insulted him. Insulted every notion of flattering fashion, and whoever had created that hue of pink was overdue for a stint in purgatory.

"You have offended no one. I'll be on my way. If Grandpapa happens by, please send him along to the library. He has imbibed quite freely and will have a sore head tomorrow if he doesn't exercise some care."

Cam did not want to return to Aunt Josephine's guests, and he did not want Alice to leave in high dudgeon. He did not want her to leave at all, in fact.

"They scare me," he said. "The young ladies, and Aunt Josephine is only getting started. In Town, I know how to repel boarders. I was a confirmed bachelor, married to my work, reeking of trade, despite being Alexander's heir. I am still a confirmed bachelor reeking of trade, but the rest of it... If Alexander had allowed it, I'd have kept the house in mourning."

Alice drifted along to the portrait of the youthful cousins. "His death was expected, and yet, his absence is still an adjustment. He was much loved and much respected. He'd made his peace with the inevitable, but I think he erred when he forbade full mourning. He was—is—worth mourning."

"Yes. Exactly." And for Lady Josephine to be flinging prospective baronesses at Cam was more irksome than all the pink ruffles in creation. Now that he'd been introduced to the young ladies, or reintroduced to some of them, they'd be free to accost him in the churchyard, to engage him in conversation at the market, or—heaven forfend—to inveigle their papas and brothers into calling upon him at the Hall.

Once that floodgate opened, Cam would be inundated with invitations and callers.

"You know," Alice said, considering him rather than the young men framed behind her, "Bernard claims that he has imposed three immutable limits on his mama. She is not to meddle in any ecclesiastical matters whatsoever, most especially not his sermons. She is not to meddle with his bachelorhood, and she has no say in the vicarage's financial matters. You might simply tell her that you refuse to look for a wife until the late baron has been properly mourned."

Simple, honest, effective. "You should consider a career in trade. You'd be formidable. Why isn't Bernard married?"

Why hadn't Bernard married *Alice*? She was nominally a gentleman's daughter, in as much as her father had been a headmaster and thus had not worked with his hands. She was astute, beautiful, smart... Could it be that Bernard was fooled by the ruffles?

"You should ask Bernard why he hasn't taken a wife. I really should locate Grandpapa. He can become querulous when he's overimbibing."

"We'll search together," Cam said, going to the door. "We might also look in the armory. This time of year, the fowling pieces want regular maintenance."

"If they're in use, they do. The only people hunting your land legally are your gamekeepers."

"And the illegal hunters?" Poachers risked hanging for the sake of a few grouse, but England's postwar economy meant that, for many, the choices were starvation or crime.

Alice took off down the corridor at a brisk march. "All the poachers I know of are local. Alexander somehow kept the gangs out of the district. Organize a shoot for the squires, and the village goodwives will be singing your praises until Christmas."

More simple, honest, effective advice. "I might not be staying long enough. We'd have to wait until after harvest, and that will go for at least another fortnight." How pleasant to walk beside a woman who didn't mince along with tiny steps.

"You'd stay less than a month?"

"If I had my way, I'd stay less than a week, but St. Didier has appointed himself my finishing governess when it comes to taking on the barony's honors and duties. He demands more than a fortnight. My responsibilities in London mean even that much will be a strain."

They approached the armory, which was part museum and part weapons cache. Alice took a key down from the lintel and unlocked the door.

"No Grandpapa. The room wants airing."

She brushed past Cam on a whiff of pungent roses. Brisk, direct, luscious, sweet.

It occurred to him as Alice relocked the door that Alice Singleton was a lady in want of *kissing*. The thought was ludicrous. She'd smack him into next week if he made the attempt, and yet... the fortified punch could not be held entirely to blame for putting the idea in Cam's head.

"I'll make a pass through the kitchen," Cam said. "If I find him snoring before the hearth, I'll rouse him and send him to you."

Alice Singleton wanted ruffling, not ruffles. Her hair free of that vile crocheted contraption, her smiles warm instead of perfunctory. She wanted laughter and affection and possibly even courting.

What was wrong with Bernard and that Blessingbody fellow or the other young man whose name put Cam in mind of jars and barrels but wasn't Jar or Barrel?

Alice cantered back in the direction of the main staircase. "You cannot *think* to intrude on the kitchen, my lord. Biblical wrath would surely follow such an invasion."

"As long as it follows by a few millennia, I will risk it. Singleton apparently did."

"You must not. Mrs. Shorer and Mrs. Bell would take it as a sign of disrespect. That Grandpapa intrudes is bad enough, but they understand that he's like an old hound who seeks the warmth of the hearth. You should be with your guests."

"Wasn't it you who told me to begin as I intend to go on? Supper at seven, if that's my wish?"

Alice paused at the top of the steps, the chatter of guests below welling up in a single tide of noise.

"I said that, but one distinguishes between establishing oneself as an independent authority and ignoring conventions that exist for good reasons. The kitchen is entitled to privacy, my lord. A buffet for two dozen people on short notice was no small feat, and you will cause all manner of upset if you insert yourself into the proceedings belowstairs."

Cam propped a hip on the banister railing. "A plain mister can wander into his own kitchen if he's peckish or thirsty."

Alice shook a finger at him. "A lord of the manor uses the bell-pull. I'll ask one of the footmen if Grandpapa has presumed on the hospitality of the kitchen. You will attend to your guests."

"I would rather have remained a plain mister." He wasn't whining, exactly. Perhaps acknowledging a loss. With Alice, that seemed permissible.

"You mean that." A gust of laughter wafted up from below.

"With all my heart. I am good at business, Alice. I understand how to balance risk and routine. I love a good, fierce negotiation, and the challenges of an international market make me feel alive. This other nonsense..." An expensive prison of protocol and public displays.

Alice touched his arm. "The title isn't all nonsense, you know. It's also your family's legacy and a community that values the traditions embodied by that history. You can negotiate the terms, provided you don't violate the trust."

She would have descended the steps before Cam did—a neglect of social protocol on her part—but he caught her wrist.

"Thank you."

That simple courtesy seemed to fluster her. "For?"

"Explaining to me what was obvious to my brother, but baffling to me."

The smile she gave him was sweet and mischievous and more potent than three tankards of the kitchen's finest summer punch. A smile just for Cam, just for that moment.

Cam offered his arm and a smile of his own. Alice Singleton wanted much more than kissing, did she but know it. She wanted *cherishing*.

Alice accepted Cam's proffered escort, and they joined the chattering, milling throng. Two minutes later, she excused herself to confer with a footman, and Cam was left to navigate the buffet on his own.

He prevailed upon Miss Halbertson to guide his choices and had the satisfaction of seeing Mr. Blessedbodywhosit's expression turn puzzled and then thoughtful.

Throughout the rest of the evening, Cam managed the small talk and the glances and the whispered news from the footmen, and even Aunt Josephine's knowing chuckles.

He avoided the punch like one newly committed to abstinence, and yet, he went to bed half intoxicated with the memory of Alice Singleton's fleeting, genuine smile.

CHAPTER FOUR

"Little Davina Halbertson," Lady Josephine said, settling beside Alice on the gig's bench. "Who would have thought it?"

"Good morning, my lady." Alice waited while the footman deposited two vast hampers under the seat. "A pleasant day for our outing."

"One does one's Christian duty regardless of the weather, Alice, but you are correct. We are blessed to enjoy high summer at its best as the new baron takes up his honors. I venture to say that is not a coincidence. 'He has made everything beautiful in its time.'"

Alice gave Cerberus—the gentlest soul on four hooves—leave to trot on. Lady Josephine would fill the morning with homilies, admonitions, and snippets of Scripture, all intended to benefit Alice's immortal soul. Her ladyship always meant well—she would assure any audience of that repeatedly—and the morning was so glorious, even Lady Josephine could not dim its splendors.

Though, to Alice, the new baron had sounded as if he were homesick for his countinghouse rather than smitten with Davina. No matter. If the gospel according to her ladyship held that his lordship was much taken with Miss Halbertson, so be it.

"How is your grandpapa, my dear? I heard he was catching forty winks when he should have been sampling the buffet. The elderly have their crotchets, but it's such a shame when they cease observing the usual conventions even when in company."

Such a shame when an exhausted steward found some needed rest? "Grandpapa is quite well, thank you. He was up and about at first light, then off to Mr. Cameron's wheat fields. The crop is coming in nicely."

"The man is entirely too ancient for his post, as is Eunice Shorer. Mark me on this, a new broom sweeps clean."

Alice drove on, nodding pleasantly, making polite rejoinders in the few places where Lady Josephine's discourse allowed room for them. The birds sang, the sheep and cattle were fat in their pastures, and the sky was a canvas of sparkling Yorkshire blue. The weekly journey to Farnes Crossing always had the same effect on Alice, a lifting of the spirits, a stubborn

welling of hope.

Despite her ladyship's diatribes.

Lady Josephine was a formidable woman in many regards. Tall, matronly, shrewd, and tireless. She was blond going genteelly flaxen, blue-eyed, and soft-spoken in the usual course. Lady Josephine had coped with much, being the wife and mother of clergymen, and she'd married down. To her credit, she'd never—in Alice's hearing—admitted to regrets regarding her choice of spouse.

One nonetheless did not make an enemy of Lady Josephine, and one could never consider her an ally. Grandpapa had observed that Lady Josephine was better suited to ruling in the shires than serving in Mayfair.

The literary allusion was more apt than Grandpapa knew.

"And about your dress, my dear? That pink business you wore last evening?"

"Yes, your ladyship?"

"Time to change the trim. We've seen that frock now for many a year, and while one appreciates thrift, and your opportunities for socializing are understandably limited, you must not, even at your age, become complacent about your appearance."

"No, ma'am. What would you suggest?"

Cerberus trotted past fields and pastures, past two crews scything wheat, and on into the village of Farnes Crossing. All the while, her ladyship held forth about the balance between upholding standards and exhibiting at *all* times the virtues of modesty, humility, and industry.

"At *all* times, Alice. Even in the privacy of our thoughts."

"You are so right, my lady." Alice turned the horse down a wide lane that led past the local house of worship. A quarter mile later, the lane narrowed, and a high hedge, likely anchored in ancient stone walls, sprang up on the south side of the road.

"You did notice the baron's interest in our Davina, did you not, Alice?"

"He escorted her down the buffet, and as far as I know, they took their meal together." Alice had withdrawn to the music room, sitting where she had a good view of the footmen's stairs. Grandpapa had taken some time to emerge from the depths of the house, but emerge he eventually had.

Mrs. Shorer would have much to say about that come Sunday morning, all of it despairing.

"You have the right of it, my dear. Camden—I must call him Lorne now, mustn't I?—Camden sat with Davina for the entire repast and had her smiling for most of it. I would never accuse my nephew of flirtation, but he did put some roses in Davina's cheeks. She's not who I'd choose to be our next baroness, but she'll be biddable. Always a fine thing in any female."

These remarks, about humble thoughts and biddability, were supposedly meant kindly. Alice had learned to ignore them, and yet, on this glorious summer morning, surrounded by sunshine and the bounty of a harvest in progress, ignoring her ladyship's patter took more effort.

Fatigue perhaps, or the aftereffects of two glasses of punch.

"And here we are!" Lady Josephine said as Alice drew Cerberus up before a solid fieldstone edifice built on spare, classical lines. Sheep nibbled at the grass flanking the drive, the fountain was dry, and the front terrace was adorned by exactly two pots of red salvia. A stately maple on each side of the house cast the yard in dappled shade, and no less than eight chimneys adorned the roof.

Not depressing, but not exactly a temple to cheerful abundance either.

"They're here!" A high, childish voice piped from inside the house. "The ladyships are here!"

Alice climbed down and assisted Lady Josephine to descend. A wizened little gnome who answered to the name Archibald shuffled around from the side of the house. Alice had never learned whether Archibald was a surname or patronym, and because the fellow was stone-deaf, the distinction mattered little.

He tugged his cap at Lady Josephine and took the horse by the bridle. "Come along, horse."

"You'll bring the hampers?" Lady Josephine called, but Archibald either did not hear her or did not regard the question, which she'd been posing nigh weekly for years, worth answering.

"We mustn't keep the little dears waiting," Lady Josephine said, squaring her shoulders. "I believe it's my week to review the menus and expenditures, which leaves you the pleasure of hearing the girls recite. Try to be encouraging, especially to those of limited understanding. Their situation is not their doing."

Another kindly barb. Her ladyship was in good form. "I will do my best, your ladyship."

"See that you do." Lady Josephine swept up the walk, stepping over the threshold without pausing, because the door opened from within as if by magic. The older girl serving as porter curtseyed politely to her ladyship, and Alice followed at a respectful distance.

Five minutes later, she was surrounded by laughing, chattering, happy little girls, two of them giggling for every one trying to shush her companions. They wore identical plain gray dresses with identical white pinafores tied in identically tidy bows at the back, and yet, Alice knew them each by name, age, and detailed biography.

"Did you bring a story, Miss Alice?" Gabriella asked. She was a study in contrasts. Flaming-red hair and a nimble mind, but careful with her words and shy of manner.

"Miss Alice always brings a story." Jeanine, three years Gabriella's junior and infinitely more accomplished at wheedling, batted big blue eyes at Alice. "I like the one about the lion with the thorn in his paw. When I grow up, I shall have pet lions."

"When you grow up," Mary said, "you will have sore knees because you shall become a housemaid like the rest of us." Mary was the voice of harsh reality among the older girls, a dark-haired, restless soul always looking out the window unless she was called upon to recite. She was smart and quick-witted, which might allow her to advance in the domestic ranks—or might get her sacked.

"A housemaid has an important job," Alice said, mindful that her words could be repeated to Lady Josephine. "If she is diligent in her duties, she has security, honorable work, a wage, and the respect of all who know her."

The habit of delivering sermons must be contagious, though Alice winced at the thought of any of these children becoming housemaids. The work was grueling in many households, the wage a pittance, and respect in very short supply. Even a housemaid's safety was far from guaranteed.

"But did you bring us a story?" Jeanine asked, making a grab for Alice's hand. "Please say you did, Miss Alice."

Silence fell, though the answer would be the same as it always had been. "Of course, and I would be delighted to read it to you, but first, I must hear your verses." The headmistress, Mrs. Dumfries, had established that sequence, and Alice deviated from it at her peril.

Mary sent Alice a disgusted look, which stung more than all of Lady Josephine's thoughtless lectures and scriptural poison darts, but what did a girl without means or family expect to have in life besides a post in service?

To foster dreams of ease or hopes of domestic bliss in such children would have been unkind. And yet, one could read them stories. David and Goliath, for example, or Daniel in the lion's den.

"Verses now, stories later," Alice said. "Gabriella, might you start us off?"

Gabriella, a walking good example, produced eight flawless verses of Proverbs, admonishing all to cling to wisdom and eschew the temptations offered by sinful men.

Mary came next with more exhortations, then Jeanine, little Penelope, and the irrepressibly boisterous Lizzy, followed by several others. Alice listened to them from the comfort of the rocking chair in the corner of the room, grateful as always for the most joyous and heartbreaking hour of her week.

∽

"I don't understand," Cam said as the morning breeze riffled the high grass carpeting five acres of good pastureland. "If you aren't using that patch for grazing, why not cut it down and make hay?"

Singleton had caught Cam riding out of the stable yard with St. Didier and attached himself to them. St. Didier had produced regular I-told-you-so looks for the next half mile. He'd then excused himself from the rest of the outing, and Singleton had commenced rhapsodizing about the water mill that had been giving excellent service since dear Queen Anne's day.

"Cut hay this late in the season?" Singleton rejoined. "*Who* would cut that hay, my lord? Every hand must be turned to scything the ripe grain, just as every hand is turned to scything hay in spring. The land has a rhythm that makes sense to those who understand it. Trust me on this."

Cam watched the old wooden wheel turning slowly and prayed for patience.

Business had a rhythm too. "We hire crews to scythe the hay, and in late winter, when nobody has any hay left to sell, we make a profit that exceeds what it cost to hire the crews now."

Singleton fussed with his horse's mane. The creature was a venerable bay gelding, white around the muzzle, and a bit slab-sided.

"But, my lord, what if we cut down that field and the heavens open up before the hay can cure? The days are shorter now than in spring, and the dew falls more heavily. The hay will take longer to dry even if we are spared rain. Wet hay is a waste at best and a fire hazard more usually. We'd spend your coin for nothing." His tone implied that wasted coin figured between mortal sins and public outrages on the scale of human wrongdoing.

"The risk of rain is true of haying in any season, and the days aren't that much shorter. I say we cut this pasture now."

Singleton sighed. He glanced heavenward as if praying for divine intervention. He even sought visual fortification from the mill wheel, turning as mill wheels were wont to do regardless of who was on the throne.

"My lord, I tell you, we lack the laborers. Having hay to sell is wonderful, but having corn to feed the livestock and grind into flour is a necessity. Besides, that grass won't make the same quality hay we'd have earlier in the season."

Cam did not intend to lose this negotiation. The grass was tall, luxurious, and in want of scything. "The hay will be good enough to sell at the end of a long winter."

Singleton's smile was pitying. "You have yet to tell me who shall cut it."

Lorne Hall was swarming with able bodies. "The gardeners are mostly idle this time of year. Their flower and vegetable beds are thoroughly weeded and will bloom and bear for at least another month, possibly two. The footmen have half days when they might enjoy earning some spare coin, as do the maids."

Women had typically joined scything crews in Cam's youth. Surely that hadn't changed?

"I'll grant you the gardeners have some feeling for the land, but maids and footmen? Does my lord expect sheep to fly as well?"

St. Didier had been right in at least one regard. The time had come to retire the old guard, not for lack of skill or knowledge, not even for lack of respect.

Singleton had lost his passion for the work, his eagerness to do not just a good job, but a better, smarter, more efficient job than he'd done the previous year.

"I'll join the crew myself," Cam said, "and we'll divide the proceeds resulting from the sale of the hay. If you're right, I'll be cutting that field all on my own. If you're wrong, we'll have some tired indoor staff and gardeners, but their labor will be rewarded."

Singleton's smile had faded to puzzlement. "Unless it rains, my lord. Unless it rains, and what is more inevitable than rain in Merry Olde?" He nudged his beast down the track that ran along the millstream, and Cam let him have the last word.

Rain was inevitable, but so was a shortage of hay at the end of winter.

Cam sent his horse after the steward's. "I'd like to see where the crews are scything today, if you don't mind."

Another huffy sigh. "Very well, my lord, but it's simply a lot of folk swinging blades, whetting and peening blades, and singing the occasional song. This late in the morning, the singing will have stopped. We mustn't interrupt the crew at its labors, though."

"Because there's a rhythm to their work?"

The sigh became a scowl. "In point of fact, there is. A literal rhythm, like a dance, with each foot moving at a precise tempo in a defined direction. I will not tolerate mockery, even from you, my lord."

"Alice said an excess of punch would leave you irritable."

"Alice should show more respect for her elders. I am merely explaining to you that the wheat does not harvest itself."

"You should have more respect for that summer punch. I wielded a scythe myself, if you'll recall. I'd thought at one point to take over your job. The old baron let me work myself to flinders for two summers before informing me that younger sons joined the military or the clergy. The post at St. Wilfrid's being occupied at the time by my uncle, I was advised to take up arms against the French."

"And that's how you came to fight Old Boney?"

"I mostly marched, drank, and fought my own temper. I also learned Spanish and improved my German, French, and Italian. After a couple years, I found things to do in civilian life that didn't involve killing or being killed." Not one letter from Papa for the entire two years, but then, Cam had limited his own correspondence to Alexander and a few friends from university. "We should replace the mill wheel with an overshot model."

"One suspected you would embark on that campaign. Undershot wheels are quieter."

"They are significantly less powerful too."

"You'd have to remodel the whole mill, my lord, and that is an expensive undertaking."

"We'd have to raise the water level in the millpond, and that's fairly simple, given the inevitability of rain you keep going on about."

They bickered and spatted and did not disturb the scything crew. Singleton declared the need for a midday meal and more or less herded Cam back toward the manor. Across the field, a gig tooled along the lane, two bonneted figures on the bench.

"Who's with Alice?" Cam asked.

"How do you know that's Alice?"

"Good eyesight, but also, Alice's posture with the ribbons is exceptionally good."

"Got that from her grandmama. She and Lady Josephine have been out making charitable calls. They have a weekly routine, and the plagues of antiquity will descend upon the fellow who disturbs their appointed rounds."

An unlikely pairing, in Cam's estimation. Both imposing ladies, but not cut from the same cloth.

"Lady Josephine favors Alice's company?" Because the reverse simply could not be true.

"When Alice arrived here as a bereaved adolescent abruptly cast into her old grandpapa's rural household, Lady Josephine exerted herself to make Alice's adjustment smoother. Alice has not forgotten that kindness."

"Lady Josephine would not allow her to forget it."

For once, the old man did not argue.

As the horses ambled back into the stable yard, Cam mentally reviewed a list, starting with the impromptu harvest of an additional five acres of hay, continuing on to replacement of the mill wheel, and including myriad smaller projects that would doubtless give Singleton apoplexies.

"How long was Alexander ill?" Cam asked before they were within earshot of the grooms.

"Too long. He'd rally and hare off to Town, then come home a wreck. Such a young man and so desperately ill. If I am a bit presumptuous about the execution of my duties, sir, it's because your brother entrusted management of the estate to me, and I take my responsibilities seriously."

"Would you say Alexander was ill even ten years ago?"

"Not so long ago as all that, but certainly five years ago he was failing, and here I am, living out my threescore and ten in roaring good form."

"And for all those years of service," Cam said, "I do thank you. Alexander would thank you, too, I'm sure, and I do recall that his will left you with a pension, which you are free to start claiming at any time."

Singleton sat very straight in the saddle. "My lord is kind and generous, but I could not think of abandoning my post in the midst of harvest."

"I am not asking you to, but I want you to know that I will honor my obligations to you and to the rest of the senior staff. You've looked after the Hall and after my brother when I could not."

Singleton halted his horse and climbed down onto a mounting block and then descended to terra firma.

"Your thanks are noted, my lord." He waved a hand, and a groom trotted out of the stable to take the reins of the old bay.

"You're Burnside?" Cam asked, swinging to the ground.

"Peter Burnside, my lord."

"You put me on a safe, sane horse, and I appreciate that, but if we have a saddle horse up to my weight who is also occasionally awake on the job, I'd appreciate that too."

Burnside grinned. "Aye, milord. I'll see what can be arranged."

Singleton was off down the path that led to the steward's cottage, a snug little dwelling just inside the embrace of the home wood. His gait was uneven and none too swift.

"Burnside, if I offered the footmen, gardeners, maids, and grooms an extra day's pay to scythe some late hay, would they hold me in contempt or take the coin?"

Burnside was in the comfortable years between having to prove his competence and having to prove his continued capability. He busied himself running up stirrups and loosening girths for a moment, then considered Cam's somnolent mount.

"Might do both, milord. Take your coin and call you daft. It's mighty late to be making hay."

"It's never the right time to waste an opportunity." If commerce had taught Cam one lesson, it was that.

"Shall I saddle you an afternoon mount now, my lord, or will you be having some luncheon first?"

Luncheon. Singleton had been maundering on about his nooning and empty stomachs making empty heads.

The sun was past the zenith and then some. "I suppose I'll have a bite to eat. Would not want the kitchen to feel insulted."

Cam had reached the edge of the stable yard when he added another task to the appallingly long list already forming in his mind.

Alice was off making charitable calls with Aunt Josephine. Upon whom and why was Alice taking on that responsibility? Aunt

Josephine could have recruited any one of her baronesses-in-waiting, but she and Alice went calling together.

Commerce had also taught Cam to heed his instincts, and that her ladyship *could* dragoon Alice into a regular weekly round of calls made Cam mildly uneasy.

CHAPTER FIVE

"I'll do that." Alice closed the library door behind her, set her basket of medicinals on the sideboard, and advanced on the baron. He sat at the library desk, a massive article of carved oak that probably hadn't been moved since Good Queen Bess had been in leading strings. Papers, inkpot, pen tray, and abacus covered the blotter. Stacks of mail three inches high sat on each side of the wax jack.

"I can open my own correspondence." His lordship nonetheless put down the letter opener he'd been awkwardly wielding and rose. "You're the estate's herb lady?"

"Not exactly. Let me see your hand. Mr. Beaglemore was most concerned on your behalf."

His lordship brandished the requested appendage. "Not very pretty."

More bruise than hand, and a livid, purpling bruise too. The fingernails weren't involved, though. "This is Gooseberry's work? That horse has had other victims."

"I was wearing gloves, fortunately. The skin isn't broken." His lordship tried to flex his swollen digits and made a poor effort. "I blame myself. Burnside warned me. Said the horse has many fine qualities—which is true—but is prone to nibbling."

Alice retrieved her basket. "You're lucky to still have all your fingers. The beast is a menace."

"I was distracted. I doubt Gooseberry will attempt similar mischief upon my person in the future."

"Good. Somebody needs to put the manners on him. Have a seat. This won't take long."

The baron propped his considerable length against the desk and folded his arms. The result was an exquisitely tailored riding jacket stretching over shoulders Apollo himself would have envied, and nobody was sitting.

"Would my lord *please* have a seat?"

"Since you *ask* so nicely, of course." He ambled to the reading table and planted himself at the head. "I wasn't aware that modern medicine offered much treatment for plain old bruises."

"If that is a plain old bruise, then Lorne Hall is a pleasant little cottage. You should keep that hand elevated and wrapped in ice."

In the depths of the basket, Alice found a blue bottle with a cork. She took that and some squares of clean linen to the table and sat to his lordship's right.

"Your hand... Might I please have your hand, sir?"

He surrendered his abused paw with an air of complete indifference, but Alice was angry on his behalf. The dratted horse had no manners, but then, the previous baron hadn't bought Gooseberry for his manners. He'd bought him for endless stamina, bravery over fences, and good bloodlines, and then promptly neglected him.

"This is arnica," Alice said, uncorking the bottle. "It isn't supposed to sting, but I have seldom seen so nasty a bruise." The discoloration described a large U enveloping the back of his lordship's hand, the knuckle of the index finger, and the middle of the remaining fingers. The shape of a horse's mouth, in other words.

Alice wet a cloth and applied it to the bruising. "You should probably be soaking the whole hand in a tincture of arnica. Bilberry can work as well."

"I do not have time to sit about soaking a hand that will heal eventually on its own."

She dabbed gently at purple flesh. "What on earth does a peer of the realm have to do that is more important than recovering the use of his hand? Arnica helps ease the pain *and* the swelling, and white willow bark tea can help with both as well. Goes down a bit easier with honey."

His lordship gazed around the library, an airy, high-ceilinged space housing a few thousand books, a half-dozen landscapes, three large hearths, and some comfortable furniture. Grandpapa's whole cottage would likely fit inside his lordship's library, with room to spare.

"I have little notion what occupies a peer of the realm," Alice's patient said. "Before the title was imposed on me, I was happily absorbed with an enterprise that trades on six continents. We're barely getting started with the Antipodes, but the potential for brisk business there is obvious."

"Trade in what?" Alice cared little which variety of commerce interested his lordship, but while he maundered on about his mercantile affairs, he wasn't grousing about his hand.

"Anything at first. When I was in the army, the old hands from India—who all claimed to have served under Wellington in every battle His Grace fought there—were of the opinion that Spain was a lovely place to wage a war, compared to India. Spain has a good supply of Peruvian bark, which can work wonders with intermittent fevers. I shipped some Peruvian bark to India and made a tidy sum."

Alice slipped one hand beneath his lordship's and bathed each finger in arnica. "Are you still shipping Peruvian bark to India?"

"When I can find a supply at a reasonable price. Willow bark tea is also in demand. The local Indian flora provides comparable and even better remedies, but the English officers and their wives want their English treatments."

"Thus you pay somebody to sail all that way, bringing coals to Newcastle, so to speak?" His hands were works of masculine art. Powerful, elegant, in proportion with the rest of him. A white scar marred the right set of knuckles, but even that was in keeping with the whole man.

"I don't pay anybody to sail my goods. I figured out ten years ago that having a valuable product is only half the game. Controlling the means to direct that product to its best market is the other half."

He said this without a hint of pride.

"You own *ships*?"

"I own three outright and shares in several others. Are you disappointed? One cannot be more thoroughly ensconced in trade than I am, and for the most part, I enjoy it."

Alice was still more or less holding his hand. She gave his knuckles a final, gentle dab and slipped her fingers free.

"But for trade, England would be bankrupt and starving," she said. "I never did grasp why polite society values idle wealth over honest labor of any kind."

He flexed his hand, winced, and flexed it again. "I can assure you, Alice, that amassing what sums I command was anything but an idle undertaking. I should not have frittered away the entire morning trotting around with your grandfather, then absented myself again for half the afternoon."

Alice collected her supplies and returned them to the basket. "If you tell Grandpapa he was frittering away his time today, he will plant you a facer."

The baron rose, smiling crookedly. "I can work with an aching jaw. This,"—he waved his hand at her—"means I will fall further behind than ever. The king's mail waits for no man. I like my work. It has meaning, it accomplishes good, and I do well with it. Keeping up with my correspondence is more than a duty, it is a necessity."

His scowl said he positively detested falling behind. To lag in his work annoyed him the way a champion racehorse was annoyed by competition at his heels.

"I can send you the underbutler," Alice said, edging toward the door. "Truckle is studious by nature and good with figures."

The scowl became a considering frown focused directly on Alice. "Truckle cannot write to my managers and applaud this one's initiative while scolding that one for sloth or carelessness. What I need..."

Alice felt a distinct sympathy for the chubby mouse espied by a hungry cat. "I'll just be going. Ice and elevation will work wonders." She extracted the blue bottle from her basket. "Bathe the hand with this every two hours. I can bring more—"

"Might you not stay for a while?" He gestured toward the letters. "As a sort of amanuensis? I'm sure you could draft suitable responses with a little guidance."

Now he turned up all polite and deferential, the varmint. "I ought to be getting home."

"Truckle will require word-for-word dictation, and in the time he and I get through three letters, you and I could plow through both stacks."

The task was simple, one Alice had been doing for her grandfather for years. As steward to a large estate, his correspondence was considerable. His penmanship, by contrast, was awful. He'd scrawl a few margin notes—*price acceptable, but delivery must be within fifteen days*, or, *no need for additional shearers this year, perhaps next*—and Alice would draft a reply for Grandpapa's signature.

She had handled Lady Josephine's correspondence when her ladyship so chose as well.

But she really must be on her way. "I can do a few. Select the more important matters and explain the replies you want."

"And you'll charge me for services rendered?"

The question was surprising and arguably insulting. "I will not, though I understand you meant no offense by asking."

"I mean to acknowledge that your time is valuable, and I have no right to it. If you won't accept coin, then at some point, you will name a favor I can do for you. Agreed?"

Put like that... "Agreed." Alice's time *was* valuable, though that seemed to be a minority opinion. Then too, his lordship's instinct for a fair bargain was a different matter entirely from implying that Alice was in service to the household.

"The favor I ask is that you sip willow bark tea, elevate your hand, and apply a cold compress for ten minutes every hour until supper."

He opened his mouth as if to argue, then closed it. "Done. We'll start with my sluggard of a French factor. I assume your French is passable?"

"Rusty—I spent only a year at finishing school—but sufficient for written purposes. My accent is atrocious."

"The French claim every English speaker has an atrocious accent. Have a seat. Ring for that vile medicinal tea and those other items you mentioned."

Alice let him get away with giving that order—she had agreed for a limited time to do as he asked, and she wanted him swilling the tea as soon as may be.

His lordship held up his end of the bargain. Two cups of willow bark tea, his hand slightly elevated on a stack of books and wrapped in a cold compress from time to time. All the while, he worked, choosing his words carefully for both brevity and impact. His French was confident and practical. His praises were sincere, his criticisms to the point and professional.

Reports were to be submitted timely. Tallies were to be accurate. Extenuating circumstances merited lenience. Flimsy excuses earned a blunt warning.

Alice penned the appropriate missives, and all the while, she was aware of the sound of Camden Huxley's voice. The depth and slight rasp that hadn't characterized the youthful version of the Lorne spare. In the quiet of the library, he created a steady discourse that spoke of expertise, focus, and commitment.

The clock ticked, the willow bark tea disappeared, the stacks of correspondence became stacks of sanded, sealed replies.

Alice ought to have gone home an hour ago.

"We have spun the straw into gold," the baron said, unwrapping his hand from the latest cold compress. "Might I have that dry towel?"

Alice fired the clean linen at his chest. "Stop flexing that hand. It might be worse tomorrow, and the day after, it will look truly horrendous, but the pain and swelling should have abated."

He gently dried his hand. "Patience is not my forte."

"If you could send your Peruvian bark to India and wait for the proceeds to come back to you, you are capable of great patience. I suspect it's taking orders that you cannot abide."

He tossed the towel onto the reading table. "A failing we share, apparently, though I am willing to take reasonable orders. Too often in the army, the orders were unreasonable. Fly across the countryside like all the demons of hell pursued us one day, wait about the next, only to be told to race back the way we'd come. Commerce is ever so much more sensible than war."

Other men preferred the racing about, the belief that their racing was heroic, however pointless in the moment.

"I'll leave you to contemplate Gooseberry's fate." Alice straightened up her side of the desk, then rose to tidy the blotter as well. "Can you hold a knife and fork, or will you take a tray of sandwiches and soup for supper?"

"Gooseberry is not a bad horse. He's nippy, and when he realized he'd chomped rather more than he bargained for, he knew he'd been bad."

"The lads likely feed him treats by hand, and that should stop," Alice said, locating her medicinals on the sideboard. "He should be fed only from his bucket, and his nipping merits firm reprimands."

"Would you like to take him on?"

Oh, to have a sizable, brave mount with the athleticism to hop an occasional stile, and the stamina for a whole day of visiting the tenants.

But what would Lady Josephine say about Alice making such a spectacle of herself? "I could improve Gooseberry's manners, and then he would be well behaved for me, but the lads would still have to teach him to be good for them. Thank you for the thought, though. Look after your hand, my lord, and I will send more arnica to Mrs. Shorer tomorrow."

He came around the desk, arms once again folded. "Might you bring it yourself?"

A tempting idea and, like all tempting notions, to be nipped in the bud. "I'll be quite busy tomorrow. Grandpapa has correspondence that I assist with, and Lady Josephine will expect me to attend her knitting circle."

A penance of an obligation. Nobody willing to share any truly interesting gossip, needles dutifully clicking for an eternal hour, and Lady Josephine selecting the dullest bit of some improving tome to inflict on her captives. The burden of reading that drivel aloud was often imposed on Alice, another well-intended cruelty on Lady Josephine's part.

"Lady Josephine can struggle along without you for one day, but I have nobody else to rely on. You have the knack for the business letter, Alice, and I mean that as a compliment."

Genuine compliments were few and far between in Alice's life, but she must not relent. "Lady Josephine expects me to attend, and I am loath to disappoint her."

"One sympathizes. My entire boyhood I did nothing but, though if her ladyship is so focused on Christian virtues and doing unto others, would she not advise you to assist me in my hour of need?"

This was teasing, or wheedling, or perhaps—from Camden Huxley—negotiating.

Alice knew a thing or two about negotiating. "You will donate a quantity of good-quality yarn to her ladyship's knitting projects."

He nodded. "Done and done. A quantity of good-quality yarn in sensible colors. Not too fancy—I suspect you ladies are knitting socks and caps and scarves and the like—but soft and durable. I know just the supplier, and you may inform her ladyship that my donation will arrive within four weeks."

Surely her ladyship would forgive a single absence when the prize earned was so great?

Even as Alice mentally posed the question, she already knew the answer. Lady Josephine would appreciate the donation and manage to be disappointed in Alice's assistance to the baron too. A lady must not put herself forward. A lady must not accept compensation for charitable undertakings. A lady must keep to her place, lest she lose the reputation that was her most precious and fragile asset.

"I'll see you tomorrow, then," the baron said, tugging the bell-pull. "Let's say around noon. You have been an inestimable help today, Alice. The whole household is in your debt, whether they know it or not. By the way, what were you and Lady Josephine doing out and about this morning?"

The instinct to prevaricate was as imperative as it was unbecoming. "We call in Farnes Crossing for charitable purposes only. Nothing of any moment, but her ladyship observes that weekly duty unless the weather is exceptionally inclement. She takes her role in the community seriously."

"What isn't taken seriously in these surrounds? Your grandpapa defends the honor of the mill wheel as if modernization were akin to moral decay. That I'd invite footmen to wield a scythe is tantamount to treason, and making hay at harvest a violation of the commandments."

Jumping Jerusalem. "Grandpapa would hear that as closer to blasphemy." Though the mill was a relic, and the footmen would be glad of a day in the fresh air. Rather late in the year for making hay, though. "Until tomorrow, my lord."

"I'll look forward to it."

For her part, Alice regarded the next day's commitment with a frisson of dread. The baron bowed her through the door, a footman materialized to carry her basket, of all the inanities, and she was soon making her way across the back terrace.

"I must develop a megrim," she muttered, having dismissed the footman at the back door. "A slight head cold. Even Lady Josephine gets megrims and head colds from time to time." Usually when Squire Huffnagel's aunt-by-marriage, Lady Euphrenia Wolling-Banner, was visiting her nephew. Lady Eu's brother was a marquess.

Maybe a megrim *and* a head cold?

The previous baron—Alexander—had been charming, intelligent, a hopeless flirt, and easily ignored. He was what Society had expected him to be, a mostly fribbling sort whose appreciation for his privileges was abstract and a little disingenuous. He'd known wealth and privilege his entire life. He expected to be treated with deference, albeit he'd been gracious about it even when he'd become quite ill.

The present baron, though... *He worked.* He chose his words with precision and intent, nothing careless about him. Problems most people would consider minor—a late report, a tally off by sixpence—merited his whole focus. He tended to stacks of mail despite a throbbing hand. He set the example he expected his employees to live up to, even when those employees were two hundred miles distant.

Those qualities in somebody who could have become the idle peer intrigued Alice, and she well knew where imprudent curiosity about a man could lead her.

～

For the first time in memory, Cam wished the day's correspondence were more voluminous, and not only because answering mail made him feel less banished from his life's purpose.

"We've been at this for an hour," he said when Alice finished the mild rebuke due to Cam's solicitors for failing to make every change he'd requested in a draft contract. "Might we break for a meal?"

In the normal course, he would have nibbled from a tray, if such a tray had appeared. Alice struck him as one who actually sat a table, consumed her food there, and probably conversed with her grandfather throughout.

"If you're hungry, you should eat," she said, sanding the page. "I can return later, though we haven't much more to do."

A pity, that. Cam wasn't keen on fine art and poetry, but he did enjoy the sight of Alice wielding a quill pen, her brows knit in concentration, her hand moving with confident grace over the page. He still disapproved of the damned snood.

"I'm not famished," Cam said, "but I'm learning that the kitchen expects me to eat regularly and well. I told them I'd take my nooning on the back terrace and to set the table for two."

That announcement earned him a scowl, though he was coming to enjoy even Alice's scowls. She could scowl thoughtfully, disapprovingly, severely, or in passing.

"Dining alone with you will create awkwardness for me, my lord. I appreciate the generosity of spirit, but you are a peer, and I am nobody."

Nobodys did not briskly correct peers in the ordinary course. "Ne'er the twain should share a tray of sandwiches? Alice, you decry the snobbery of a Society that values idle wealth over everyday gumption, but you disdain to break bread with me."

They were in rural Yorkshire, for pity's sake, not Mayfair, and a midday meal on the terrace was hardly a clandestine tryst. More to the point, she was Alice Singleton. Who in the entire shire would suspect her of putting on any airs, much less airs above her supposed station?

Alice sat up very tall. "I will visit in the kitchen while you enjoy your meal, sir. I can return to the library in, say, an hour?"

He liked watching her write, he enjoyed her turn of phrase on the page, and he seemed to be developing a taste for her negotiations.

"Very well, Alice, consign me to a solitary meal. Leave me to the pitying glances of every domestic gawping out a window, when I could instead be seeking your counsel about that dratted Gooseberry. I vow he looked penitent when I went down to the stable this morning."

Alice directed a considering glance at Cam's abused hand. "What were you doing in the stable?"

"Conferring with the stable master. You are right that the horse is a menace, and had I not been wearing gloves, I might be missing some fingers."

The scowl became thunderous. "Or *worse*."

"Or worse, hence the need to teach the beast better behavior. Burnside says you do well with difficult creatures."

"I've had some success with ailing or injured dogs and cats, but that's mostly Grandpapa's expertise combined with Mrs. Shorer's herbal remedies."

"About Mrs. Shorer..." Tiny, aging Mrs. Shorer, who had no designated understudy. "Why isn't she in charge of tending to the minor ailments here at the Hall? Why bother you to see to my hand?"

"Your hand needed seeing to."

That was an opening. "Alice, I am all at sea here. In his final months, Alexander had no interest in acquainting me with my prospective duties. Only a ghoulish younger brother would have asked him for assistance as he lay dying. If I seek Lady Josephine's guidance on the smallest matter, she will invade like ivy climbing a southern wall. She's planning an invasion anyway, but taking my measure first. I cannot manage the Hall, much less manage it from London, without a firm grasp of who is on my staff and where their capabilities lie."

"From London?" Two words, but they had a satisfyingly plaintive ring.

"My business is in London. My life is in London. That cannot change just because a brother I'd seen little of in the past ten years finally went to his reward."

"London is so far away." Alice organized the newspapers on the reading table, then rose and dumped the quill shavings in the pen tray into the dustbin. "You cannot move your business here?"

Novel thought. "Not easily. Have lunch with me, and I'll explain why." He knew she was tempted. She wanted to see the horse put to rights, of that much he was sure. "Deny me the next hour of your time because of what the staff might think, and I will call you a hypocrite."

Such a look she gave him. Brooding, disapproving, considering, and ever so slightly relenting, like the silver lining shining about a thundercloud.

"We will discuss your business over sandwiches and soup. It is my charitable duty to aid your transition into your new role, and the less said about returning to London, the better."

Victory. Cam knew better than to gloat. "You may tell Lady Josephine that none of my correspondence from Town is personal. She'll want to know that."

Alice winced. "She will, and that is certainly none of my business—or hers."

"Placate her with a few crumbs, and she's less likely to snack on my peace or invade my citadel. Let's eat, shall we?"

Having put on a show of reluctance, Alice nonetheless consumed a hearty meal and asked insightful questions about the business. When a tray of pears and cheeses was brought out, Cam wandered back around to the delicate topic of his senior staff.

"Why are you wielding the medicinals, Alice?" Why was she Aunt Josephine's preferred familiar? Why was she the veterinarian recommended by the stable master?

Why wasn't she married?

"Mrs. Shorer's eyesight isn't what it used to be. Grandpapa pointed out that she doesn't write her recipes down. I started asking her about her herbal so her wisdom might be recorded."

Cam's hand was painful, but it wasn't throbbing. Much. "Isn't that something for the under-housekeeper to take on?"

"The under-housekeeper found other employment in a household to the south. She was not very well lettered in any case, and it's a short step from writing down Mrs. Shorer's remedies to following her directions for their use. The pears this year are marvelous."

The sight of Alice savoring a pear was marvelous. That Cam

would entertain such a thought must be the invidious influence of fresh Yorkshire air, a painfully bright blue sky, and a breeze that bore the scents of green grass and scythed wheat.

"You stepped into Mrs. Shorer's shoes by default?"

"Grandpapa calls it stealing a march on the enemy. Some of Mrs. Shorer's remedies are nearly as unpleasant as the ailments they purport to treat, as Grandpapa has learned firsthand."

"Others are quite effective, as I can attest. What else occupies your time?"

Alice finished munching her pear. "A bit of this and that. Shall we get back to work?"

"In a moment. Tell me of Beaglemore. He's moving slowly, and St. Didier says colder weather will result in worse symptoms of rheumatism."

Alice patted her lips with a table napkin. "The problem is as much stubbornness as sore joints. If Mr. Beaglemore would keep a proper fire in his bedroom and allow himself some willow bark tea or ginger tea or even a drop of the poppy, he would be plenty comfortable."

Said with some asperity, meaning Alice's efforts to offer relief had been rebuffed.

"He doesn't want the footmen thinking he's wasting coal, in other words, and he doesn't want the maids delivering him trays of ginger tea at the end of the day. They will all say he's getting on."

"He most assuredly is getting on," Alice observed, "but he needn't be getting on in such pain. One thing I will say for your brother, he willingly availed himself of relief from pain or fatigue. He accepted what care we could offer."

This was news. "You did duty in Alexander's sickroom?" Did every responsibility at the Hall fall upon Alice Singleton's sturdy shoulders?

"I sat with him from time to time. He liked me to read to him. Novels, plays, anything light and humorous. He became self-conscious of his appearance and spent more time in his apartment toward the end. If you've felt guilty for not coming to see him, forgive yourself. He did not want to be seen."

"He wrote to me to that effect." And yet, Alice's words brought some comfort. "I thought I ought to come see him anyway, but a man should be taken at his word."

"In this case, yes." She helped herself to another slice of pear. "He also asked that Lady Josephine be kept from the Hall to the greatest extent possible. He found her hovering ghoulish, to use your word. Bernard told Lady Josephine to let the man die in peace, and she did, for the most part."

"While she counted his silver and the porcelain?"

Alice nodded. "Alexander didn't care about that, as long as she didn't inflict... As long as she didn't interfere with his privacy."

Alexander? "Alice, were you in love with my brother?" Was that why Alice hadn't married? She pined for the charming, wealthy, witty, tragically declining baron?

She shook her head. "I liked him. I suppose we were friends of a sort. We were not in love, and you will never ask such an impertinent question again. I will meet you in the library."

She rose, taking a slice of pear with her and leaving Cam to enjoy the lovely day in solitude.

Or as close to solitude as could be had when half the curtains on the first floor were still twitching, and a procession of three different footmen had found it imperative to bring a single dish to the table or take one away.

Worse than a lot of junior clerks.

Cam put the remaining pear and cheese slices on a plate and followed Alice into the house. She hadn't been in love with Alexander, but Cam would bet his next shipment of Peruvian bark she was, or had been, in love with somebody.

And Peruvian bark was worth a *great* deal.

CHAPTER SIX

Alice finished her ablutions, retied her snood, and made her way back toward the library, ignoring the questioning looks from the footmen.

No wonder the baron did so well at trade. He gloried in every aspect of it, from knowing the seasonal shifts in ocean currents to keeping track of which clerk had an ailing mother. His business was his passion, almost like a composer who became enthralled with the creation of a great symphony.

In the context of mercantile activities, his voracious curiosity and restless mind were assets.

They were positively bothersome when aimed at Alice's past.

The library door was open, *of course*. Alice stopped in the corridor, consulted the watch on her sleeve, and made a silent vow that she would decamp in one hour. The day's mail was light, and she was developing an instinct for how to fashion a reply consistent with the baron's preferred tone.

"You are displeased," Alice said upon returning to the library. The baron's expression was nigh thunderous.

"The ruddy blighter is quitting. I cannot believe..." He rose from the desk and paced along the tall windows. "That varlet. That unreliable, ungrateful, unimaginative... He'll be back, but of all the times to jump ship. And he knows that. He's doing this when I'm stuck up here in Yorkshire, and nobody's stopping him."

The baron had turned his back on Alice, and what a fine view of manhood in its prime that was. "Who has given notice, sir?"

"The person I have trained, educated, and supported for five years, whom I have entrusted for the past two years with overseeing North American trade, our most lucrative market... Profanity falls short of the mark, Alice. I'd like to see him blackballed from his clubs, turned out of his house, and left with only the coins in his pocket, which is where he'd be if I hadn't spotted his potential."

Ah, betrayal wrapped in abandonment. A very serious hurt. "You want revenge."

He sent a fulminating glance over his shoulder. "Do you blame me?"

"Certainly not." Alice took the seat behind the desk and picked up a quill pen. "I suspect the best revenge is simply to wish him well. Send him your hearty congratulations on having secured an exciting new post. Promise to keep him in mind if an opportunity to benefit him professionally comes along. I trust he took up with a competitor?"

"Of course, and for what he claims is more pay. I paid him what he was worth and turned a blind eye when he went running home to his wife three times a day."

"Coin of the realm is not the only valuable compensation. If this fellow has less responsibility and less authority to act independently, he will not last long at his post, no matter how lucrative. If he's henpecked at home, then his business acumen will mean a great deal to him."

The baron turned as Alice began sharpening his pens. "You do have a point. Worth Kettering hovers over his clerks like a cat with one kitten. I can't imagine a new factor will be permitted much initiative, not that Armendink has much initiative."

"Who is Worth Kettering?"

"A man of business, in every sense of the term. We sometimes cooperate for mutual gain. Kettering married recently. Perhaps he's looking to step back from trade. Found an earl's daughter to take him on. Armendink will have to toe the mark."

London gossip was no doubt part and parcel of London trade, but Alice found it tiresome. Who had just married whom two hundred miles to the south did not interest her in the least.

"Oddly enough, Kettering is an earl's younger son," his lordship went on. "In trade and enjoying every minute of it. When I first mustered out, I found significant consolation in Kettering's example."

At least he'd found consolation in something. "Make Armendink miss his old job," Alice said. "Cite all the projects you had hoped to delegate to him, but now cannot. Mention how you'd enjoy having his opinion on this or that prospect, then dismiss the topic. Make him wish his new employer trusted him with as much responsibility as the previous one did after five years."

The baron stalked to the desk and took the chair opposite. "You have a diabolical streak, Alice Singleton. This is a singularly attractive quality and profoundly useful in a commercial context. I will do as you say. Let's draft a reply for our Mr. Armendink, shall we?"

The baron favored hearty good wishes, while Alice advocated a touch of wistful regret.

"'What a shame you won't be on hand to help us name the next ship,'" Alice said. "That sort of thing."

"You want me to take a leaf from Aunt Josephine's book?" Dark brows rose. "Half my boyhood was that woman lamenting my shortcomings. 'Such a pity little Camden isn't very bright.' 'What a shame Camden struggles so with figures.' 'A very great mercy that Camden is the younger son, considering how little talent he has for witty conversation. A peer must be charming, after all.'"

"Oh dear. You struggled with figures?" The reading table boasted no less than six open ledgers, and a seventh sat on the desk before Alice. "One cannot credit that."

"I have never struggled with figures, unless I admit that looking away from them is often difficult. I was several years younger than Alexander and Bernard, and thus my grasp of mathematics lagged behind theirs. Little Cam grew up, and his ability with numbers has improved significantly."

A toothy smile accompanied that observation.

"I can vouch for little Cam's brightness," Alice said, wanting to take her parasol to Lady Josephine Huxley. In some sideways version of caring, Alice might deserve her ladyship's criticisms. Young Camden Huxley should never have suffered such insults. "Little Camden has grown perceptive and shrewd. He is quite the man of the world and more than equal to a peer's responsibilities."

"Perceptive and shrewd? Alice, you will put me to the blush."

"I am stating the obvious."

"Stating it a bit fiercely."

The smile in his lordship's eyes said he was pleased with her defense of him, though his joy was a subtle, sweet thing to behold. He radiated secret satisfaction, and Alice's soul answered with reciprocal happiness.

"Bad of me," she said, "but the notion that Lady Josephine was so very, very wrong is gratifying. She meant well, I'm sure, but—"

"Stop. You needn't print a retraction in *The Times*. My aunt is a disappointed woman and cannot reconcile herself to a situation most ladies would delight in. She was nasty to me as a boy. I can only imagine what Bernard has had to put up with from her."

Bernard, among *many* others. "She wants him to become a bishop. You will be expected to assist in making her ambitions a reality."

The baron crossed his legs at the knee, which a gentleman ought not to do in polite company. On him, the posture was relaxed and sophisticated. He folded his arms as well, putting Alice in mind of a castle garrison raising the drawbridge and manning the arrow slits.

"Does Bernard want to be a bishop?" he asked.

"Put the question to him. I do believe he wants to be free of his mother's hovering, but she refuses to use the Yorkshire town house."

"I'd banish her to the London property, except that I bide in London, and she would make my life merry hell."

Alice considered the very sharp point on her quill pen. "You could alternate. You spend spring and fall up here, send Lady Josephine to Town for those seasons." Was it lovelier to contemplate Lady Josephine's absence or the baron's presence?

Dangerous question.

"I suspect," his lordship said, "Aunt Josephine cannot afford Town, which means I am safe there from her meddling. I will query Bernard regarding his ecclesiastical ambitions. I have no sort of pull with the archbishops, but I do occasionally have some spare coin."

Little Camden had also acquired a grasp of irony, apparently. "Coin works well at securing heavenly favor, I'm told."

"Then Bishop Bernard will have to be patient. My means at present are mostly tied up in inventory. Later in the year, I should be quite flush, but as the cycle of revenue and expenses stands now, it's the vicarage for Cousin Bernie."

"You are honestly pockets to let?" Alice ventured a question she would not have considered even a day ago.

"No. I am personally solvent and then some, but the business is a trifle overextended. It gets that way from time to time, then products sell, ships journey to lucrative destinations, and the next season's inventory can be procured. We manage a cycle of having either plenty of inventory or plenty of cash, but seldom both in abundance. All of commerce operates on a similar pattern."

Alice did not like the sound of this pattern, but at least his lordship was personally secure. "Have we more letters to write?"

We. The slip was forgivable, given that the baron had just been freely discussing his finances with her.

"Only one." He passed her a sealed missive. "That's from my Irish factor. The news is neither terrible nor joyous."

Alice slit the seal with a letter opener. "How can you tell?"

"His penmanship varies with his mood, or perhaps with his

consumption of spirits. The man is utterly reliable, though, and knows the linen trade like Gooseberry understands green grass."

"You buy Irish linen?" Prized for its quality, especially for summer bedding.

"I grow Irish flax, or I do unless the weather is disastrous, and I have my flax turned into linen. What does he say?"

Alice scanned a short, tidy epistle. "Harvest will be adequate if the weather holds, though a bit late. Some time might be made up in the retting and hackling, but weavers will likely be unavailable by the time the fibers are ready for spinning, owing to earlier crops absorbing capacity."

"Meaning we won't be first to market with this year's batch." The baron steepled his fingers and tapped them against his lips. "Tell him... tell him to secure weaving capacity now with small deposits paid directly to the women. He is not to pass the coin to the menfolk, who are likely to drink the unforeseen bounty or squander it at the cockfights. The women will reserve capacity for us in exchange for some coin. Tell him to send additional dispatches as needed, much appreciation for his hard work. Regards to his dear Brigid. Cordially, Camden Huxley."

"Cordially, Lorne," Alice said, penciling notes on the margin of the epistle. "Tidy up your ledgers. This won't take but a moment."

They apparently had moved past the need to spat over requests and imperatives. The baron saw to his ledgers and stacked them one-handedly on the side of the desk.

"I don't suppose you have any interest in seeing London?" he asked as Alice penned regards to the factor's lady.

"None. I am content here in Yorkshire." Not exactly true.

"I wanted to see the whole world when I was younger." His lordship began a prowling circuit of the library. "A few years in uniform sufficed to quell that urge. You never want to leave here? Never want to see Paris?"

Of course Alice wanted to see Paris, and Edinburgh, and Hyde

Park, and the baron's London establishments. "My current surrounds are beautiful. I am fortunate to dwell here." Two true statements.

Alice lifted her pen and surveyed a neat little missive. "Have you no wish to remain at your boyhood home?"

He wandered to the atlas and peered at whatever map it was opened to. "None."

A single, simple, honest syllable that disappointed Alice inordinately. His lordship wasn't even protesting too much. He was merely stating reality.

"Lorne Hall is lovely in its way," he went on, turning a page, "but I was made to feel like a guest here pretty much from birth, an uninvited guest. Alexander was as good a brother to me as he could have been. When my father bought my colors, it was Alex who wrote to me, Alex who admonished me to take care. I miss him, but I have never, ever missed this place."

"Perhaps you'll miss it when next you leave," Alice said a bit too brightly. "You can sign this one, and I believe we're through. Let me see your hand."

He came over to the desk and held out an appendage still discolored, but the purple was already beginning to fade, and the yellow wasn't so ghastly. The swelling had abated entirely.

"You heeded my advice."

He tucked both hands behind his back. "I am not so foolish as to disdain your wisdom, Alice Singleton. Will you miss me when I return to London?"

Alice was not so foolish as to mistake that for a simple, teasing inquiry. His curiosity had been piqued, and Camden Huxley's—*Lord Lorne's*—curiosity was formidable.

All the same, he'd gallop back to Town, to his countinghouse, to his disloyal clerks and Peruvian bark, and never think of her again.

Temper goaded Alice to imprudence. "I will miss you very much. I believe you are sufficiently recovered from Gooseberry's bad behavior to manage without me. Good day, my lord."

She rose, curtseyed, and departed, and was half running by the time she'd cleared the terrace steps.

Not until she'd returned to the cottage to find Grandpapa asleep in his chair by the hearth did she realize she'd forgotten her dratted shawl in the dratted library where she must never, ever again be alone with the dratted baron—even with the double-drat-dratted door open.

∽

"Dinky has deserted his post," Cam said. "I lift my glass to the freedom of bachelorhood. The poor fellow was doubtless goaded into rash measures by that wife of his. She is acquisitive by nature, and Dinky would do anything to keep her in gloves and bonnets."

St. Didier shifted in his wing chair. "Perhaps Mrs. Armendink is increasing. One views the future differently when bringing children into it."

"As one damned well should." Cam sipped his brandy and tried not to envy Armendink, who stood six feet tall in his stockings. True, Dinky was smitten with his wife, and Mrs. Dinky regarded her dear Dink-Dink as the zenith of masculine perfection. She gushed so profusely over every flower and token Dinky brought her that it was a wonder they ever got round to the procreating part of the business.

St. Didier visually consulted the clock ticking over the sideboard. "You are thinking of your pickpockets."

"They aren't pickpockets any longer. They are junior clerks."

St. Didier tasted his drink, though how did he make even that mundane activity look elegant?

"They are clerks," he said, "but they never sit at a desk for longer than thirty minutes. You send them haring all over London like your personal arsenal of pigeons. You set them to watching the docks and Doctors' Commons, to sentry duty outside Carlton House, and to the very trees of Hyde Park. Oddest sort of clerking I've seen."

"Boys like to climb trees and lurk and spy, and they are good at it." *I miss them* almost slipped out on a brandy-fueled impulse toward sentimentality. "I lied to Alice today. To Miss Singleton."

"She probably sensed the falsehood. I would not be too concerned that you've deceived her."

For all his elegance, St. Didier could be a dunce. "I did not advise her to buy the wrong reticule, St. Didier. I told her I did not miss Yorkshire. I half lied." And Cam did not entirely understand his own motivations.

"Then you half told the truth, I suppose."

"You are an utter failure at wheedling confidences, St. Didier." And somebody had drunk Cam's whole serving of Alexander's good brandy.

"Perhaps you need to work harder at sharing them. How does this prevarication trouble you?"

Cam got up and helped himself to another half serving. St. Didier shook his head when offered more.

"I told Alice I never missed my boyhood home—Miss Singleton, rather—and that was only technically true. I do not miss Lorne Hall as a dwelling. I have no fond memories of hiding behind bannisters to eavesdrop on the adults, no favorite hiding places where nobody ever found me. I was delighted to go off to public school and spent every holiday with a school chum rather than return to the Hall."

"It's a house," St. Didier replied. "When I admit to missing my family's former seat, I am not expressing a longing simply to return to that rather drafty edifice."

Cam considered his meager drink by the light of the fire in the library's main hearth. "The Hall itself could go up in flames tomorrow, and provided no lives were lost or injury suffered, I would honestly be relieved. Damned place is impossible to heat. But this little corner of Yorkshire...?"

"Quite lovely, I agree."

"Heartbreakingly lovely, incomparably lovely. The light here in any season, the roll and majesty of the land. The beautiful vistas in spring, summer, and fall, the uncompromising bleakness of the winters... The people who can weather anything and relish the challenge. I worked very hard not to sound like a Yorkshireman when I went off to public school, but I hear the accent now, and..."

"And?"

"I am,"—Cam spoke softly—"homesick. Homesick for the beauty and even the bleakness, for the feel of the place. As a youth, I could not leave Lorne Hall fast enough or often enough, but now... I understand why Alexander chose to end his days here rather than amid the blandishments and conveniences of Town. This little piece of creation nourishes the spirit."

"Do you miss London as well?"

The honest answer was no. Summer, winter, and every season in between, the metropolis stank. London was increasingly filled with people who could find no work, no housing, no means to keep body and soul together.

London was also full of matchmakers, peers, and politicians. Who on earth would choose London?

"I am not homesick for Town, though I am concerned for my business affairs. Besides, the boys would hate it here."

"The boys who love to climb trees and roam and spy and lurk. They'd be miserable, I quite agree."

"Not subtle, St. Didier. My business is in Town, and from every appearance, the Hall will run like clockwork with or without a baron in residence."

St. Didier finished his drink. "Clocks invariably need winding. How's the hand?"

"Looks ghastly and is quite tender, but I can hold a pen." Carefully. "I don't suppose you need another horse? The fellow who did this to me isn't a bad sort, but he wants consistent handling and a real job."

St. Didier toed off his boots and put his feet up on the leather hassock before his wing chair. "Do you see every wayward creature as an orphaned boy in need of shelter and support?"

Alice Singleton was not a boy, and she was the furthest thing from wayward, but Cam worried about her needs for shelter and support.

"Why isn't Alice Singleton married, St. Didier?"

St. Didier crossed stockinged feet and settled lower in his chair. "Why does the sun rise in the east? Is your mind never idle? She's a formidable woman without substantial means. Perhaps she prefers the unwed state to risking her life in childbed every two years. Perhaps she prefers to be a human being in the eyes of the law, rather than some husband's chattel. Perhaps she has been unlucky in love."

"That was my thought. She's reached the sadder and wiser phase of the proceedings." Much sadder, though she hid it well. "She said she wasn't in love with Alexander."

St. Didier sighed. "You did not ask her. Please, my lord, say you did not."

"She could have inspired him to marry her, and then she'd have been the widowed baroness, but she didn't make the effort. She said they were friends. Why be friends when you can be baron and baroness? It's not as if Alex would have importuned her for conjugal favors."

This puzzle had a compelling quality. Alice needed marrying. An aging grandfather was all that stood between her and destitution. She was sensible, kind if a bit tart, shrewd, and pretty when she didn't truss her hair up in its little woolen corset thingum.

Gorgeous, in fact. The local bachelors were blind and...

"She pushes men away." Cam cast his mind back to Aunt Josephine's buffet, when he'd watched one fellow after another try to strike up a conversation with Alice. She knew them, and she knew how to manage them, because the exchanges she'd permitted had been exceedingly brief.

"Shame upon you," St. Didier said. "You are speculating on the personal motivations of a lady who deserves both privacy and your respect. I am off to seek my slumbers before you make a complete cake of yourself."

"I cannot make a complete cake of myself in the short time we'll be here. With Dinky's departure, I am needed in Town. I also received word today that my Irish flax will be late to harvest, and I am likely to miss the advantages of being early to market."

"Why not hold back until all the best linen is bought up and then be the very last of the high-quality goods available?"

"I've done exactly that in some years, but this year finds my enterprises hungry for cash. I have been trying to ever so gradually increase the volume of goods we ship, which means I take a prudent degree of risk every time I acquire my inventories. I buy a little more than I can afford and typically make a little more profit as well."

"You're in the window between the buying and the profiting. An uncomfortable place to be."

"I should be used to it by now. Expanding the business requires taking the occasional risk, and for the most part, my risks have resulted in reward."

St. Didier took his feet off the hassock. "Why expand? Why not keep what you have, content yourself with whatever wealth results. You aren't a greedy man."

That was the sort of question Armendink used to ask. Simple enough on the surface.

"I enjoy the bustle and hum of business. I relish the wins and see the losses as inspiration for further wins. Failed experiments, not failures. I'm good at commerce, and I make a gift of that admission to any who'd insult me by it." Not quite an answer to St. Didier's question.

Other motivations applied too. The boys had to eat, they needed to be taught useful skills, and when the present lot gained their feet, others were just as deserving of a chance.

St. Didier rose, stretched, and pulled on his boots. "You excel at commerce, but methinks you need to spend more time roaming the countryside and perching in trees while you still can. Will you rent Lorne Hall out to some obliging banker who longs to boast of his country retreat?"

The mere suggestion sparked a peculiar sense of indignation. "No, that is... It's too soon to make that decision."

"Right. I'll bid you good night and leave you with a suggestion."

Cam rose as well. Would not do to be found dozing by the ashes when the footmen came in at dawn to clean the hearth.

"You have my undivided attention, St. Didier." The part of Cam's attention that wasn't still dwelling on Alice Singleton's unwed state, anyway.

"Leave Miss Singleton in peace. You have spent two days closeted with her in the library, and that has been noted. Her reputation cannot recover from even the mildest bruise in these rural surrounds, and you treat her carelessly at your peril."

St. Didier was no prude and not exactly a high stickler, though he was personally circumspect.

"You'd call me out for accepting some assistance with correspondence?" The library door had been open the entire time, and on both occasions, Alice had been at the Hall for a handful of hours. Though, in truth, Cam had asked for that assistance.

"If you misstep with Miss Singleton, I shall have a long and pleasant chat with Worth Kettering and others of his ilk. You would suffer the consequences of your ill judgment for at least the next five years." St. Didier paused to yawn behind his hand. "Don't stay up too late. I suspect you have plans to ride out on that demon horse who tried to snack on your bones. One wonders if the beast has suffered a tummy ache for his bit of mischief."

Cam did not know whether to be amused or appalled at St. Didier's threat. "Good night, St. Didier. And you need not fear for Miss Singleton's reputation. She's been deflecting bothersome bachelors for years, and she would make short work of me as well."

"Relieved to hear it, but nonetheless, my lord, you *will* behave yourself."

Cam bowed rather than stick out his tongue. St. Didier was only offering a reminder of what honor required. "As will you."

St. Didier nodded and left on silent feet.

Cam considered the wing chair, considered the hour, and considered that dawn was mere hours away. He left his unfinished drink for a footman to enjoy and took himself up to bed.

St. Didier knew something or suspected something regarding Alice Singleton's circumstances, something that explained her curious situation. Cam made up his mind to keep his eyes and ears open where the lady was concerned.

He was returning to London, and he had no business prying, but if she needed assistance, if she needed an ally, he was prepared to offer what aid he could.

Though perhaps all she needed was a friend. Cam was perplexed to admit that even that role appealed to him, though not as strongly as some others he could name.

CHAPTER SEVEN

"Alice, my dear." Lady Josephine adopted the long-suffering, faintly pitying expression Alice loathed. "Of course you meant well. I would never imply otherwise. A fellow creature is wounded and in need of assistance. You are capable of providing that assistance. The generous and compassionate impulse itself is laudable."

Now comes the but. Alice focused on the ticking of the vicarage parlor's mantel clock. Lady Josephine's *buts* were always delivered in gently chiding tones and with the loftiest of stated intentions. They could go on interminably because Lady Josephine had the knack of blending a small portion of truth with a very large helping of innuendo, opinion, and Scripture.

"But, Alice, you of all women, *of all women*, must be mindful of how you are perceived in local Society. Your grandpapa will not live forever, and then what is to become of you? Lorne Hall's new steward will need the use of that cottage. You have no family to take you in, poor thing. I daresay you lack independent means, and you aren't getting any younger."

Her ladyship took a dainty sip of tea and shook her head minutely. "My dear, my very, very dear Alice, you cannot risk the only asset you have left, the most important asset any lady has—her good name."

My good name is not my only remaining asset. Tick, tick, tick. Next would come her ladyship's current favorite mangled quote.

"Scripture tells us," Lady Josephine went on, "that nothing is so delicate as the reputation of a woman. It is at once the most beautiful and most brittle of all human things, and in your case, it is also the sum total of your worldly possessions."

Mrs. Burney would be surprised to learn she had joined the exclusive company of the evangelists.

"I do apologize," Alice said, "for causing you any concern, but the baron requested my assistance, and we were at no time private while I served as his amanuensis."

Lady Josephine sighed again, closed her eyes again, and shook her head yet again. "That is the conundrum, isn't it? You had to remain in plain view—I'm told his lordship even expected you to join him on the terrace for a meal—and thus the entire household saw you reduced to the role of an unpaid clerk. The only thing worse would have been if his lordship had passed you coin while the housemaids gawked from the windows."

So many retorts begged to be shot into Lady Josephine's hot-air balloon of judgment and condescension.

I could use a bit of coin but didn't have the nerve to admit as much.

Are you implying the maids become somehow fallen because their hard work is rewarded with wages?

So the library door should have been closed for hours on end?

"I was caught in a quandary, your ladyship is quite right. The baron's request surprised me, and his injury is considerable. He needs a secretary."

"Of course he does, but in the absence of such a fellow on the premises, you should have sent for me. I have quite a tidy hand. You know I pride myself on maintaining a voluminous correspondence with my connections in the church. I am the baron's aunt, and my assistance would have provoked no discussion among the gossips."

The gossips would have started placing bets instead of merely gabbling. His lordship's imperiled sanity would have figured prominently in the wagering. More to the point, Alice handled most of her ladyship's voluminous correspondence, and her ladyship had the penmanship of a fidgety schoolgirl.

"Ma'am, you are entirely correct, and I can only plead a lack of imagination on my part. That you would serve as his lordship's clerk simply did not occur to me."

"If you want for imagination, that's just as well. A fanciful woman pleases nobody. Another half cup, if you please."

Agreement in principle did not necessarily signal an end to the lecture. Her ladyship was capable of second, third, and fourth winds.

Alice obliged with the teapot nonetheless. Alice was in the habit of obliging Lady Josephine, but the impulse to refuse, to rebut, to rebel had lately become unbearably tempting.

Alice's hostess sipped her libation plain, sugar and milk being extravagances, according to her ladyship. Alice had it on the authority of the vicarage cook that her ladyship swilled sweetened tea liberally laced with cream when consuming her drink in private.

"Now, then, Alice, let's consider your options, shall we?"

Oh, not this again. "If your ladyship would like to."

"You can go into service. A tragedy, when you enjoy the nominal standing of a lady. Your father was a headmaster, and we must admit that qualified him as a gentleman of sorts. At least according to some. You could become the housekeeper for the next steward, assuming he's unmarried. A housekeeper must fill her hours with labor, her wages are modest, and her time is not her own."

Lady Josephine peered over her tea cup at Alice. To miss the weekly knitting meetings would be no hardship, but Lady Josephine's innuendo pointed in another direction.

"I am happy to work for an honest wage if need be," Alice said, which was nothing less than the truth, "but to have an employer commanding my every waking hour would be... onerous." Heartbreaking, really, given Lady Josephine's portentous looks and ruthless streak.

"Precisely. Every waking hour. You would lose your gentlewoman's standing, no matter that all and sundry would sympathize with your loss of station, but one must be realistic. You know how to keep house. The work is honest. Not an ideal resolution to your dilemma, though. We are agreed."

What precisely is my dilemma? Alice had never asked Lady Josephine, though the situation/dilemma/circumstances received regular allusions from her ladyship.

"Which takes us to the logical, realistic, and readily obtained alternative of marriage. Do not wince, my dear. Do not retort that age has rendered you unsuitable for the office. You are not yet thirty."

Not yet six-and-twenty.

"Once dear, darling Davina brings the baron up to scratch, matrimony will be in the air, and autumn weddings are quite the thing. If you put your mind to it and exerted yourself to be agreeable, I'm sure Blessington Peabody would offer for you. He's fundamentally lazy, and you are to hand. A bit of blunt speaking, for which I do apologize, but he's also quite the catch by local standards."

He was quite the prig, too, and he'd be more tyrannical about Alice's free time and independent pursuits than any employer.

"Ma'am, I do not wish to marry."

"What woman does? Oh, I know there are the so-called love matches, but infatuation fades, and then one is still quite married and wishing a bit of infidelity on the husband's part would come along to lighten the wifely load, so to speak. More blunt speaking, only because I am so very worried about you, Alice, and you are not without experience of the world. You nonetheless have no mama to guide you, your grandpapa has one foot in the grave, not a penny to your name. I positively fret about you."

I have seventy-six pounds, six shillings, four pence, thank you very much. Alice's life savings consisted of a small inheritance from a maternal grandmother augmented by pennies saved from the pin money Grandpapa had doled out over the years.

"You are kind to worry, ma'am, but I wish you wouldn't. Are you truly convinced that Davina Halbertson will suit the baron better than Dorothea Considine?"

"Alice, you are changing the subject, which is naughty of you."

Alice had been trying to be polite. "One does wonder how Dorothea would take having to address Davina as 'your ladyship.'"

"The humiliation would do that one good. I know my nephew, and Camden is not possessed of a particularly penetrating mind. His perceptions extend no further than the nearest ledger or shipping schedule. The poor dear hasn't the mental nimbleness to keep a restless creature like Dorothea from making all in her ambit unhappy. Cam will bring sweet little Davina the occasional bouquet and think himself quite doting. So will she, and all will be well."

"Do you expect them to bide at Lorne Hall?"

Lady Josephine considered her cooling tea. "At the Hall? Goodness me, Alice. A peer attends the social whirl in Town, and a responsible peer votes his seat. At least Camden has some familiarity with London Society. We might see some of him when the shooting season comes around. Davina will have her hands full parting him from his commercial pastimes, though. I will abet her in that necessary undertaking to the fullest possible extent."

Camden Huxley's interest in trade was a passion, not a pastime.

"Perhaps I could succeed Mrs. Shorer as housekeeper at the Hall," Alice said, though she had no intention of doing so. Lady Josephine would object at length, though, and then Alice, after being suitably instructed, chastened, corrected, harangued, and pitied, could be on her way.

"Alice Singleton, if you are jesting about succeeding Mrs. Shorer, I must protest the nature of your humor. A household of that size is no mere cottage to be kept up between morning prayers and tea. Lorne Hall is a great monument to history and tradition, an edifice of immense consequence. You are neither capable nor experienced enough to undertake such a post."

Her ladyship galloped on, citing noble households brought to the tragedy of creeping damp by incompetent housekeeping. She railed against the hubris that gave rise to even speculation that Alice might aspire to such responsibility and leaped forth to conclude that if the baron left such a one as Alice in charge of his family seat, then the man had surely taken leave of his modest senses.

She knows. Alice hunched meekly over her tea cup and listened with growing dismay to a genteel tirade. Somehow, Lady Josephine had divined what Alice herself had only reluctantly admitted: Alice had *enjoyed* those hours talking business with Camden Huxley. She respected his expertise, his commitment to his enterprise. She liked that he didn't take himself too seriously, though he took his obligations very seriously indeed.

The word Alice had spent half the night avoiding was *respect.* She respected Camden Huxley, in part because he had respected her first. Not her fine figure, her hair, or her complexion—her.

Her mind, her capability, her temper, her judgment. Camden Huxley, by his words and deeds, had made it plain that he respected Alice, and she was helpless not to find that aspect of him attractive.

The less said about his shoulders, his voice, his subdued smile… All very lovely, but so was the way he looked Alice in the eye, paused before he fashioned replies to her arguments, and laughed when she caught him out in convenient illogic. Why had his hand healed so very swiftly?

"Alice, are you attending me?"

"Every word, ma'am. Your guidance is most appreciated."

"Then you will exert yourself to charm Mr. Peabody?"

Heaven forbid. "I will be as charming to him as I know how to be, though my best efforts might never bring his sisters around."

"Once you are his wife, you will be in line to become the female authority in the household. The Misses Peabody will understand their places."

Lady Josephine would delight in assuring that result, though Alice had no intention of encouraging Bless Peabody's affections.

"Ma'am, look at the hour! I really must be going, though I do so appreciate moments spent with you. I would love to stay a bit longer, but Grandpapa is very particular about mealtimes, and his temper has been rather short lately, what with all the extra effort of harvest."

Alice rose, dipped a curtsey, and took the first of the twenty steps that separated the parlor from the front door.

"Be off, then, if you must," Lady Josephine said, waving a hand. "Give the bell-pull a tug while you're on your feet, and I will see you at services on Sunday."

Eighteen, seventeen, sixteen... Alice was at the parlor door when Lady Josephine's voice stopped her.

"By the way, Alice, I have arranged with Mrs. Dumfries for the girls to use Tuesday morning for an outing. You may consider yourself excused from your usual duties in Farnes Crossing. I know you will appreciate a few more hours to yourself, particularly when your grandpapa is in one of his more difficult moods. Don't thank me, my dear. Even the Almighty permitted Himself a respite from the labors of creation."

She beamed placidly from her well-cushioned sofa, and never had Alice felt such an impulse to do another human being an injury.

"My regards to Mrs. Dumfries and the children, then, your ladyship. I will put that time to good use. Until Sunday." Alice saw herself out as a maid hurried past with a fresh tea tray.

By sheer force of self-discipline, Alice traveled the path that led behind the vicarage, past the glebe acreage, and onto Lorne Hall land. The harvest crews had already taken the wheat off the glebe fields, and from there, the path wound through Lorne Hall's home wood.

The way was beautiful, bathed in waning afternoon sunshine, saturated with the peace unique to a late-summer day. Alice's path was also devoid of other travelers, which was convenient when a lady needed to cry most of the way home and then some.

"His lordship's head is buried in his ledgers even as he has one foot out the door," Mrs. Shorer said. "Beagle tells me that the daily correspondence from London could fill a bookstall."

Thaddeus Singleton kept up with the small woman at his side, though it took effort. "This is no business of ours, madam. You meddle with the young people at your peril." Hadn't Vicar just half an hour past preached a sermon on 'blessed are the meek'? Or maybe that was last week.

"If you sit back and do nothing, Thaddeus Singleton, Alice will be left with nothing. You've turned her into your drudge. The brightest, most thoughtful, prettiest young lady in these surrounds, and she spends her days waiting on you hand and foot."

Thaddeus wasn't quite sure how Alice spent much of her days. "She waits on Lady Josephine nearly as much. Deprive her ladyship of Alice's companionship, and we will all suffer for it." Thaddeus was also not quite sure how her ladyship would exact retribution. Good Christian soul that she was, Lady Josephine would never burden the Almighty with exacting vengeance. She'd tend to that task herself.

"The baron and our Alice laugh when they're together, Thaddeus. He has a nice laugh, and he makes Alice sparkle."

"Alice does not sparkle. Next, you'll be claiming that he puts roses in her cheeks and stars in her eyes. We'll be having none of that, Eunice Shorer." The blasted woman was tireless, while Thaddeus was nearly puffing with exertion.

"Nature herself put the roses in our Alice's cheeks, you dunderhead. Though I vow, when the poor girl came back from her year of finishing school, I feared she'd turned consumptive."

"Madam, I remind you that the Sabbath is a day of rest, not a day to go sprinting across half of Yorkshire. Moderate your pace, if you please, and Alice was at finishing school for two years, thanks exclusively to Lady Josephine's generosity."

Mrs. Shorer glowered up at him, which always put Thaddeus in mind of a displeased pantry mouser. A small creature exuding sheer disdain wrapped in regal indifference.

"Thaddeus, we are not long for this earth. What will become of Alice when you go to your reward?"

The question troubled Thaddeus, when he wasn't troubled by the water level in the millpond, the slow progress of the harvest crews, the baron's outlandish plan to make autumn hay, and the pervasive aching of joints no longer happy to spend hours in the saddle.

"Alice will manage. Alice always manages. She excels at managing." Thank the heavenly powers somebody was inclined to manage Lady Josephine, else the shire would have no peace.

"The most brilliant female on the planet cannot manage without coin, sir. Alice yet claims the status of lady, and if we don't do something, that conniving Considine harpy will snatch the baron right out from under Alice's nose, with Lady Josephine applauding loudly."

Alice claimed the good, proud Singleton nose. Everybody could see that. "Eunice, I am in great good health, and Alice will inherit all I have to give her."

Finally, the dratted woman paused at the stile between the home wood and the mares' pasture. She wasn't remotely out of breath.

"And how much do you have to leave her, Thaddeus? Three hundred pounds? Four hundred? You like your brandy and pipe tobacco, you indulge your taste for good fashion, and you have a fine collection of books and pamphlets. I don't begrudge any man some creature comforts, but a young woman cannot live for the rest of her long life on four hundred pounds. *Alice must marry*, and before you and I are no longer on hand to see the thing done properly. Do you want Priggy Peabody for a grandson-in-law?"

Bless Peabody was slated to come into some good land. He ought to be draining more, though, because he hadn't enough grazing for how many sheep he was running. Sheep could be harbingers of destruction if improperly husbanded.

"He's not a bad person, Eunice, just because he's somewhat high in the instep. Young people today aren't as open-minded as we were."

Eunice hopped up the steps and down the other side as nimbly as a nanny goat.

"Bless is not a bad person, but he'd be a penance of a husband, to say nothing of what his sisters would contribute to Alice's misery. Thaddeus, I'm telling you, we must give nature a helping hand here. The baron is smitten with Alice, and that confirms my opinion that Camden was always a sensible boy. The old baron agreed with me, but one could not get him to admit it."

That much was true. "You doubtless did not allow Baron Leland the privilege of a word in edgewise, and Baron Alexander fared even worse. You will not meddle, Eunice. Promise me."

Off she went across the mares' pasture, the horses pausing in their placid munching, doubtless to wonder at such energy on a summer Sabbath morning. Eunice Shorer put Thaddeus in mind of a comet streaking across the heavens, leaving all who beheld her dumbstruck at her sheer momentum.

"I promise you," she retorted, "that I shall do all in my power to see our Alice and Baron Cam happy. You don't want her to go off to London and take her place in Society, and that is shameful of you, Thaddeus. I thought better of you."

Nobody could deliver a scold like Eunice Shorer. Lady Josephine overshot the mark with sighs, biblical allusions, and buckets of disappointment. Eunice fired off a flaming arrow of outrage and went about her business.

"Alice would hate London." London would love Alice, though. She was smart, sensible, kind, quietly beautiful and not vain with it. Cam had always been Thaddeus's favorite of the three boys.

"You don't know how Alice would fare in Town," Mrs. Shorer retorted. "You would hate coming home to an empty house, nobody to grouse to, nobody to ask you how the work is coming along and if the Bladens have finally come up with some rent."

Truth be known, Thaddeus had come up with the coin more than once to keep the Bladens on their little farm. Good people, but they needed time for their boys to grow up enough to help out. Each year, they did a little better and were less dependent on Alice's baskets.

Alice herself approved of Thaddeus's little rent-abatement maneuvers, though whenever he surrendered his own coin to the Bladens' cause, he felt guilty for slighting Alice's inheritance.

"I would miss Alice, true, but I managed on my own quite well before she was thrust upon me, and I'll manage should she accept Bless Peabody's offer." Though, really, Bless Peabody was no prize, and he would not improve with age.

Camden Huxley, on the other hand...

"Thrust upon you? You claim Alice was *thrust upon you?* Thaddeus, your memory is deserting you. She rescued you from a lonely and cantankerous old age, sees that you have proper meals, a tidy house, and clean clothing. She preserves you from premature senility and relieves you of inflicting your miserable handwriting on half the merchants in the shire, *or* driving Lorne Hall into debt with your indolent attitude toward the ledgers."

All true. When had the mare's field become such a wide expanse? "Eunice, you are in fine form today. One must ask if some sort of brain fever stalks you?"

Her steps mercifully slowed. "A brain fever. Now there's a notion. I am not in fine form, Thaddeus. I am worried."

She stopped and gazed at the majestic edifice rising up across the ornamental lake. Lorne Hall showed well from this perspective, though not as well as from the curving main drive.

Alice was worth more than ten Lorne Halls and lacked the sense to appreciate her own value. That was the trouble with her. Thaddeus's granddaughter did not appreciate her own value, and that was no sort of legacy to bequeath to her.

Eunice Shorer, on the other hand, spent her days scrubbing and polishing and conducted herself with more dignity than any queen. Always had.

"You do not appear worried, Eunice. You appear to be deeply

absorbed with the process of plotting mayhem. I beg you, don't do anything stupid. The baron will hare off back to London, taking his uppish friend with him, and we will be left to deal with Lady Josephine and her endless displeasures. Step carefully."

Lady Josephine, a new mill wheel and mill design, a lot of footmen thinking themselves experts on the land because they'd spent a day or two wielding a scythe, and Alice in Lady Josephine's bad books.

Though Eunice had a point, as usual. The baron might not go haring off to London without having chosen a baroness.

"I quite like Mr. St. Didier," Eunice said. "He's proper without being stuffy. So few bachelors can manage that balance." She emphasized this opinion by brushing Thaddeus with a passing scowl.

"I was a widower, not a bachelor."

"And forty years on, you still miss your first wife." Eunice wrapped her fingers around Thaddeus's forearm as she continued her progress. "I still miss my Harold, though sometimes I forget what he looked like."

"Janette always smelled of honeysuckle, and she…"

"Yes?"

"Made me laugh."

Eunice did not hoot out an I-told-you-so. Thaddeus did not shake his arm free. Instead, they shared the sort of old soldier's smile that was not for airing before witnesses.

"I will be careful," Eunice said. "You mind you get enough sleep and don't neglect your tucker, old man. Harvest is no time to go spare with yourself."

"Yes, ma'am." He endured her surreptitious half squeeze and bowed to her retreating form as she marched across the pasture. Only when she'd passed through the gate and onto the main drive did Thaddeus turn his steps back toward the home wood and his own abode.

Janette would have liked Eunice Shorer, and Thaddeus well

knew that he would have heartily enjoyed the company of Eunice's long-departed Harold.

Ah well. Time for a nap, because the Sabbath was good for that, as well as for a weekly scolding from one of the finest, most contrary women Thaddeus had the pleasure to know.

CHAPTER EIGHT

"Mrs. Shorer claims the ankle doesn't hurt much." Alice tipped up the abacus on the windowsill, making all the beads slide to one side. "In truth, I can't see much bruising or swelling. More puffiness than bruising, really, but if Eunice Shorer admits to discomfort of any sort, the situation is to be taken seriously."

"When did this happen?" Cam asked, more than a little alarmed. Mrs. Shorer had been ancient in his youth, and a twisted ankle might lame her for life. He did not return to his desk, because he was in the presence of a lady. Also because one wanted to be on his feet when Alice was prowling about the library.

"She took a tumble this morning after divine services." Alice bustled along, straightening books on the shelves, tidying the newspapers on the reading table. "She and Grandpapa usually walk home from services together, doubtless airing differences they don't want the rest of the congregation to hear. Grandpapa had parted from her in the mares' pasture—Mrs. Shorer does not permit him to escort her all the way to the Hall—when she lost her footing. I gather finishing the journey to the Hall was poorly advised, but Mrs. Shorer is not one to sit about in the grass, waiting for aid."

"Will she be mortified if I peek in on her?"

Alice looked up from rattling newspapers. "Of course, but a small dose of mortification can work wonders on one recovering from an injury."

Alice was so pretty, in her staid, reserved way, and capable of conveying such mischief with just a gleam in her eyes. The snood was still an affront to fashion, feminine pulchritude, and nature, but it was *Alice's* snood.

Though Cam wasn't fooled by it. He propped his hips against the desk and folded his arms.

"This turned ankle is bad news for Mrs. Shorer, Alice, but I'm sure her iron constitution will soon rally. It's a disaster for me."

"For you?" Alice snapped the last of the newspapers open and folded it neatly atop the stack. "How so? The staff will continue cosseting you and Mr. St. Didier within an inch of your lives, hoping desperately to persuade you to put off your return to London. Mrs. Shorer will command her underlings from her bed, and you will hardly know she's laid up for a bit."

"She needs to be resting, not commanding a performance from the wings, and after this morning's ordeal in the churchyard, I am tempted to slip away to London under tonight's waning moon."

Alice became absorbed with pleating a burgundy velvet curtain hanging in perfectly symmetric folds to the left of a tall window.

"What ordeal?"

Cam eyed the open door and decided a few reporters belowstairs might be a good thing. "Lady Josephine all but insisted that I escort Miss Halbertson to dine at the vicarage, and when Dorothea Considine just happened to overhear that salvo, she attached herself to my arm like a long-lost poor relation. Miss Dingle was bound by the rules of matrimonial combat to seize my other arm, and Hercules facing the Mares of Diomedes could not have felt a greater sense of peril."

Alice peered at him over her shoulder. "The ladies don't want to eat you up."

"Yes, my dear, they do. They want to seize me, take me captive, deny me the commercial pursuits I enjoy, and fence me into the venerable institution of wedlock—emphasis on the *lock*—all on their dubious terms. Lady Josephine appears to abet Miss Halbertson's chances, but she'd in truth support any one of them who could bring me up to scratch."

"Davina Halbertson is perfectly sweet and sensible. She's just a trifle timid." Alice started on the second curtain, which also hung perfectly straight.

"Miss Halbertson would be the proverbial soft clay in Lady Josephine's hands, and I would know no peace. London, Yorkshire, the Antipodes, no place would I be safe from my aunt's generous guidance of my wife, and that's why you must drop in over the next few days to ensure Mrs. Shorer is recovering as swiftly as possible."

A fine plan. Simple, practical, logical even.

"But, my lord, that will not be necessary. Mrs. Shorer herself knows more about injuries and illnesses than I can ever hope to learn, and all her situation wants is rest."

Of course Alice would resist an application of irrefutable logic. "You said yourself that Mrs. Shorer is ancient. She is also stoic, and if she says her ankle pains her, then she's likely in agony. One modest dose of the poppy, and as small as she is, she'll sleep the day away, and what do you think her staff will do?"

"Dust? Polish? Sweep?"

"The weather is beautiful, the household has recently endured months of mourning. If the martinet overseeing your labors took an extended nap, would you resist temptation?"

Alice straightened, and some shadow passed through her eyes. "The maids are not a lot of schoolgirls who can't wait for their holiday."

"When is the last time they had a holiday?"

"Beltane, I suppose."

"Months ago. If Lady Josephine should stop by and see dust on the foyer windowsills, I will be besieged."

"My lord, you will be besieged in any case. You've accepted an invitation to dine at the vicarage. It's well known that your visit to the Hall will be brief, and Lady Josephine has already seen to it that you've hosted your neighbors here at the Hall. You are now honor-bound to make reciprocal calls upon your guests. You escaped the Sunday roast at the Halbertsons only because Mrs. Halbertson hasn't had sufficient time to order delicacies from York."

The situation was worse even than Cam had suspected. "I did not, as it happens, accept an invitation to dine at the vicarage." He pushed himself away from the desk, took Alice by the wrist, and led her to the wing chairs by the empty hearth.

She came without protest, no doubt keeping her powder dry.

"Let's sit, shall we?" Cam suggested, gesturing to a chair.

Alice perched on the edge of the cushion. "I really should be going. Grandpapa likes his Sunday meal rather early."

"Singleton is either enjoying a pipe on the porch or snoring over an agricultural pamphlet in his study." Cam sat, though Alice hadn't given him explicit permission to do so. He took that as progress of a sort.

"Your grandfather," Cam went on, "is an adult and capable of holding off starvation for twenty minutes or so here and there. Please say you'll look in on Mrs. Shorer and have a word with Cook and the maids when you do."

Alice looked around the room. "Mr. Beaglemore might be the better resource, my lord."

"Beaglemore would sooner expire of mortification than tell female staff what to do. Cook doesn't venture out of her domain, and Mrs. Shorer has no assistant. I no longer even know most of the maids by name, Alice, and yet, somebody must keep order in the ranks for the next few days. If Lady Josephine senses an opportunity, she will move into the baroness's suite, and a trebuchet would be insufficient to dislodge her."

Ah, a hint of a smile, possibly at the image of Lady Josephine being launched over the gateposts like a load of rocks hurled from a catapult.

"Not the baroness's suite," Alice said. "She would never be that presuming."

The hell she wouldn't. "She's an earl's daughter. The baroness's suite is the least she'd feel entitled to. If you won't have a word with the staff, then have a word with me."

Alice shifted back, and it occurred to Cam that his guest was tired. Today was the Sabbath, the ordained day of rest, and Alice looked short of sleep. Why?

"I cannot be seen to intrude here at the Hall, sir. Bad enough I served as your clerk for two days. Your aunt was wroth with me because I did not summon her to support you in your hour of need. She will take a very dim view of my usurping Mrs. Shorer's authority. That would be putting myself forward."

Cam knew the impulse to curse. Simple logic was a two-edged sword. "But if Josephine puts herself forward, that's Christian charity toward a dim-witted nephew?"

Another gleam in Alice's eyes. "According to her ladyship, your perceptions are limited to ledgers and shipping schedules. She does not call you dim-witted."

Alice drummed her nails on the arm of the chair while Cam waited, because as surely as storms rose in the North Atlantic, Alice Singleton had more to say.

"I shall be blunt, my lord. I am a lady, according to your aunt Josephine, because my father was nominally a gentleman, and my grandfather qualifies as the same by only the most lenient definition of the term. Papa did not and Grandpapa does not labor with his hands."

"Why do I feel there's a but in the offing?"

"With Lady Josephine, the buts and nevertheleses and notwithstandings abound. *But* I have no means, I am beyond the first blush of youth, and between impending penury and my own foolishness, I am staring destitute spinsterhood in the face. Grandpapa will leave me a little something, but only a little. Lady Josephine is concerned that I safeguard the good name I enjoy and avoid a descent into the lower orders, such as, say, by becoming a housekeeper myself."

Cam considered what Alice had said, what she'd omitted, what she'd delicately implied.

"Whom does she want you to marry?"

"Blessington Peabody, at present, though she'd accept any one of several others on my behalf. If Lady Josephine could see me married to Mr. Peabody, her fears for me would be quieted."

An odd progression of sensations assailed Cam. Heat, queasiness, a sinking in the gut... He recognized these discomforts as the physical manifestation of a perception of injustice, of *wrongness*. He'd felt it before, when he'd seen a chimney sweep terrorizing a small boy unwilling to go up a hot flue.

The small boy was a few inches taller now. The sweep was no longer employed in the metropolis.

"Alice, I would not allow you to dwell in penury. Out of respect for your grandfather and respect for you, I will see a sum settled upon you such that you can tell Lady Josephine to go to perdition if you want to." What could be simpler?

Alice blinked. She swallowed. She stared at him, then at her hands. "That is very sweet of you, sir. Very kind, but I do not want your pity."

"Then give the money away to your favorite charity, provided it's not St. Wilfrid's church. I would excuse Lady Josephine's infernal meddling if she had no means herself. One could reason she was attempting to be useful, trying to be appreciated, and was simply bad at it. She has ample wealth, but that's not enough for her. She must have power in addition, and thus she plays skittles with the little misses' marital aspirations.

"She has apparently done her bit to inflict misery on you too," Cam went on, "and she doesn't quibble at playing God with the lives of local bachelors. Well, in your case, I can thwart her mischief, and I wish you'd allow me to. If nothing else, you might find a way to use the money to preserve other people from Josephine's pious cruelties."

Alice peered at him, her brows knit. "You really don't care for your aunt, do you?"

The boot had long since been on the other foot. "Alice, who would be the baron now, if it weren't for my humble existence?"

"Ah. Interesting point. Alexander was never all that robust, was he?"

"Born early, according to my uncle, and sickly as an infant. I am not sickly."

Alice gifted him with a slow, warm sunrise of a smile. "And you are not an infant."

"Haven't been for some time. Promise me you will not fret about penurious spinsterhood, Alice. If you want to marry Blessington Peabrain, then I wish you every measure of earthly bliss in his loving if undeserving arms. If your aspirations lie elsewhere, don't let Lady Josephine bully you into compromising."

Cam did rather hope Alice's aspirations lay elsewhere in his very direction. The thought should have surprised him, should have disconcerted him, except that it didn't. He not only liked Alice, he respected her, and he was prepared to deal summarily with any who would becloud her happiness. As for the rest of it...

He had some thinking to do. A lot of thinking, and then some serious negotiating that Society sentimentally labeled *courting*.

"I will consider what you've said, my lord. If you'd drop by Grandpapa's cottage shortly after noon tomorrow, you and he can confer regarding the progress of the harvest and this mad notion you've presented of making a late hay crop."

She scooted forward, and Cam was on his feet instantly, hand extended. "Allow me."

She accepted the assistance she did not need, and Cam was careful to step back and release her hand rather than presume.

"You'll stop by the cottage tomorrow?" she asked.

"Shortly after noon, and if I have any queries regarding dusting, sweeping, or polishing, I can relay them to you in your grandfather's hearing."

Alice stepped nearer, put a hand on Cam's shoulder, and spoke close to his ear. "Grandpapa naps after his nooning. You mustn't be offended if he doesn't receive you personally."

She eased away, and while Cam was still mentally groping for words, thoughts, anything coherent, Alice passed through the open door. He stared at the empty doorway and wrestled with the urge to call her back. Had Alice Singleton just kissed his cheek, or had he wished that sensation into existence?

∼

"I did not quite kiss him." Alice had informed the cat of this sorry failure—or sorrier success—twice already.

Cassandra, a calico queen, yawned, showing exquisite feline indifference and a pink mouth full of sharp teeth.

"To have money, Cass. To have real, adequate money. I envy the maids their wages, you know." Alice collected the lunch dishes from the breakfast parlor and took them to the kitchen. Today was half day for the daily cook/housekeeper, not that Mrs. Patrickson did a great deal even when on the job.

The cat followed Alice into the kitchen, tail high.

"I cannot accept money from the baron, but even to think of having means..." Alice put the dishes into one half of the divided copper sink and worked the pump handle until the sink was half full. She dumped a kettle of hot water over the lot and watched the steam rise.

Her imagination had had the evening, the night, and the morning to consider what a difference funds would make. The magnitude of that difference still fascinated her. How limited her life had become, how circumscribed by *cannot, will not, and must not*, all pronounced in Lady Josephine's genteel, censuring tones.

Money meant freedom, for Alice and for those she cared about. Money meant...

Cass stropped herself against Alice's skirts.

"Right. The dishes won't wash themselves." She unfastened her cuffs and rolled up her sleeves, swabbed a rag in the soap dish, and picked up a plate.

Lady Josephine would never change. Grandpapa would at some point go to his eternal reward, though Alice hoped not for many long happy years. Gabriella was growing up.

Something would have to be done, the sooner the better.

"I knocked, and nobody came to the door."

Alice whirled and beheld Camden, Lord Lorne, hat in hand, peering about the kitchen and making the whole room seem half its usual size. Cassandra sniffed at his boots and gave him her best won't-you-pet-me-please? purr.

Shameless beast. "My mortification is without limit, my lord. You will please wait in the parlor, and I'll bring a tea tray. I believe you'll find Grandpapa there."

The baron hunkered down to pet the cat. "My steward is making a contented journey through the Land of Nod. I hadn't the heart to disturb him. Mrs. Shorer was also said to be asleep when I had the audacity to stop by her apartment earlier today. The maids are guarding her slumbers like a lot of mobcapped dragons defending their hoard of gold."

"You were not permitted to see her?"

His lordship stood and put his hat on the table. "I was nigh tossed bodily up the steps by the first footman and the head porter. I left them muttering about 'London addling the poor lad's wits.'"

None of this insubordination appeared to bother the baron. He used the water in the sink to wash his hands and appropriated a towel draped on a peg over the hearth.

"Best tend to that plate," he said. "The food gets sticky if you let the dishes sit, and then it's twice as much work to wash them."

He apparently meant to dry the dishes. Alice was torn between appreciation for the assistance and the voice screeching in her head that he was seeing her in an apron *and* without her snood.

Hysterics would not do. Alice returned the plate to the sink. "Grandpapa dined early. I wasn't expecting you to call quite so soon."

"Rain on the way," the baron replied. "I came on foot. Didn't want to get a soaking. I can wash if you'd rather. I know ladies like to keep their hands dry."

How would he know that? "I'm fine. You really should not be here."

"You all but invited me."

Alice scrubbed the plate within an inch of its little, ceramic life. "To the cottage, not into the very kitchen."

"You are having cold feet, because we talked about money, and Blundering Peahen, and the abomination against the natural order who is my aunt. Why haven't you married Bernard? He's a good sort, if a bit stodgy."

They were to discuss marriage instead of money? From bad to worse. "He hasn't asked." Then too, a life spent under the same roof as Lady Josephine would be akin to torture. "Why aren't you married?" Alice set the clean plate in the empty half of the sink.

"Stubbornness, mostly. I would like to be married. To have a partner in life, a loyal friend and lover, an affectionate ally... I have always approved of that notion. That aside, I am aware that my prospects were evaluated by the matchmakers in light of Alexander's illness. A purveyor of Peruvian bark or sailcloth would never merit their notice. A baron's heir poised to come into forty thousand acres and a tidy income? That fellow was worth an introduction."

Alice dealt with plates, glasses, and utensils. The baron pumped rinse water over them and arranged them on the counter on a dry towel, all the while regaling Alice with the social gatherings he'd endured in Mayfair.

"They all but counted my teeth," he said, "and when it became apparent Alexander would not rally, the Huxley family solicitors were besieged with invitations to lunch and supper by their colleagues."

The same solicitors who handled Lady Josephine's affairs, no doubt. "Grandpapa says the estate is not as profitable as it once was. That you ought to consider some enclosures if you have the capital."

"And yet, he hasn't mentioned enclosures to me. I brought up replacing the mill wheel with a more efficient design, and he nearly had an apoplexy. I brought up taking off a second cutting of hay from fallow pasturage, and he importuned heaven to relieve me of my fanciful notions. Have you thought about my offer of coin, Alice?"

She'd thought about not-quite kissing him nearly as much. She took the towel from him and replaced it on its peg over the hearth.

Thunder rumbled in the east, and a spattering of raindrops hit the kitchen window.

"Tea, my lord?" Alice couldn't send him out into a downpour, could she?

"Why not? Don't suppose you have any biscuits on hand?"

Alice set a tin on the table, refilled the kettle, and hung it on the pot swing. To apologize for a near kiss or to pretend it hadn't happened? To allow discussion of her lack of funds or to pretend coin of the realm did not exist?

Even to ponder these dilemmas pleased Alice in a perverse, refreshing way.

The baron sniffed the contents of the tin. "Cinnamon. I came to the right kitchen. Talk to me, Alice. I offered you money yesterday, and you were not offended. I surmise Aunt Josephine has been terrorizing you, else you would have slapped my face. I meant you no insult. I want that understood."

Alice rummaged in the tea drawer, measured out enough for a strong pot, and began assembling the humble, everyday wooden tea tray. The temptation to confide was nigh overpowering, and yet, the need to protect, to exercise caution won out.

"Your aunt terrorizes everybody. Times are hard. She mentions to one of the poorer tenant families that she might be able to find a domestic post in some parsonage up near Thirsk for their daughter, but then the son presumes to ask the wrong young lady to dance at the quarterly assembly, and no post is forthcoming. She's a tyrant, and Bernard overlooks her behavior or excuses it as well intended, if he even notices it."

Alice had not discerned the tyranny behind the gracious words until much too late.

The baron gestured with half a biscuit. "How does she tyrannize you?"

The kettle began to whistle, and Alice grabbed it before the noise could wake Grandpapa. He would not be scandalized to find Alice offering the baron a cup of tea in the kitchen, but he'd be worried. Grandpapa had enough to worry about.

More than enough.

Alice poured the boiling water into the teapot and for one moment entertained the notion of telling the baron the truth. Such a relief that would be, assuming he wasn't horrified.

"Her ladyship gently hammers on my destitution, my lack of a husband, my great and ever-increasing age. My precarious station, which is related to all of the above. How strong do you like your tea?"

"Strong, not bitter."

Like his lordship. Alice put the honey pot on the tray and, in a fit of rebellion, poured out a small pot of cream from the clay dairy crock. She even put a few drops on the flagstone floor for the delectation of the cat and to blazes with what a lady must not do.

Cass readily agreed.

"I prefer strong tea myself," Alice said, bringing the tray to the table and sitting opposite the baron. "You should look out of place here in the kitchen. You don't." He looked relaxed, not too overdressed, and very intent on his biscuits. "Save some for me."

He held out the tin, and Alice took two, then a third.

"Tell me, Alice. Is there anybody you might consider marrying?"

She pretended to examine the tea, which was not yet strong enough. The startling answer to his question was that, yes, she might consider marrying *him*. He did not put on airs. He saw right through Lady Josephine. He was generous to the point of causing awkwardness—at least with Alice—and he had no patience with hypocrisy.

To say nothing of a quick mind and an appetite for hard work.

And an excellent, robust physique, too, of course.

And yet, he was the baron. He would marry a woman who was a lady in every particular, rather than aspiring to the label under false colors.

"I am not contemplating matrimony to anybody at present," Alice said, though the subject was none of his lordship's business.

"Anybody ever?"

"You are no respecter of privacy, are you?" She arranged cups and saucers, grateful to have something to do with her hands.

"When negotiating, it helps all parties to reach a satisfactory conclusion if they are dealing from adequate, accurate information. If my opponent needs three ships to haul his cargo, and I have only the one available, we both need to acknowledge that."

"I have never considered marrying anybody who might have entertained a reciprocal notion about me, so please desist from this line of inquiry. My prospects are not your concern."

He demolished another biscuit. His fourth, and yes, Alice was counting. Also making a note to let Cook at the Hall know of his lordship's fondness for cinnamon.

"I have in mind a little project," he said, lifting the lid of the teapot and inspecting the contents, then pouring out two cups. "I'm thinking of sending Josephine to London to refurbish my town house."

"Don't. She will bankrupt your exchequer and festoon your parlors in gilt and silk." Though the prospect of weeks free of Lady Josephine's hovering presence... Nearly as attractive as having some means.

"A little gilt and silk for show might not go amiss."

"My lord, heed me on this. Alexander had to forbid Lady Josephine, in writing, from making any changes to the Hall, and he told me he put that provision in his will. The problem is not her ladyship's excessive taste, it's that she will use the redecoration to spy on your staff, your neighbors, and you. If you have ledgers that aren't under lock and key, if you keep any sort of journals..."

Alice fell silent before she said too much, though apparently she already had. The baron was regarding her over the last bite of his fourth biscuit.

"She has spied on you, hasn't she?"

The tea and biscuits, the cat purring on the hearth, the rain pattering down, that note of quiet exasperation in the baron's voice... The kitchen had become a confessional.

And yet, his lordship would return to London, while Lady Josephine would remain on her throne at the vicarage.

"She spies on everybody. One of those maids who so fiercely kept you from looking in on Mrs. Shorer will pass along to the housekeeper at the vicarage that Mrs. Shorer has taken to her bed. I'm surprised Lady Josephine was not on your doorstep this morning, bearing tisanes and insisting on bothering the patient herself."

The last bite of the fourth biscuit met its fate. "Did she spy on Alexander?"

"Tried to. I did what I could to protect his privacy, as did the rest of the household staff. A dying man should have a right to some dignity. We could not stop her from sorting through the mail on the sideboard or reviewing the household books with Mrs. Shorer."

"Aunt has a nerve, prying into the ledgers like that."

"She was doing her Christian duty, given the seriousness of the late baron's indisposition."

And now that Alice had a sympathetic ear, the enormity of Lady Josephine's meddling took on its true proportions.

"She invites confidences," Alice went on, "presents herself as the soul of understanding and sympathy. You are astonished that such a fine lady is actually so approachable and kindhearted. Perhaps you confide that you're worried about your poor granny, who is going vague and lives all alone. The next thing you know, the young man you were walking out with cools toward you. Eventually, you learn that he became aware of raving insanity dangling a bit higher up on your family tree, though forgetfulness assails us all at times."

"You describe the fate of Mrs. Shorer's understudy?"

"Lady Josephine is adamant that domestics must not be permitted to marry, even though in this case, the couple could have stepped into the respective shoes of Mrs. Shorer and Mr. Beaglemore. To their credit, they saw past Lady Josephine's lies. She'd told Maryanne not to fret over Henry's defection, because a man with a wandering eye made a poor husband."

"Henry's eye never wandered."

"Of course not. The point of this parable is to admonish you to mind your back where your aunt is concerned. You underestimate her at your peril."

The baron finished his tea, poured himself another half a cup, and topped up Alice's serving as well.

"You have given me much to think about, Alice, and adroitly changed the subject from money and kisses. Of the two, I find—somewhat to my surprise—that the latter topic interests me more than the former."

They had not been discussing kisses, though admittedly, Alice had been thinking of kisses. Near kisses.

"I was overly familiar with you yesterday," Alice said, looking the baron straight in the eye. "I apologize for my presumption. Your generous proffer was unexpected, and my manners deserted me."

He patted the fingers of his right hand against his left palm softly. "Bravo, Alice. Nicely done. A fine apology for not much of a kiss. My turn." He rose and moved toward the hearth, stooped to pet the cat, and stood again. "Miss Singleton, I have been remiss. The lady ought never find it necessary to take the initiative when it comes to kissing, and if you would allow me this opportunity to remedy my oversight, I would be eternally in your debt."

Was he being humorous? Daft? "I don't understand, my lord. I got a bit above myself, I've apologized, and now..."

She rose, intent on putting the tea things away while the baron regarded her.

"I want to kiss you, Alice. If you are not of like mind, then simply say so, and we forget I ever presumed to make any overtures."

Did he negotiate everything? But then, was it such a bad thing to be *asked* about one's preferences? No, it was not. Not a bad thing *at all.*

"You are so matter of fact, as if we're discussing bolts of cloth or barrels of pickled herring." While Alice's insides had gone widdershins in eight directions at once.

He stepped closer. "We are discussing my growing regard for you, my attraction to you, my interest in forging a closer bond with you, and—I hope—your reciprocal interest in me."

Alice scrabbled mentally for any vestige of common sense. "You are returning to London as soon as possible."

"I will always have obligations in London."

That was a concession, but what sort of bargain were they striking?

"Alice, might I kiss you?"

No, no, no. The only possible, sensible, safe answer was no. If Alice refused him, his offer of coin would not be rescinded. She knew that as she knew every footpath on Lorne land. If she refused him, Lady Josephine would not acquire one more potential increment of leverage over Alice's dwindling sliver of happiness.

If Alice refused him... She would regret that cowardice for the rest of her life. She would concede some battle that hadn't yet been entirely lost.

"I would like to be kissed by you," Alice said. "But you mustn't get untoward ideas."

His smile lit up the gloomy kitchen with affection and glee. "Too late for that, but you can trust me, Alice. I have few friends in London, and no small store of competitors, but to a person, they would also say that my word is reliable."

Alexander had said as much too. Camden was in trade, feckless fellow, but he was an honest tradesman.

"Don't make me regret this," Alice said, feeling at once determined and foolish. "And don't be all day about it. Grandpapa's naps tend to be short."

"Yes, ma'am." The baron wrapped her gently in his arms, and the fit was perfect. Alice, whose height had been the subject of many of Lady Josephine's laments, rested her head on the baron's shoulder, sighed, and tucked close.

Wonderfully, scandalously close.

CHAPTER NINE

One of the worst blunders a negotiator could make was to hurry. Conveying a sense of urgency, even sometimes a false sense of urgency, could be a useful tactic, but to hurry—to ignore details, to rush headlong—was invariably a mistake.

With Alice in his arms, Cam found the self-discipline to treasure the moment and the woman. She honored him with a snug embrace, no missishness, and no mistaking the abundance of her curves.

Untoward ideas galloped around in Cam's brainbox with a rambunctiousness he'd not enjoyed since his soldiering days. He acknowledged a fleeting sympathy for Dinky, hopelessly enthralled with his wife and heedless of his own dignity.

Over Alice's shoulder, Cam spied the cat, basking in the warmth before the hearth, flicking her tail lazily. Patient creatures, cats.

Alice stroked a hand down Cam's back. "Does your version of kissing—?"

He brushed his lips over hers. "My version of kissing involves patience and pleasure." He repeated the gesture. For such a tart-tongued woman, Alice's lips were sweet and lush. "Heaps of both."

She sank her fingers into his hair. "More pleasure, less patience, please."

Well, then. He sealed his mouth over hers and felt her smile in response. Good. Kissing should be a joyous undertaking for all concerned. He nonetheless kept to a leisurely pace, until Alice's grip on him had become quite firm, and Cam's untoward ideas had migrated in a southerly direction.

"You're good at this," she said, resting her cheek against his chest. "Maybe too good."

Whatever did that mean? "If I say you are equally accomplished, will I get my face slapped?"

She patted his chest. "No, because I can tell you in all honesty that my expertise seems to have come over me all of a sudden. Perhaps I excel at kissing only you. We ought to sit."

They ought to find a nice, comfy bed and put a rainy afternoon to its best possible use. "I notice you aren't following your own suggestion, Miss Singleton."

"I'm all in a muddle, *your lordship*."

"Cam, or Camden when you are vexed with me."

Alice loosened her hold and would have stepped back, but Cam gently prevented her. "This kiss happened, Alice. Please don't pretend otherwise. I would like other kisses to happen, and more than kisses, to put my objective in plain view."

She perused him suspiciously, putting him in mind of a much younger Alice. "More than kisses?"

"I want to hack out with you first thing in the day, not because I enjoy trotting about at an ungodly hour, but because I long to start my morning with you. I want to walk you home from services—we'll take a different route from your grandpapa and Mrs. Shorer—and I want you and your grandpapa enjoying Sunday supper with me at the Hall. I want—"

She pressed two fingers to his lips. "Be sensible. A stolen kiss is lovely, beyond lovely, but my reputation will not survive a dalliance."

No dalliance in Cam's experience involved walking home

together from divine services. "My heart would not survive a dalliance. I intend to ask Thaddeus for permission to court you, if you'll give me leave."

Alice slipped free of Cam's embrace, which was not the reaction he'd hoped for, but then, he hadn't presented his request in the manner he'd planned to. Forever after, in Cam's mind, cinnamon would be an aphrodisiac.

"Who is being impatient now, my lord?"

I have waited years for you. "I am being forthright. A different matter entirely."

Sadness limned Alice's smile. "You are being ridiculous. Peers don't wed penniless spinsters."

Had her mind all made up, did she? "Are you telling me what I may and may not do, Alice? I know of at least one baron who married his mistress, and two of her sisters are leading lights of the demimonde. In your grandfather's day, the Duke of Chandos acquired his second duchess through the barbarous institution known as the wife sale. What is ridiculous is a mind closed to happy possibilities."

Russet brows drew down. "Then you are being precipitous, at best. Call upon some of that patience you recently cited. I barely know you, and you aren't even planning to dwell at the Hall."

And yet, she'd allowed him that kiss. "You know me. When you were fourteen years old, you joined your grandfather's household, and we became more than passingly acquainted. You'd started putting up your hair, and you wore it in the same style as your late mother because you wanted to keep her memory close. Two braids twined in a coronet, no damned snood."

Alice sank onto the bench at the table. "I told you that. You caught me playing truant from my lessons, and I... You were playing truant too."

Cam sat beside her rather than across the table. "My French was already better than my tutor's. Yours needed work."

"I was better read than you."

"You still are, unless we're talking about the financial pages. Your

Latin was surprisingly good." Humiliatingly good to a boy intent on outstripping his elder brother in at least one subject.

"My father was a headmaster, you'll recall. He made Latin a game, and there was none of this 'now you pronounce the letter, now you don't' that makes French so beastly. You walked or rode across every corner of the estate, even then."

"Alex prided himself on his horsemanship. I learned to not compete, and that meant taking my exercise in solitude." Once Alex had gone off to university, Cam had become beyond competent in the saddle. Knowledgeable enough to realize that Alex had been given superb mounts, while Cam had been expected to make do with inferior hacks.

Alice regarded him slantwise. "You are very competitive now. You love to best your business rivals and turn a coin where nobody else will dare try."

Cam very nearly told her that he had half a dozen mouths to feed, that growing boys were bottomless when it came to food, clothing, tutoring, boots, hats... That his own father had taunted him to make something of himself, and Papa's ghost had not yet been exorcised.

He was competing with shades and haunted by the notion that he might somehow betray the trust the boys had placed in him.

But Alice herself had counseled moderation. Patience.

"In business, yes. I am competitive and, thus far, largely successful at it. I hope I am not greedy, though. You would have no use for me if I were."

She opened the tin of biscuits, broke one in two, and passed him half. "No use at all. You could house a regiment at the Hall. For it to sit in rural splendor, ignored by the one person who has the right to dwell under its roof should bother you."

"It does bother me, but I'm not about to let Lady Josephine establish herself at the Hall." The biscuits were scrumptious. Buttery, fresh, sweet... A bit on the small side, though. "I don't suppose you're ready to kiss me?"

"I thought you said... oh. We're to take turns?"

"Seems equitable. Share the pleasure, share the patience?"

Alice nibbled her half of the sweet into oblivion. "I must give this whole peculiar notion of yours some thought. I did not intend that you..."

"Kiss you?"

She brushed an imaginary crumb from the table. "Involve yourself with me. First, you offer money, and now, you're bent on this other notion. What if tomorrow you're away to London and inclined to trade kisses with somebody else?"

A wave of tenderness assailed Cam, followed by a sense of having been brought up short and deservedly so. He put an arm around Alice's shoulders and considered how best to reassure a lady who'd lost both parents and her home at a young age. Who'd been sent off to finishing school, but who'd never found anybody with whom to finish the race to the altar.

All that French and Latin served no purpose at Lady Josephine's command knitting sessions.

"I must seem impulsive to you," Cam said. "I was a broody boy, prone to sulks and sighs, but that was half a lifetime ago." He'd been a miserable boy. Never good enough, never worthy of praise, never even satisfactory.

"You rarely laughed," Alice said. "I don't recall that you sulked so much as you were simply quiet."

"I sulked, pouted, and plotted. But I also learned to govern my impulses. Alice, I am not paying you my addresses out of some passing notion. I am heeding my instincts, applying common sense to my subjective inclinations, and trusting my own judgment."

She rested her head on his shoulder. "Hard to do when you're told your judgment is poor."

What fool...? Lady Josephine, of course. "Hard *not* to do when I'm the one who must live with the consequences of my decisions. Will you let me walk you home from services?"

She straightened. "No. I need time to consider this... this development. I esteem you, Camden Huxley, and I like you, and I find you attractive."

"But you are entitled to ponder the ramifications and to gather information pertinent to the negotiation. I agree."

Because his arm was around her shoulders, he felt the tension ease from her.

"I will not be rushed. I'm glad you understand that. The rain has let up. You'd best be going while you can dodge between showers."

A frigid deluge or two might have been helpful, given the state of Cam's animal spirits. "I'll look in on your grandpapa on my way out. You need not see me to the door." Where he'd be inclined to kiss her, despite the fact that it wasn't his turn to initiate such festivities.

Cam rose and extended a hand to Alice, who had been getting up and down from kitchen benches unassisted for her entire earthly span.

She squeezed his fingers when he would have offered a bow. "I do like you, Camden Huxley, but my situation is not as simple as it appears. I, too, have obligations, and I must think carefully."

Alice deserved to consider Cam's suit at her leisure. He understood that she was citing duty to her grandfather as the pretext for further deliberations, but if she cast a favorable eye on Cam's courtship, they'd ask the old boy to dwell at the Hall.

Some solutions were both simple and easy.

"I'm inviting you and your grandpapa to Sunday supper, Alice. See that you don't turn an ankle or come down with an ague between then and now, and mind Thaddeus doesn't either."

"Be off with you." She bussed his cheek. "You doubtless have correspondence to tend to, and somebody has eaten the last of the morning's biscuits. I'd best bake another batch."

Cam tapped his hat onto his head, blew a kiss to the cat and one to Alice. Patience was a harsh taskmaster. He nonetheless spent a few minutes in the parlor chatting with Thaddeus about rain delaying the harvest and the cost of installing an overshot mill wheel.

Before Thaddeus could bellow for Alice to bring a tea tray, Cam was out in the chilly drizzle, thinking hard, and not about his correspondence.

~

Alice reassembled the tea service she'd just washed, made a fresh pot, brought it to the parlor, and set it on the side of the desk.

"You just missed his lordship," Grandpapa said. "I would have rung for the tray, but the lad bustled off as if the last coach to London might leave without him. Haven't we any cinnamon biscuits?"

Alice moved to the mullioned window and pushed the curtains wide open. "The shortbread should be eaten before it goes stale." The day looked dreary—a sopping home wood, gray skies, drops sliding down the panes—but to Alice, it felt merely cozy.

Special. A day for contemplating possible miracles.

"Do sit, Alice. Your bustling about will destroy my peace. We might as well get some correspondence tended to if the rain will insist on bucketing down."

Alice pushed the second set of curtains open and turned a gimlet eye upon her progenitor. "What about *my* peace, Grandpapa? What if keeping order on Mrs. Patrickson's half day is a pleasure and a joy?" Lady Josephine, knowing exactly when the cottage had no staff, usually left Alice in peace on half days.

"Then you are a contrary female, albeit not as contrary as some others I could name who have a penchant for housekeeping. You come by your disposition honestly, though." Grandpapa sipped his tea. "Rather contrary myself sometimes, but I do believe I've met my match in the present baron. The boy will have his overshot mill wheel, and there's an end to it."

Alice had the distinct sense that this outcome pleased Grandpapa inordinately. "Aren't undershot wheels growing old-fashioned?"

Grandpapa selected a piece of shortbread and dunked it into his tea. "Not old-fashioned so much as indicative of lesser means. An overshot wheel requires a significant drop in height between the upper sluice and the millpond. Unless the terrain is fortuitously designed by the hand of the Almighty, one must engineer such a drop, and engineering requires funds. The lad has funds. His father would be pleased. Alice, for the love of threshed wheat, please sit. When you insist on dusting and straightening, I feel as if I ought to climb into the saddle and make some tenant calls."

"Not in this rain, Thaddeus Singleton. I cannot have you coming down with an ague."

With anything, other than the occasional testy mood.

"You sound like your dear grandmama. The baron tells me Eunice Shorer has turned her ankle. The daft woman insists on a forced march from divine services, the one day of the week when rest is ordained from on high. I don't suppose you could look in on her?"

Alice took the seat across from the desk. "I already did. She hasn't sent for me since."

"Of course not. She's too proud. You ought to nip up to the Hall tomorrow anyway. If she's back on her feet, she'll need a stern lecture about not overdoing. If she's still abed, the end times are approaching. The sooner we're aware of our imminent demise, the sooner some of us can turn to the immediate repair of our celestial accounts."

Grandpapa was in a good mood. His truly sour moments were marked by silence, a closed parlor door, and much staring off into the home wood beyond the windows.

"Hadn't you best reconcile yourself to making the acquaintance of Old Scratch?" Alice asked, pouring herself half a cup.

"To hear Lady Josephine tell it, we're all headed down to the pit. Be nice to have the company of one's neighbors in the afterlife. We will fortunately be spared her membership in our infernal shire. She will be too busy instructing the angels on the latest fashion in halos."

"You don't care for her ladyship?" Why hadn't Alice brought this topic up with Grandpapa previously? He groused and muttered about the many hours Lady Josephine demanded from Alice, but Grandpapa groused and muttered about nearly everything.

He paused with half a piece of shortbread poised over his tea cup.

"She thinks she bought your soul by sponsoring you for those two years at finishing school, Alice. But why send you off to learn all that deportment and folderol just so you can rusticate into old age at her ladyship's beck and call?"

Alice swished her tea in its little cup. "I suspect she will make a companion of me when you have no more use for me. A bit of French, some ability with watercolors, a touch of refinement are required in a lady's companion."

Grandpapa set down his cup. "Alice Singleton, you must not allow that... that *troublesome harpy* to steal the rest of your life. I forbid it. Common sense forbids it. You were all that stood between her ladyship and the late baron's wishes for a quiet demise. She would have driven the poor man barmy, praying by his bedside when he wanted to laugh at some bawdy play. She tried to turn the Hall into a temple of mopery upon his death, directly contrary to his wishes. You shall not allow her to make you her familiar any more than you already have."

Perhaps this was why the topic of her ladyship hadn't come up. Absent a convenient pot of gold materializing in Alice's cedar chest, the issue had had no resolution.

"What do you propose I do to support myself when this cottage is no longer available to me?"

"When I die?" Grandpapa dunked his shortbread and munched contentedly. "The baron will give you a life estate, and I won't even have to ask him. You'd be better off marrying him, though. The lad wants a wife. You can see that from twenty paces away in a dense fog. He'll immure himself in his damned commerce otherwise. Getting and spending, laying waste his powers. Is that Scripture?"

"Wordsworth. *The world is too much with us, late and soon...*"

"Oh, right. The fellow was in a dreary mood when he wrote that one, or perhaps he was contemplating years serving as Lady Meddlesome's companion. Will you drink that tea, Alice, or stare it into submission?"

Alice downed her serving. "The baron cannot marry me."

Grandpapa topped up his cup. "Tell him that, and he'll be down on bended knee before you can say, 'You do me great honor.' You never met a more contrary fellow in your life. If his tutors told him Caesar's Gallic letters were too advanced, Camden set about translating them at once. If the boy's father noted that the lad was easily winded, Camden charted a course of hikes over every bridle path and lane on the Hall's land."

"He's competitive." And that meant, if the steward said an overshot mill was out of the question, or making fall hay ridiculous... *Ah*. Alice smiled into her empty tea cup.

"Camden is determined," Grandpapa said, punctuating the air with half a piece of shortbread. "A quality Alexander never exhibited. Our present baron would make you a good husband, Alice. He asked me to give you his regards."

"You have never suggested I marry anybody before. Why him?" That Grandpapa, who needed looking after and would need more of the same as time went on, was abruptly shoving Alice up the church aisle was as suspicious as it was touching. "Are you having heart pangs again?"

Grandpapa thumped a fist against his bony chest. "Never felt better. That damned tisane works wonders. Digitalis, of all things. A ruddy weed, and Eunice Shorer swears by it."

And Grandpapa started his day with a serving, meekly consumed without fail. "So why present the baron to me as a marital prospect now, Grandpapa? I like him well enough, but marriage requires more than liking, and a union between us would be considered a mésalliance."

"Marriage, my girl, goes down a good deal easier if the parties like each other. Mark me on that. I know of what I speak. The baron has taken notice of you, and marrying a woman he esteems would spike Lady Josephine's cannon nicely. Two birds with one stone, if we include your need to elude her dismal plans for you. Put the Considine minx in her place, too, and before the girl becomes truly obnoxious."

Alice took up the letter opener and the top item in the day's stack of mail. "Grandpapa, you surprise me." She slit the seal on an epistle from an assistant land steward employed by the Duke of Northumberland.

"If I have thwarted your expectations, then my day has been a success. I do see what goes on around here, Alice. When I'm not discussing the advantages of rutabagas over mangel-wurzels, I listen to what the tenants and their wives tell me. I talk to the Hall's gardeners, and my weekly forced marches with the Queen of Dustmops and Tisanes are informative as well."

Alice had wondered why two confirmed adversaries insisted on that weekly show of civility. The habit had initially struck her as akin to opposing generals dining together the night before a battle. In recent years, she'd sensed more of a comrade-in-arms quality to what had become a tradition.

"Grandpapa, are you truly feeling well?"

"The rain looks to be never-ending, we're in the middle of harvest, and you ask if I'm well."

"We get rain every year during harvest, and you say the respite is always timely, and the crop is always brought in anyway."

"I say a lot of things. Who is plaguing me by mail today?"

Alice passed over the letter, allowing the change of subject. "Mr. Delauncy, reporting developments from Alnwick Castle. I gather they've had a difficult summer."

Grandpapa donned his spectacles and perused the letter. "Poor man has his hands full. A new duchess underfoot, one with ideas. A mere barony masquerading as a dukedom and all that land to be managed."

"Wasn't there an earldom somewhere in the succession?"

"Details, details. Let's see what other laments the day's correspondence has brought us."

Alice worked through the stack, a much smaller pile than the baron dealt with, and the rain eventually slowed to a drizzle, then drips.

"Well, at least that's done," Grandpapa said. "Time to catch up on my reading. You will look in at the Hall tomorrow, won't you, Alice? Mrs. Shorer is difficult and demanding, but she means well and will allow you to fuss over her when lesser mortals would be sent away with their pride smarting."

Lesser mortals such as Grandpapa?

"I suppose a short visit won't be out of the ordinary. Mrs. Shorer is always happy to confer regarding her recipes and remedies." Alice gathered up the tea things, lit a candelabrum with a spill from the jar on the mantel, and set the candles near Grandpapa's elbow. "Don't strain your eyes, sir."

"Bossy wench. Be off with you."

That was as close to an endearment as Alice had ever heard from her grandfather, but it confirmed his high spirits. Some scheme known only to Grandpapa had been hatched and was coming along nicely. A cross-breeding of sheep, perhaps, or a patch of ground put into Italian clover two years ago, bearing a whacking great crop of maize this year.

Grandpapa was not indifferent to her—far from it—but he had never been demonstrative, much less affectionate.

Alice left him to his reading and returned to the kitchen. Cassandra yet dozed on the hearth, the picture of calico contentment.

"I am not content." As Alice put another load of dishes into the sink, she pondered the nature of her restlessness and decided that discontent was an improvement over the resignation that had gripped her prior to the baron's arrival.

His discontents had propelled him to commercial success and—at least based on appearances—happiness.

And yet, the baron would not take lightly the news that Alice had egregiously misstepped nine years ago. He might take that news very badly indeed, but Alice would not abandon her daughter to Lady Josephine's machinations.

Not for all the handsome, ardent barons in Mayfair would Alice contemplate that course, and yet, she wasn't quite sure how she'd convince his lordship that she really, truly did not want to be courted by him either.

Because in the weak and wanton corner of her heart that had no use for resignation, Alice was very interested in having Camden Huxley pay her his addresses.

CHAPTER TEN

"I was uncertain of my lord's whereabouts," Beaglemore said, taking Cam's damp coat. "I told her ladyship you were out, and she declared that no man of sense was abroad in the middle of a rainstorm for long. She ensconced herself in the family parlor and has been making free with the tea and cakes for the past half hour."

No man put off by a little rain could transact much business in Old Londontowne, unless he preferred to rely entirely on supernumeraries, which Cam did not.

"I paid a call on Thaddeus Singleton," Cam said, fully aware his late father and even his charming late brother would not have explained an absence to a servant. "I knew the rain meant our steward would be holed up in his cottage, and if we're ever to have an efficient mill, Singleton needs to be brought round to the notion."

Beaglemore's white brows rose. "A new mill, my lord?"

"New mill wheel. Overshot instead of undershot. Not complicated." While Lady Josephine's presence was not simple. "I am tempted to slip into the library and wait her ladyship out."

Beaglemore accepted Cam's high crowned beaver. "I would not advise evasive maneuvers, my lord. Take the time to put yourself to rights, though I'd be quick about it, and greet her ladyship properly. She is patient by nature, but if you elude her now, she will only reappear on the morrow, twice as determined on whatever errand brought her here."

The butler gave away nothing by his expression, save disapproval for a slightly wilted hat. Did Lady Josephine hold some long past peccadillo over Beaglemore's head? A penchant for gambling beyond a butler's modest means? Alice had been very clear that her ladyship had elevated meddling to domestic extortion.

"Then I will deal with the old besom now," Cam said.

"My lord, a gentleman does not wear somewhat muddy boots when greeting a lady, much less his lady aunt." Beaglemore sounded as if he were pleading with Saint Peter on behalf of a truant schoolboy.

"We are thus left with a logical conundrum. Either I am not a gentleman, or the person seeking to ambush me in the family parlor is not a lady. No fresh tray, Beaglemore, and feel free to lurk at the door. The exchange may prove lively."

Beaglemore looked as if he'd offer further admonitions, then nodded solemnly. "Best of luck, my lord."

You'll need it remained unspoken.

Cam caught his reflection in the pier glass outside the library, deemed himself sufficiently rumpled and wrinkled, and entered the family parlor without knocking.

"Aunt Josephine, good day." He bowed. "What could be of such pressing importance as to bring you out in this weather?"

She smiled faintly and remained seated in the center of the sofa. The fire threw off good heat, and the silver tea service sat before her on the low table, two cakes left on the plate.

"My lord, clearly something compelled *you* to brave the elements. While I appreciate that, as a conscientious host, you did not wish to keep me waiting, I will understand if you'd like to take a moment to," —she paused delicately and swept Cam with a head-to-toe appraisal — "tend to your toilette."

"I'd rather not keep you from whatever appointed rounds you're on, Aunt." Cam seated himself in the wing chair flanking the sofa, though a gentleman ought not to take a chair without a lady's permission.

Her smile became mildly dismayed. "Camden, dear, did you leave all your manners in Mayfair? I have yet to invite you to sit."

Nor had Cam conferred upon her the honor of serving as hostess at the Hall. "I left any insistence on silly protocols in Mayfair. I am in my own home, humoring a family member who chose to make an impromptu call. It is you, in fact, who made yourself comfortable without asking permission from your host, and Beaglemore is too gracious and good at his job to thwart your presumption. Have you come to discuss Bernard's stipend?"

"Gracious me, of course not. Such a topic... Honestly, Camden, the weather has affected your humors."

Not the weather, unless weather had dark red hair, an impish smile, and a gift for slow kisses. Cam had been determined to hold the line with Aunt Josephine for his own sake, but knowing how shabbily she dealt with Cam's staff, tenants, and neighbors—to say nothing of her presumption where Alice was concerned—his determination to remind Aunt of her limitations had taken on the nature of a vow.

"My lady, I am a busy man. If you must intrude here at the Hall without notice, then please respect that I might not have much room on my schedule to spare for whatever discussion you hoped to have with me. I have obligations that I must see to in a timely manner. Inheriting the barony has only added to their number."

She sat forward, spine very straight. "But that's the very thing, Camden. *The very thing.* I am here to help. I am at your disposal in oh-so-many ways, and you must believe me that one who had the honor to be the helpmeet of a distinguished clergyman under consideration for a bishop's see is well versed in tasks that might surprise you. I am a talented and tireless amanuensis, for example."

Cam's most junior clerk would doubtless be her equal, but Lady Josephine was only getting started.

"I am adept at managing correspondence," she went on. "I would be happy—well, willing, in any case—to resume reviewing the household books with Mrs. Shorer, and I daresay the estate books could use a thorough inspection too. All of this I could take from your overburdened shoulders. Not to state the obvious, but I am also more than capable of organizing your social calendar such that you will call upon and entertain the best local families in the optimal order. I daresay you have no other resource competent to undertake that challenge."

Beaglemore, Mrs. Shorer, Singleton, or Alice could all have managed the same feat in twenty minutes flat. Miss Considine might need closer to thirty.

"My brother went to his reward barely three months past, my lady. A furious round of socializing is beyond me, particularly given my ongoing London obligations. I appreciate your kind offers and will take them into consideration. If you will excuse me, I'll have Beaglemore see you out."

That last rudeness, failing to see a family member to the door, was heavy-handed. Not a miscalculation, but rather, an outright mistake resulting from temper.

Had Alice not warned Cam, he might well have capitulated to Lady Josephine's apparently generous offer to review household books with Mrs. Shorer. A tedious little ritual Cam might have delegated with some relief, thinking he'd placated his aunt's need to meddle and freed up a little of his own time.

Cam rose and offered Lady Josephine his hand. She took it and struggled to her feet as if impersonating a woman twenty years her senior.

"One must admire your industry, Camden. Even as a boy, what you lacked in discernment or quickness, you could somewhat make up for in diligence. I must warn you, though, that here in the shires, particularly the northern shires, we hold to the quaint notion that gentlemen—much less peers—do not engage in trade. You may dabble on 'Change, discreetly, you may have your investments and even hold shares in a bank or two, but conducting yourself like a senior clerk in a countinghouse..."

She dropped his hand and advanced toward the door. "It won't do, my boy. It simply won't do, especially not with the wealthy gentry. Families such as the Considines, Halbertsons, and Dingles are higher sticklers than your typical duchesses, and those families have long memories."

Aunt Josephine would have to do much more than threaten the cut direct in St. Wilfrid's churchyard, and yet, Cam admitted that she'd retreated from the skirmish with her head held high and managed to imply a vague threat on her way out the door.

"Beaglemore, if you'd see her ladyship out? Aunt, thank you for calling. I ought to next be receiving on Thursday afternoon at two of the clock. My regards to Bernard."

She shook her head and exchanged some sort of long-suffering glance with Beaglemore. "You will at least invite the Halbertsons for the Sunday meal, won't you? Or begin with the Considines and invite the Halbertsons next week, if you'd rather. Even you ought to grasp the necessity for such a basic show of manners."

Aunt had been on a matchmaking mission as well. She'd never lacked for ambition.

"I'm conferring with Singleton when the Sabbath meal rolls around. We're in the midst of harvest, and unless I take advantage of the Lord's Day to snabble my steward, he'll elude me until Yuletide. I cannot afford to absent myself from London for nearly that long. Good day to you, Aunt."

This visual inspection was a bit less condescending, a bit more speculative. "Until Thursday, my lord." She dipped the hint of a curtsey and took herself off at a regal pace, Beaglemore at her side.

Cam waited by a window until he saw a largish carriage pulling away from the front steps before seeking out his butler.

"My lord?" Beaglemore had retreated to the library, where he was making some sort of inventory of the decanters on the sideboard.

"Did she say anything noteworthy out of my hearing?"

Beaglemore put down his pencil and regarded a dozen crystal bottles, each holding a vintage for which Alexander had paid dearly.

"She inquired after Mrs. Shorer and assured me she would keep our housekeeper in her prayers."

"No attempt to look in on Mrs. Shorer?"

Beaglemore took out a plain linen handkerchief and wiped the stopper of a decanter of calvados.

"Her ladyship posited a desire to wish the patient a speedy recovery in person, but I allowed as how Mrs. Shorer was resting a great deal and refusing all callers. I implied that dignity was more the issue than any serious incapacitation, which is the truth, my lord. Her ladyship contented herself with assurances that I would pass along her felicitations to our housekeeper."

"Will her ladyship exact revenge for your rebellion?"

Beaglemore gave the stopper a last swipe. "I don't know, my lord. If I might speak freely?"

"Always."

"You underestimate Lady Josephine at your peril. According to her own late husband, she is a walking incarnation of the woman scorned and deserves a wide berth. She can be quite pleasant and then, without warning, quite *un*pleasant."

For Beaglemore to offer that warning both touched and alarmed Cam. "I will tread carefully, now that battle has been joined, but you and the rest of the staff should know that nothing in Lady Josephine's power can affect the pensions or the loyalty that I owe you. Nothing."

"Thank you, my lord." Offered in a perfectly uninflected tone.

Cam was deep in thought as he left the library. He'd meant to begin his negotiations with Josephine as he meant to go on—as the sole authority over the Hall, its local relationships, and staff. Josephine's return salvo had been cleverly couched.

She'd used the tried and true tactic of presenting Cam with

options—surrender control of the estate books, his correspondence, his social calendar, or the lowly household books. A little buffet of tempting opportunities to delegate tedious chores.

Such an approach often meant that the option not listed—in this case, surrendering *nothing*—might well slip from Cam's awareness.

A man less steeped in commerce might have fallen for her ploy, and two trustworthy sources—Alice and Beaglemore—had warned Cam not to underestimate her ladyship.

Did they both speak from experience, and if so, what would Lady Josephine try to use against Cam to similarly maneuver him under her thumb?

∼

Lady Josephine's coach took the long sweeping drive back to the village, though a shorter route ran through the home wood. That she had leave to call at the Hall whenever she pleased needed to be taken as holy writ. Despite Camden's atrocious rudeness, Lady Josephine had no intention of being relegated to milling about the Hall's formal parlor on Thursday afternoons.

She made a graceful descent from the coach, assisted by the sole footman employed at the vicarage, and mentally organized her resources for the next item on her agenda.

Bernard was, as usual at midafternoon, toiling away over some bit of theological arcana in his study. Lady Josephine detested the look of him at his desk, cuffs turned back, glasses perched on a patrician nose, the picture of the local parson embarking on the transition from handsome to distinguished.

A complete waste of an earl's grandson. "If you need material for this week's sermon, might I suggest 'blessed are the meek'?"

Bernard looked up. "Mama, greetings. I covered 'blessed are the meek' less than a fortnight ago. That was a very short round of calls."

Bernard's disappointment would have stung Josephine to the

quick had she not long ago reconciled herself to disappointment in her only offspring.

"I dreaded to think of our poor coachman up on the box in the abysmal weather, and the rain makes the going harder for the horses. I had quite a nice chat with dear Camden, who sends you his regards."

Bernard set his quill pen in the pewter tray and rolled down his right cuff. "Should you be bothering Cam when he's here for only a short inspection tour?"

Lady Josephine took the wing chair closest to the hearth, though the fire wasn't giving out nearly enough heat.

"Camden is here in search of a wife, my dear. His chosen occupation makes him unfit for Mayfair's best drawing rooms, despite the title, and his surly disposition means the die-away misses on offer in Town will have nothing to do with him. He doesn't need an heiress, ergo he's looking for a baroness who hails from the old, respected families of his home shire."

That reasoning should be simple enough to appeal to Bernard, who apparently enjoyed life in rural obscurity.

"You proposed to assist him in selecting a bride?" Bernard, who had no valet, tucked his sleeve button into place. "Please assure me you did not presume to such an extent."

Since turning thirty, Bernard had become a bit harder to manage. More outspoken, less inclined to accept advice given with only his best interests in mind. The right wife would settle him down, but that project would have to wait until Josephine had matters at the Hall under control.

"I did not mention marriage, Bernard. Really, credit me with some tact. I have been told that Eunice Shorer came to grief on her way home from services yesterday. Took a tumble, turned an ankle, had to make her way across field and fen on an injured foot. I was most concerned, given the woman's advanced years, and thought it would be rude to look in on the housekeeper while ignoring my nephew. Camden was happy to receive me, and I can report that Mrs. Shorer is mending apace."

Eunice Shorer had been a thorn in Lady Josephine's side since the unfortunate day Josephine had joined the vicarage household. The impertinent woman had a cure for every ailment, knew Scripture from Genesis to Revelation, and gave lowly parlor maids far too good an opinion of themselves. Fortunately, Lorne Hall's housekeeper was of such venerable years that time was on Lady Josephine's side, thank the immortal powers.

Bringing Camden up to scratch was imperative, but installing the right successor to Mrs. Shorer was nearly as pressing. A problem for another day, but what the staff needed was a firm and pious hand to enforce the discipline that Beaglemore had allowed to grow so lax.

"I will make a point to visit Mrs. Shorer tomorrow morning," Bernard said. "She would not take to her bed for anything less than a serious injury."

"And yet, she prides herself on her ability to heal others. Such a paradox, isn't it?"

Bernard took off his spectacles and pinched the bridge of his nose. "One does not want to be rude, Mama, but this translation is giving me fits, and whatever small talk you made with Cam is between you and him."

Bernard was a good man and very bright in a bookish way, but he lacked both ambition and vision.

"If you ever want the bishopric that fate so cruelly denied your father, Bernard, you had best take an interest in his lordship's affairs. His sponsorship will mean the difference between moldering away here in the shires for the rest of your days and making a real difference among churchmen of note."

Bernard put his spectacles back on. "Mama, do you miss the late baron even a little? For I confess I do. Alexander was the closest thing I had to a friend in these surrounds. He'd known me since birth and ensured I was well situated here at St. Wilfrid's. He was a good, dear person, and I still feel his absence far too keenly to be bothering about bishops or churchmen of note."

What an inconvenient moment for Bernard to indulge in an outburst. "Of course I mourn the late baron deeply. He was my nephew and the best of fellows. But now we have Camden to deal with, a lesser article by any measure, and how he goes on will matter to the whole shire, just as Alex's generosity and graciousness mattered. I have a duty to introduce Camden to his responsibilities in a manner that befits the tradition he must now uphold."

Bernard rose, dumped half a scoop of coal onto the hearth, and poked up the fire. "I will pay my respects to Cam when I look in on Mrs. Shorer tomorrow, but, Mama, you meddle with the Hall at your peril. I ask you to note my strongest disapproval of such actions. Leave Cam in peace. Do not harass him into courting Davina Halbertson or Dorothea Considine. He would make either woman miserable, assuming you could hoodwink him into marrying one of them."

"I was actually leaning toward the Dingle girl. She's not as catty as Miss Considine and not as uncertain as the Halbertson girl." Until that moment, Lady Josephine hadn't given Miss Dingle one serious matchmaking thought.

"Annabelle Dingle is also quite enamored of Horace Doonenburg. Perhaps you haven't noticed that they are walking home from market together?"

"The little baggage is toying with him, else she'd walk home from services with him." Though Annabelle was also astute enough to avoid letting Lady Josephine note her interest in Doonenburg, a widower with some acreage and a small daughter.

The match would be solid, as the locals said, but Lady Josephine was disinclined to reward deviousness with connubial joy. The late Mrs. Doonenburg had run up debts in the York shops, and a husband could be imprisoned for what his wife owed.

The law was so unforgiving in many regards.

"Please take my warmest regards to Camden when you call

upon him tomorrow," Lady Josephine said, "and my best wishes for a full and speedy recovery to Mrs. Shorer. The dear creature should long since have been pensioned off, but one did not want to press Alexander to tend to such matters when he was so clearly declining."

And when Alexander had nearly snarled at his aunt for even raising the topic. Such ingratitude, but then, the baron had been staring eternity in the face, and that might blight the mood of many a lesser man.

"Mama, did you have a specific reason for intruding on my sermon preparations?"

To be referred to as an intruder twice in one day... The younger generation needed a serious lesson in manners.

"I wanted to ask you a question. Have we any parishioners who are considering emigration?"

Bernard removed his right sleeve button and began folding his cuff back. "Why raise this topic, Mama? Your usual circle in our surrounds will remain by the Dales until their stately homes are ruins overrun by sheep. They would consider emigration as a fate worse than purgatory."

"As would I, and yet, for the tenant families, the shopkeepers, the lesser folk, leaving Albion's shores often appeals." And good riddance to them if they were so unhappy in such a green and pleasant land.

"Mama, I must ask again, why do you raise this question?"

"Because such families are often in difficulties, Bernard, and it is our duty to aid those in difficulties. Use the wits I know you to possess. Such unfortunates leave home because their land can't produce, their shop goods aren't selling, their children can find no work. They will maintain appearances as well as they can for as long as they can, but when a family begins to approvingly refer to cousins in Nova Scotia, a conscientious vicar takes note."

Bernard put his sleeve button in a pocket. "The Colcannons have mentioned her brother and sister in... Pennsylvania, I believe. They do not appear to be struggling."

I have raised a dunderhead. "Well, do let me know if you hear of an impending emigration, or somebody saving up for passage money."

"Of course, Mama." Bernard set the pen in its tray and resumed his seat behind the desk. "I'll see you at supper."

Truly, men were to be pitied. Completely at the mercy of their moods and animal spirits.

Perhaps Miss Halbertson ought to marry Bernard, but no. Better to have the meeker resource installed at the Hall. Bernard would just have to endure another year or so of bachelorhood, and by then Miss Considine might have learned sufficient humility to become a vicar's wife. Handsome, solvent bachelors were hardly thick on the ground, a lesson she had yet to take to heart.

Lady Josephine ordered a tray in her sitting room and turned her mind to her long list of acquaintances and correspondents. The right party would be discreet, resourceful, and pragmatic, as all the best clergymen's wives needed to be. Connections in the wilds of Ireland would be helpful, or even—duty demanded stern measures—the former colonies.

A name popped into her head like a heavenly inspiration. "Ah, the very one."

Lady Josephine subjected herself to the laborious process of composing an epistle. Gracious, tactful, and polite, but also a concise statement of need and ability to pay. Kendra MacDougal was all that her ladyship could desire, also a bit of a schemer. Her designs were all in aid of her husband's advancement, and nobody should fault a clergyman's wife for harboring ambitions that would allow him to better serve the church.

Dear Camden could spout off all he pleased about mill wheels, harvest, and Thaddeus Singleton's stubbornness, but the lord of the manor did not brave the pouring rain to talk about mill wheels, much less sacrifice his Sunday feast for more discussion of same.

"He's smitten," Lady Josephine murmured, sealing her letter. "Camden has ever been one to take the wrong road, to disdain the blessings he's done nothing to earn."

To be fair, Alice was likely blameless. She could not help that she was a walking invitation to sin, what with that awful hair and such an unfashionable figure. She doubtless had no idea the baron was harboring ungentlemanly thoughts about her. The girl was curiously dull-witted in some ways. Even Blessington Peabody was hesitant to take her on, and he was no great intellect himself.

Alice must nonetheless be inspired to dissuade the baron from foolishness.

And really, if he wasn't offering the poor girl marriage—even Camden would not be that daft—then entangling herself with him would be the most foolish path Alice could pursue. Josephine's duty —to Alice and Camden both, much less to the spiritual welfare of St. Wilfrid's parish generally—could not be clearer.

She scrawled the direction on the outside of her epistle and slipped it into her reticule. She'd mail that letter from Farnes Crossing and send it by express.

CHAPTER ELEVEN

"Wiggle your toes," Alice said.

Mrs. Shorer obliged. "I told you, nothing was broken. I simply wrenched it. I should be up and about tomorrow."

Alice slipped a thick wool stocking over the small, veined foot. "What are you up to, madam? You could be bustling about now, but you continue to rest. You are no better at resting than I am."

Alice and her patient—or sham facsimile thereof—enjoyed the cramped but absolute privacy of Mrs. Shorer's sitting room. The baron's dressing closet was twice the size of the housekeeper's parlor, but not half so full of memories and mementos. Sketches on the wall told of nieces and nephews, as well as great-nieces and great-nephews. One of several frames above the mantel depicted a couple no longer in the first blush of youth, their Sunday finest suggesting a humble station.

Maryanne and her Henry, the couple who'd seen through Lady Josephine's nasty lies and eloped. Alice had made the drawing at Mrs. Shorer's request, and a fortnight later, the couple had decamped for better prospects.

"You must promise me your discretion, Alice," Mrs. Shorer said, taking the slipper from Alice's hand and tucking it over her foot. "Most of all, you must not discuss my little ploy with your grandfather. He will lecture me until kingdom come, as only Thaddeus Singleton can lecture."

Interesting. Grandpapa was not prone to lengthy discourses in Alice's experience. He was more one to brood, expostulate, and be done with a topic.

"Your confidences are safe with me."

"Of course they are. I ought not to have implied otherwise. Be a dear and pour us a bit more lemonade."

An extravagance, by Mrs. Shorer's standards, but she believed fresh fruit aided healing, and who was Alice to argue?

"We'll not run out of ice this year," Mrs. Shorer said, sipping her drink. "No baron on hand this summer to help us use up our stores. And toward the end... I do miss Baron Alexander, but Camden is making a good start on matters. He personally demanded that I explain the household books to him."

Why announce that? The baron was Mrs. Shorer's employer, and he ought to inspect his own household books. "His lordship is very comfortable with figures and ledgers."

"He always was. The brightest of the lot, according to your grandfather, and let it be noted that for once, he and I agreed." She peered, birdlike, at Alice over the rim of her glass. "You mustn't tell him that. Thaddeus delights in believing himself to be the sole diviner of Camden's potential, despite the way Lady Josephine slandered the boy."

"Slandered him?"

Mrs. Shorer set her glass on the side table with a soft thump. "There he was, years younger than his brother and his cousin, and all her ladyship could notice was that his studies were not as advanced, that he was not as nimble, not as strong, and she always spread this bile in the hearing of other adults."

"Camden heard enough of it too," Alice said, thinking back. "I did as well. I recall..." The memory was vague, but not gone altogether. "The older boys were playing chess, and Alex was losing. Cam came along and moved one of Alex's pieces to get him unstuck. Bernard howled, Alex gloated, and Cam was just beginning to smile when Lady Josephine remarked that only a little barbarian would interrupt a gentlemanly game in such an unmannerly fashion."

That long-ago day had been sunny, the hour early. Alice had accompanied Grandpapa on a call to the Hall and been consigned to tarrying on the back terrace while the adults conducted their business. What Lady Josephine had been doing among the infantry, Alice did not know.

Spreading bile.

"Her perishing ladyship is a plague on the shire," Mrs. Shorer said. "Tried to catch me making errors in the ledgers, tried to accuse me of a lack of thrift. That woman would not know thrift if it bit her beringed finger. She found nothing—not a sum rounded the wrong direction, not tuppence in the wrong column. You be careful, Alice. You be very careful of her."

"I try to be, but none of this old news explains why you are malingering with a perfectly spry ankle."

Mrs. Shorer grinned. Alice had seldom seen her without her mobcap. To behold Mrs. Shorer at her leisure, snow-white hair in a soft bun, humor lighting her eyes, was to realize that even the elderly could be full of surprises.

Eunice Shorer was pretty, as pressed flowers were pretty. More delicate than the fresh specimen, the color subdued, the foliage faded, but still very much a blossom, and all the more precious for having so long outlasted the lavish beauty of springtime.

"Dearest Alice, you might not have noticed, but I have grown old."

Alice assumed a puzzled expression. "You have? I was not aware of this. You flit about this house like a sparrow looking to free itself from a disobliging barn. The maids trundling in your wake are invariably panting with exertion. The Hall sparkles or you know the reason why, and your linen closets are the envy of all Yorkshire. Nobody's sachets and soaps smell as divine as yours, and the staff enjoys robust good health in part because of your expertise with the herbs. What is this 'I have grown old' nonsense you refer to?"

"You are such a sweet person, Alice Singleton. I am elderly, and Saint Peter has plans for me. Heaven is undergoing a thorough cleaning in anticipation of my arrival. You may depend upon that. Because I value my post, I must choose a successor from among the maids."

"The baron will make the choice."

"The baron has a good head on his handsome shoulders—the rest of him is rather splendid too. Don't look shocked, Alice. I am not blind. He will choose the party I nominate as my successor. I don't suppose you want that honor?"

"Lady Josephine would be horrified." Then too, the post of baroness might be offered, a notion Alice could barely credit, much less accept.

Mrs. Shorer patted Alice's wrist with cool fingers. "You and Camden would suit, you know. Marry our baron, and you might give that demon in Christian clothing an apoplexy."

What cataclysms were portended when both Grandpapa and Mrs. Shorer were making a match between Alice and Camden Huxley?

"Eunice Shorer, you blaspheme."

Mrs. Shorer took a placid sip of her tea. "I have contemplated slipping a lethal dose of belladonna into her ladyship's cordial, my dear. Not a pleasant death."

This disclosure was made without a scintilla of humor—or shame. "Now you sound as if your wits are wandering, and I know you are trying to distract me from my earlier question: Why pretend you turned your ankle?"

"We will get to that, but first, you may be assured that my vengeful impulses are under control for the nonce. Her ladyship was most in peril when you wrote to me about the difficulty you endured when you were parted from the baby."

Sore breasts. Terribly sore and swollen breasts, after three months of nursing an infant multiple times daily. The problem had begun to subside even before Mrs. Shorer had penned a reply.

"Gabriella. She has a name." And she was no longer a baby.

"You were in pain and had nobody else to advise you. Why you and the baby could not simply stay on with that vicar and his lady, I do not know."

"The vicar and his lady wanted a child of their own. I understood that. I was glad of it. They were good to her too." Good to Alice as well. "Mrs. Frampton wrote to me on several occasions. She sent me a lock of Gabriella's hair. You know that."

Mrs. Shorer had been the correspondent of record, lest Lady Josephine get wind that the clean break *demanded by both common sense and kindness* had not been so clean after all.

Mrs. Shorer helped herself to a candied violet from the dish on the side table. "A pity Mrs. Frampton was taken to her reward so soon."

Alice had always found candied violets to have an underlying bitterness. "And a blessing that Mr. Frampton wasn't willing to take Gabriella with him to Cathay."

He had suggested the orphans' home in Farnes Crossing, and Lady Josephine had capitulated, in part because she'd had no choice. At that point, Mr. Frampton had been Gabriella's only surviving parent of record. A good, kind man who apparently saw more than he'd let on and who'd loved his wife dearly.

Three years ago, Bernard had casually imparted the news that Reverend Frampton, former shepherd of the flock in Kettleham out on the Dales, was among the missionaries who had succumbed to some tropical disease. Alice had dropped half a row of stitches as

Bernard had maundered on about some bishop's son who was said to be in the sponging house again.

From that point forward, Alice's life had been balanced between dread and hope. For any legal purpose, Gabriella was an orphan, and Alice had no claim on her.

While Lady Josephine was the patroness of the orphanage.

"Tell me about your ankle," Alice said, abruptly out of patience with ancient history. "Why dissemble like this?"

Mrs. Shorer selected another violet. "Somebody must take up the reins here, Alice, and I must have time to teach that person how to deal with Lady Josephine. Her kind aren't prone to premature death. Their sheer bitterness sustains them, and—the Lord, He knoweth— she has the means and mentality to make life miserable for the present baron's entire household. Both your grandfather and Beaglemore warned me when I was new to my post, and they are not fellows to speak ill of a lady, whatever other faults they might possess in abundance."

"Then you are allowing the maids to choose your successor amongst themselves?" What an odd, inspired notion.

"We have a good bunch here at the Hall, Alice. Hard workers, smart without getting above themselves. Beaglemore can say the same about his lads, and I'd put our outside staff above any, including those jumped-up buffoons at Alnwick. My girls will sort themselves out."

"How?"

"I am watching for who tattles. Who holds her tongue despite the temptation to gossip. Who notices that this time of year, all the scything east of the Hall puts a fine dust in the air that ends up all over the library. I will see who whispers behind her hand to stir the pot and who uses my supposed absence to linger over her nooning."

"Beaglemore will report to you?" Another odd notion.

"We keep each other informed, Alice, and look out for each other. Not the same thing at all. Why aren't you at Farnes Crossing this morning?"

"Lady Josephine wanted to remind me of my place." As cruelly as possible. Alice would admit that much, to herself.

Mrs. Shorer smiled benignly. "Won't she be surprised when she finds that your place is in the baroness's suite, hmm?"

"Please don't speculate in that direction and certainly not aloud." Alice had been speculating in that direction, also dreaming and wishing. "And you'd best make a miraculous recovery soon, ma'am. Nobody believes you'd stay abed for more than three days."

"Suppose I'd better." She popped to her feet and hugged Alice tightly, which was both similar to and very different from the rare hugs Gabriella had given Alice. "Take care, child, and be bold. Camden understands the need to be bold sometimes. Why don't you depart through the herb garden? One can always use a bit more mint or lemongrass, can't one?"

Alice dipped a curtsey and exited the Hall by virtue of the door between the china and porcelain closets. She'd put on her bonnet and gone halfway across the herb garden before she realized that she and the bees were not the garden's only occupants.

Camden Huxley sat on a bench in the shade, eyes closed. He opened them and treated Alice to another one of those subdued smiles.

"Caught you fair and square, Alice Singleton. Let's walk, shall we?"

He had caught her, well and truly, but how fast would he uncatch her if he learned she had a daughter born out of wedlock who lived only a few miles away?

∼

A war had begun inside Cam, between the directive by which he conducted most of his life and the directive by which he'd earned most of his coin. The first commandment was: Do not rush.

Whether negotiating the sale of lucrative cargo, allowing a new boy to find his way among the others, earning trust from horses or cats, or training a new clerk, haste could be fatal to success. When investigating a business prospect, haste could result in risks overlooked or competition underestimated.

With the boys, trying to steer a lad toward clerking when he was a groom at heart only resulted in misery, unless the boy himself made the decision.

And even then...

Watching Alice Singleton stride across the garden, all business in a wide-brimmed straw hat and plain brown walking dress, Cam stifled the urge to spring over the herbaceous borders and tackle her amid the lavender.

He'd take off that straw hat, letting his fingers brush her chin and neck as he undid the ribbons, and he'd brace Alice against the birch tree in the corner, and froth that ridiculous ruffled hem over her knees...

Do not rush.

He rose slowly. "It's a pleasant day for a stroll, and you can tell me how Mrs. Shorer is getting on."

Alice regarded him balefully. "Were you spying on me?"

"Miss Singleton, you wound me. I used to come out here as a boy because the scents are so lovely and the gardeners never tattled on me. I'm wrestling with a conundrum, and this is a quiet place to think."

"What manner of conundrum?"

She was tallish, wary, and possessed of quick wits that she could hide behind half a glass of punch and a simpering smile.

Cam winged his arm. "Several different puzzles vex me. I must promote somebody to Armendink's place, but that person will be resented by all whose ambitions I frustrate. I have three candidates in mind, none ideal and all sufficiently qualified."

Alice slipped her fingers around the crook of his elbow. "You could hire somebody."

Preferably somebody Worth Kettering had relied upon for years.

"Time is somewhat of the essence, and here I am, lost in the wilds of Yorkshire and likely to remain here for at least a fortnight."

"A fortnight?"

"At least." Not much time to get a courtship underway, but Cam's latest trek along the Great North Road had actually been a pleasant respite. He could make the journey again and have an even better sense of how to make time in a coach productive. "What did Mrs. Shorer have to say?"

"She claims her turned ankle—the ankle she pretended to turn—is a ploy in aid of choosing a successor, oddly enough. While she's tucked away in her parlor, the maids are sorting themselves out. Some are slacking a bit. Some are working as hard as ever. A few are yielding to the temptation to gossip. Others are cheerful without lapsing into idle talk."

Cam held the door in the garden wall for Alice and followed her out onto the lawn bordering the park. The sun sparkled on lush green grass. The sky arched achingly blue above. A border of hollyhocks along the wall added tall stalks of pink, white, and yellow joy to the scene, and Alice Singleton was allowing Cam to escort her.

Truly, Yorkshire was lovely in the summer. "Is Mrs. Shorer holding auditions?" Cam asked.

"So she claims."

The urge to take Alice's hand, to lace his fingers with hers, to brace her back against the old wall and kiss her until they hadn't a functional wit between them...

Alice resumed her grip of his elbow. "The path to the cottage starts among those maples."

"I know that. You aren't convinced Mrs. Shorer was honest with you?"

"She was in some regards. Not in others. She knows her staff, my lord. She knows who carries tales and who quietly takes initiative. Some of those women have been in her employ for half their lives. Three days of idleness on Mrs. Shorer's part won't yield any great insights, and besides, you might decide to send your London housekeeper up here rather than promote from among the Hall's staff."

"My London housekeeper would never leave Town." Nor would she abandon her *wee, wicked laddies*, bless her rather stern, Scottish heart. "Do you fear Mrs. Shorer needed the rest for some reason more serious than a sprained ankle?"

Alice's steps slowed. "My lord, she was matchmaking."

Cam nearly said, *Between one of the maids and a footman?* But he caught himself as the notion meshed with his unacknowledged hunches.

"I suspect Thaddeus was doing the same, with yesterday's protracted postprandial nap. I don't know whether to be alarmed or pleased, but I suppose their support is better than their disapproval."

Touching, in a way, to have a vote of confidence from the old guard. Also… unsettling.

Why had they taken up the cause almost before Cam himself had decided upon his course? What was the urgency? Would Alice be put off by their intrigues?

Do not rush.

"I fear both Grandpapa and Mrs. Shorer want to see me settled before they die, and that… I don't want them to die, and I don't want to be an obligation they must tend to on their way out the door. More to the point, I cannot abide meddling in any fashion. Well-intended meddling is still meddling."

For Alice, that was a tirade, and in the vicinity of Lorne Hall, all tirades led to… "Lady Josephine is a champion meddler."

Alice picked up her pace, her atrocious ruffled hem rustling over the grass. "Oh, precisely, my lord. Her ladyship has no shame when it comes to manipulating others, always for their own good, and yet, nobody seems able to manipulate her."

Interesting observation. "Alice, I can have a word with the elders, tell them that their machinations are likely to have the opposite of the intended result. I don't care to be treated like a pawn on a chessboard either."

Stop fidgeting, Camden. Speak up, young man. Huxley, recite.

"They would be hurt," Alice said. "They are only trying to help."

Alice would not for the world offend people she cared about. "But they have upset you?"

Cam had escorted Alice to the towering maples that enjoyed the sunlight at the edge of the home wood. The path winding deeper into the woods lay mostly in shade, and though Cam had traveled it often in boyhood, the prospect was lovelier with Alice at his side.

This part of the woods, so close to the Hall, had been undisturbed for generations. The trail wound beneath ancient maples, around sprawling oaks, and through dappled clearings. Greenery sprang up where the occasional sunbeam penetrated, with herb Robert providing splashes of pink and dog violets adding tiny dashes of purple to the palette.

Alice stumbled slightly against his side.

"Careful." He took her hand and expected to be rebuked.

"I'm in a hurry. I know better than to hurry," Alice said. "That root has been tripping me since the day I arrived on Grandpapa's doorstep. Grandpapa has told me to take my time more often than he's told me to stop chattering or be still."

"You don't chatter." How pleasant, how deeply gratifying, to hold her hand and stroll through the woods. How frustrating that Alice was wroth with the elders and annoyed rather than pleased with their schemes.

"I chattered when I was younger," she said. "I seemed to be the only girl of my age in the entire shire, and I had to learn that Grandpapa did not want to hear about every new litter of kittens or pair of fawns I'd seen on the way to market."

"And thus you became bookish." Perhaps Cam had trodden this path with Alice and hadn't known it at the time.

"Your uncle, Vicar Ambrose Huxley, was kind to me. Generous with his books, not at all prone to spouting Scripture. He said I was smart. I was astonished because I knew the vicar would not lie to me, and what few indications I had suggested I was the wrong size, had the wrong hair color, the wrong interests and proclivities, the wrong everything."

"Uncle said the same thing to me," Cam said, brushing his thumb over Alice's knuckles while setting a more deliberate pace. "That you were smart." At first, Cam had pushed the observation aside as just another backhanded slight to a boy who was not smart, or quick, or charming, but Alice was right—Uncle had been kind and honest.

Lady Josephine had doubtless thought she could manage Uncle into a bishop's robes. She, or life's many frustrations, had managed Uncle into the brandy decanters and an early grave instead.

"My lord?"

"Cam."

"I am not feeling very bright right now. I am feeling..."

Cam stopped and took her other hand in his. *Let her say amorous. Please let her say she's feeling amorous.* "Yes?"

"Muddled. I am quite, quite muddled, and when I am muddled, I make foolish choices."

What was she going on about? "You could not possibly be foolish, Alice."

She looked at their joined hands. "You are so wrong. You are so wretchedly, abysmally wrong."

Never argue with a lady, particularly when she appeared to be contemplating mischief.

Alice shook a hand free and wrapped it around Cam's nape, then pressed her lips to his. "It's my turn. I want to take my turn."

Cam put his arms around her waist and waited until, take it, she did.

Alice was as thorough and energetic about her kissing as she was about everything else. She explored, she tasted, she investigated and invited Cam to take reciprocal liberties. This was no spinster tolerating a few chaste overtures. Alice *taking her turn* was like a Valkyrie taking to the skies, determined on achieving victory over every inhibition and prohibition.

By the time she rested her forehead on Cam's shoulder, he was breathing heavily, and his back was braced against—of all things—a half-grown white birch.

"Not here," he rasped, tunneling his fingers into the warmth of Alice's bun.

Alice peered up at him. "Beg pardon?"

"Not... I cannot believe I said this out loud. Not here. Not among the bracken and rocks, in the forest damned primeval, where any village boy could come along..."

Alice brushed her hand over his hair, her eyes alight with amusement. "I was only kissing you."

"*Only*. Woman, you have no idea." Except, she did, apparently. Alice was no innocent, and the relief of that realization was enormous. The best negotiations were between equals, between parties with similar degrees of confidence, skill, and determination.

Somebody had afforded Alice the opportunity to develop the skill. Sheer determination was hers by right of birth. Confidence had been less in evidence. If pressed, Cam would have said that Alice's kisses, while passionate, also bore an edge of desperation, of anxiety.

Who was he? Cam would no more ask that question than he would have laid Alice down among the ferns and commenced rutting. The temptation was there, but so was the common sense—and the respect.

Do not rush. Perhaps Alice had had a succession of disappointments or frolics—Cam had certainly had a few of the latter—but her past was not his concern.

"I need..." He breathed in attar of roses and shut his fool mouth. He did not need to step away from her, regain his dignity, and saunter out of the forest as if nothing had happened.

He needed *her*. He needed to hold her, to feel her, to be hers.

"I need time," Alice said. "If I was muddled before, I am completely at sixes and sevens now. You kiss fiendishly well, my lord."

"Cam. You provide fiendishly spectacular inspiration."

She brushed a hand over his falls and muttered something about spectacular being in the eyes of the beholder.

"Alice, please don't tease."

She withdrew her hand immediately. "Sorry. I presumed…"

Cam seized her fingers and kissed them. "You did not presume, and were we guaranteed privacy and time, I'd be… naked, for starts, and teasing you right back. Let's leave it at that, shall we?"

She smiled that beguiling, sweet, infernal smile. "So would I—be without clothing." She paced off a few steps, head bowed, then rounded on him.

"I was planning to tell you that while your overtures are very flattering, and I am tempted, that we would not suit and to please take yourself back to London."

All the bubbling, warm, amorous sensations inside Cam froze in an instant. "You did not tell me that, and I hope you aren't about to embark on such a hopeless announcement now."

Her smile faded to something infinitely sadder. "I should."

No, she should not. "Alice, we got a little carried away, I agree, but courting couples kiss. They do more than kiss." Wonderfully much more.

"I haven't given you leave to court me."

Cam rather thought she just had. "Trying my paces, were you?" To his chagrin, he was not enjoying this negotiation, if that's what it was. Not at all.

"Or testing my own." Alice sighed, closed the distance between them, and winnowed her fingers through his hair again. "I love touching you. Nobody touches me, but with you… I am in very great trouble, my lord. You really would simplify my life by returning to London."

"I will soon enough. I'd like to take you with me." A complicated undertaking, given that they were not married—*yet*—but some chaperone or other could be hired for the duration.

"Not possible. Harvest has some weeks yet to go and there's still a great deal of work to do before winter arrives."

Cam tucked a strand of hair behind her ear. "Are you tempted anyway?"

She caught his wrist and cradled his palm against her cheek. "Of course. I am besotted with you. I have no dignity and less than no sense where you are concerned. I know better. I know how fragile my reputation is, and—"

Cam kissed her busy mouth. "I know that I care for you as I have never cared for another, ever, and that conclusion is closed to debate. The feelings are there, as real and substantial as the Dales, and I make a gift of them to you. Let me court you, Alice."

Her scrutiny was nearly solemn, and Cam braced himself for a rejection. A setback, rather, and only a setback, because he'd spoken the plain truth.

"I want to be courted by you," she said, "but I have much to consider, and we must not be hasty. Other people will be affected by the decisions we make, and haste has never served me well. Please consider that I might be toying with your affections and exercise appropriate caution."

She was warning *him*? Confirmed spinster, parish do-gooder, all-around over-competent, dowdy, nobody martyred to Lady Josephine's pious conceits? *She* was warning the man-about-London turned peer?

And yet, Cam could not dismiss Alice's words or the foreboding they dashed all over his unruly desire.

"You be warned," he said, once again offering his arm. "I am determined to a fault, Alice, and I can be both endlessly patient and ruthless when necessary. I have never sought permission to court a lady previously, and if you refuse my addresses, then Lady Josephine might well be the mother of the next baron. You would not want that on your conscience, would you?"

His attempt at humor—albeit humor based in fact—did little to lighten the moment.

Alice took his arm, and when they emerged from the trees, she stopped, dipped a curtsey, and left him standing in the shadows without another word, and certainly without another kiss.

Which meant... it was now *his turn,* and the second commandment Cam kept ever near his awareness, the directive by which he had become modestly wealthy and enviably successful, was: Once the course is set, do not hesitate.

He watched Alice disappear into her grandpapa's cottage and had to force himself to leave rather than stand about like a gormless boy hoping for a glimpse of his adored as she passed by a window.

And Alice believed *she* was besotted.

CHAPTER TWELVE

"Might I carry that for you, Miss Singleton?" Bernard Huxley, blond, smiling, and utterly inconvenient, fell in step beside Alice as she marched along the high street of Farnes Crossing.

"You absolutely may." She passed him a small burlap sack. "Grandpapa says now is the time to stock up on whetstones. At the beginning of harvest, they're dear, then the prices drop."

"Whetstones." Bernard hefted the sack. "Does nothing escape Singleton's notice?"

The question bore a hint of innuendo, which might have been real, but was more likely the product of Alice's overly active imagination. Bernard had never been given to hints or veiled threats before, and she was being ridiculous—probably.

"Grandpapa claims his eyesight and hearing aren't what they used to be, but I can detect no signs of diminished faculties." He was religious about his morning dose of digitalis, though Alice would not disclose that to the vicar.

Because the vicar might accidentally mention what he'd heard to his blasted mother.

"Alice, I confess I am not pleased that Singleton would send you after his whetstones. Might not one of Jonesberry's underlings from the home farm have made this trek?"

Alice had left her gig at the livery, and she was walking in the opposite direction. Bernard would notice that.

"I come here every Tuesday with your mother, sir. It's hardly a trek, and Cerberus enjoys the exercise. Besides, every able-bodied man is needed to bring in the wheat, and the baron wants some haying done as well. Grandpapa is in high dudgeon over that suggestion, and telling him to have somebody else fetch his whetstones would have required fortitude I lack."

Grandpapa had, in fact, intended to send one of Burnside's grooms. Alice had offered to go instead.

"What does the baron know of haying?" Bernard asked. "I thought his lordship had eschewed all things rural and plighted his troth to the countinghouse."

Was Bernard *bitter* to have his younger cousin in residence at the Hall? "The sweet shop is two doors up," Alice said. "Will you join me in an ice? You are sworn to secrecy, of course."

"As are you. I haven't had an ice... Well, yes. I will join you. Tell me about Cam's haying project."

"You aren't lordshipping him?"

"Mama is, at least in the hearing of anybody save myself. I would never disrespect my cousin publicly, or privately for that matter, but to me, he has always been Cam. A solemn little boy who grew into a quiet adolescent and then a broody young man. Took a first in mathematics, much to everybody's shock. I'm not surprised that he's immured himself in commerce. He likes complicated puzzles, and I gather commerce is that."

The present Lord Lorne liked slow kisses and cinnamon biscuits too. Alice hoarded that knowledge like a first edition copy of Wordsworth's poetry.

"The baron saw the old yearling pasture standing two-feet deep in grass and told Grandpapa we might as well make hay out of it.

Grandpapa protested vociferously, but the baron threatened to scythe it himself or put the gardeners and footmen to the job."

"*Footmen* making hay? Mama would be scandalized."

What scandalized the vicar's mama should matter not at all to anybody, but instead mattered far too much.

"Grandpapa won't let it come to that. The gardeners know how to wield a scythe, and they will doubtless be asked to help, but I suspect his lordship brought up the footmen simply to inspire Grandpapa to action."

Cam was that clever, that strategic.

Bernard held the door to the sweet shop and saw Alice settled at a little table in the shop's side garden. No market was in progress, and thus the garden had only two other occupants. A pair of older ladies in widow's weeds occupied a table in the shade, their laughter merry and frequent.

What did it signify when Alice envied widows their joy?

"What flavor for you?" Bernard asked.

"Cinnamon. You?"

"Barberry." He strode off, too handsome not to catch the eyes of the older ladies. They beamed at Alice and nodded, as if congratulating her on some accomplishment.

Of all times and places for Bernard to appear… Drat the luck. Drat the rubbishing, perishing luck.

Bernard emerged from the shop, followed by a maid carrying a tray. She set the treats down, cast an appreciative eye over Bernard, and bobbed a departing curtsey.

"Does being a handsome, single vicar ever grow burdensome?" Alice asked.

Bernard picked up his spoon and smiled wanly. "Conceding your compliment for the sake of argument, I hardly know how to answer. Would being a homely single vicar be worse? You might better inquire if it's burdensome having my mother at the vicarage, but you are too diplomatic for that. I could ask you how Mrs. Shorer is faring —one heard she was in bed with a sprained ankle—but you will choose your words carefully on even that subject, knowing I might repeat the news to Lady Josephine."

Alice took a spoonful of frozen sweetness, the better to give her time to frame a reply. Bernard in a mood this forthright was a new and disconcerting experience.

"Your mother is much respected."

"Much resented, you mean. Annabelle Dingle and Horace Doonenburg walk home from market together and studiously avoid each other in the churchyard. I made the mistake of informing Mama of this when she began considering Miss Dingle for the baron. Horace and Annabelle don't want Mama doing to them what she did to Henry and Maryanne last year."

"Your mother is the reason Henry and Maryanne found the courage to marry and leave here."

"Not in that order, which is a blight upon my care of the flock. What do you make of the new baron, and no, I will not parrot your words to my mother."

"Nobody believes you bear tales." Some of Alice's pleasure in her treat waned. "We know how her ladyship is, though. She could winkle secrets from a stone saint."

"All in the name of somebody's best interests or the greater good." Bernard ate a small spoonful of his ice. "She's trying to find a bride for Cam, and I cannot see that ending well."

To be honest, neither could Alice, if the prospective baroness was local. "I thought his lordship was returning to London soon."

Bernard regarded her over his empty spoon. "You are privy to his plans? He's told me nothing."

"I spent hours with him tending to correspondence, Bernard. The whole shire knows as much. His commercial enterprises are demanding and require his presence in Town. Only St. Didier's prodding got his lordship up here before winter."

Bernard set the spoon back in the bowl. "St. Didier bothers me. What is he doing here, and why do I have the sense I've seen him somewhere before?"

Probably because the man was capable of spying in disguise. Alice would have to ask Cam about that.

"St. Didier's family title reverted to the crown exactly one generation ago. Mr. St. Didier has developed the habit of encouraging reluctant peers to attend to their duties."

"Cam told you that."

Well, yes. Between a thank-you to the Paris factor and a query regarding timber from Sweden, St. Didier's lot in life had come up.

"It's no secret. Your mama's London correspondents probably know more than that about him."

Bernard gathered up another spoonful of ice. "She doesn't have many connections in Town, except for those related to the church. I doubt there's a corner of Britain where she hasn't some parson's widow, wife, mama, or sister to write to. Very industrious."

Very burdensome, when Alice was called upon to rewrite Lady Josephine's epistles to all those pious ladies.

"Bernard, what brought you to Farnes Crossing today?"

If he took offense at the abrupt change of topic, he didn't show it, which was fortunate. Alice wanted, rather urgently, to know what he was about.

He saluted with his spoonful of ice. "I'm conducting an epistolary romance, in the opinion of the innkeeper's wife. Or several of them. Have been for some time, but such is my discretion that I come to Farnes Crossing to send and receive my missives."

"Bernard, what are you talking about?" The whole discussion, Bernard's very presence in Farnes Crossing, made Alice uneasy. Would he report seeing her to his mother? Could Alice ask him not to? Buying new whetstones at harvest was hardly urgent enough to justify driving miles across the countryside, and Bernard was shrewd enough to conclude as much.

"I'm looking for another post," he said. "Accepting the living at St. Wilfrid's was a mistake, but Mama was insistent. Said I owed Papa's legacy that show of respect. The result has been a curse upon the congregation."

And a curse upon Bernard too? "You don't want your mother to know you're unhappy?"

"I am not particularly unhappy, or no more unhappy than usual, but others around me are. Mama has become a problem, and she's my problem. That business with Henry and Maryanne went too far, Alice. That constituted interference under Alex's roof as he lay dying. I cannot overlook it, and thus I'm taking what steps I can to remove Mama from the scene of her crimes."

Alice took another spoonful of melting ice. "You are seeking another post."

He nodded. "Cornwall appeals."

The Antipodes would be better, if Lady Josephine accompanied her son. "Your mother will hate Cornwall." Her ladyship would hate Bernard for dragging her there, but then, Lady Josephine was no more likely to dwell in Cornwall than Alice was to become a baroness.

"She will never let you take another post," Alice said, surprised at her own blunt speech. "Her ladyship thrives here, in her fashion, and Cornwall—anywhere else—would be purgatory for her. Here, Lady Josephine has the consequence of being the baron's aunt and, at least for now, the heir's mother. Elsewhere..."

"Elsewhere, she will still be an earl's daughter, still have her courtesy title and all the airs and graces she wields so well, but I can better thwart her. I am the *vicar*, Alice, which honestly doesn't matter to me as much as it should, though I am also a *gentleman*. Something must be done about Mother, and it's my fault she's been allowed to become so irksome. Nobody will say it to my face, but she's growing worse—flinging women at Cam when Alexander has barely gone to his reward, insisting on those weekly knitting sermons—and the time to act is now.

"How many times," Bernard went on tiredly, "have we heard her cheerfully admonish others to 'bloom where they are planted' as she has so selflessly bloomed after marrying my father? She can jolly well replant herself nearer to Land's End and astonish a whole new congregation with her wisdom and resilience."

Did Bernard know *how* Lady Josephine wielded her power? How she collected confidences and secrets and then extorted obedience in return? The general assumption about the shire was that he could not possibly grasp what a venal, underhanded, cruel woman he had for a mother.

Somebody needed to warn him. "Bernard, she will fight you, and you cannot imagine the low tactics she willingly employs." Alice was certain—almost certain—that Bernard knew nothing of Gabriella's situation. In the local surrounds, only Mrs. Shorer had been taken into Alice's confidence. Not even Grandpapa suspected what Alice's protracted absence had really entailed.

Though, of course, Lady Josephine knew all.

"Mama will fight me, but I am the one person she will not destroy, aren't I? If she casts me into disgrace, the scandal would reflect on her too. I am not entirely without means, Alice. I have been investing in Camden's ventures for years, modestly, of course, and anonymously, but steadily. Seemed the least I could do, and my faith has been rewarded, as it were. I can make a go of a post in Cornwall."

He sat back, looking more like a prosperous lordling than a rural vicar. "Are you finished with your cinnamon treat?" he asked. "My ice is now a cold wet mess in the bottom of my bowl. Not very appealing, I'm afraid."

"Bernard," Alice said. "Be careful. Be very careful." She had not considered previously that he'd regard his mother as anything other than a doting busybody, a fixture in his household by virtue of both filial duty and affection, but no very great imposition.

He'd been carrying a burden in silence, and Alice knew how such heartaches could increase in weight. One grew reckless, using a dozen whetstones as a pretext for spying, for example.

Bernard rose, took her hand, and bowed over it. "You be careful as well, Alice. I know Mama has made a particular pest of herself to you, and yet, you bear her company without complaint. Exercise extreme caution. She will turn on you in an instant if you come between her and her plans for the baron."

Her ladyship had long since turned on Alice—and Gabriella. "I will exercise utmost care."

He hefted the sack of stones and put it on the table. "You never saw me today. I was not here. I never come and go from the Farnes Crossing posting inn."

"Tall blond men abound in Yorkshire," Alice replied. "At a distance, they look much the same."

The vicar was asking her to lie for him. That sad realization was also a little reassuring. Alice was not Lady Josephine's only victim, not the only party baffled by her ladyship's ceaseless bullying.

Bernard favored Alice with a smile that put her in mind of the late baron. Charming, kind, even genuine most of the time. Then he was off, crossing the garden at a good clip and leaving Alice to ponder the puzzles multiplying under her nose.

"I wanted a glimpse of Gabriella," she muttered, spooning the mostly melted ice from the bottom of her bowl. "I wanted to sit up on the hill behind the orphanage and watch for her helping to hang out the wash."

Bernard's scheme was doomed. His mother would simply write to the wife of whatever vicar was retiring or vacating his post and gently, regretfully, explain why Bernard, though such a fine man, really, was not at all suited to the new position.

Her ladyship might already be on to his scheme, intercepting his mail at the posting inn. She was that devious and that determined.

That devoted to her son, she'd say.

Mrs. Shorer's remedy for the situation flitted through Alice's mind, though where would Gabriella be if Alice were hanged for murder? Emptying chamber pots in some lowly inn, vulnerable to every drunken lout with perverted fancies.

"Don't do this." Alice gathered up her effects, including the sack of stones, and made for the livery stable. Brooding and fretting never solved anything.

As she steered Cerberus in the direction of home, Alice wished she could lay Bernard's situation at Cam's feet. Cam dwelled in London. He might not know bishops or well-placed churchmen, but he knew the sorts of people who held the livings churchmen most coveted.

He knew how to negotiate with a rival, he knew... He knew Lady Josephine.

He did not, though, know about Gabriella, and Alice couldn't envision a way to inform him.

∼

The song came to an end, the windrow came to an end—or what would become a windrow when raked—and Cam glanced behind him.

"Not bad work," he said, accepting the tankard St. Didier passed him and draining half. "Straight enough, and we kept up."

"The rest held back so as not to disgrace us. They don't know whether to be scandalized or amused." St. Didier had kept his shirt and waistcoat on, but like everybody else on the haying crew, he had chaff in his hair. The toes of his boots were also covered with fine green detritus, and his complexion was ruddy.

"The rest," Cam replied, "will be able to boast next spring that Lorne Hall had plenty of hay, unlike some other estates."

"Unless it rains," St. Didier said, doing a fair imitation of Thaddeus Singleton's Yorkshire accent. "Unless it rains, sir, and then ye'll be nobbut a laughingstock." St. Didier looked almost approachable in a humorous moment.

"A tired laughingstock at that, but each acre we bring in is another ton of fodder, St. Didier. A ton of fodder can feed a large horse for a month, give or take."

"You would know these things." St. Didier finished his tankard. "Ten thousand cuts per acre. Did you count them out once upon a time in your misspent youth?"

"That figure is as old as Yorkshire, I'd guess, but I tested it. Counted cuts per pass across a field, times number of passes, divided by acres, that sort of thing. Ran the experiment over several fields. The length of the scythe can compensate for variations in the height of the scyther, provided the handles are adjusted correctly."

St. Didier regarded him with some puzzlement. "You can't help it, can you? You think like a banker."

"Like a clerk, you mean? A good farmer has a thorough grasp of numbers. Thaddeus Singleton told me that when I aspired to be his understudy. He said the ciphering part came naturally to me, and I should be grateful for it."

A rare compliment, handed out as a seemingly casual observation, but Cam had taken it to heart.

"He was right," St. Didier said, passing his tankard to the boy collecting them.

"Parkin, isn't it?" Cam said, handing over his empty tankard as well. "How is the kitchen managing without Yorkshire's best potboy?"

The lad grinned. "Cook says if the gardeners can go for farmhands, the potboy can mind the ale and water for an afternoon and no shame in it. You made a proper job of your row, my lord."

"High praise. Mind you have an occasional drink yourself, young man. That sun means business."

"Aye, milord. Best get your shirt on, sir. That's Miss Alice with the nooning."

"From the mouths of babes..." St. Didier murmured as a gig pulled up in the shade of the hedgerow, two wicker hampers tied behind the bench.

Alice wore a wide-brimmed straw hat that had seen better days, a simple maroon walking dress, and dusty ankle boots. Her arrival was greeted with a ragged cheer as the rest of the crew pulled off hats and donned shirts, waistcoats, and even jackets.

"No ruffles," Cam said. No ruffles, just the simple, sweet wonder of Alice Singleton brightening an already brilliant summer day.

"Shirt," St. Didier muttered. "Your shirt on, now."

Alice looked up from wrapping the reins and went still.

"Half the Hall's outside staff is watching," St. Didier went on quietly, as Parkin looked from Alice to Cam.

Cam made a production out of shaking the chaff from his shirt before pulling it over his head, then doing up two of the four buttons.

"Waistcoat." St. Didier spoke through clenched teeth. "Unless you want me to strangle you with it. Do not make a spectacle of yourself that involves the lady."

Somebody yelled for water, and Parkin scampered off.

"You told me to get dressed," Cam said. "I am getting dressed."

Alice accepted a proffered hand and hopped down from the gig. She disappeared amid a throng of hungry men and women who crowded around the back of the vehicle.

"I cannot emphasize strongly enough," St. Didier said, "that you trifle with that woman at your peril and hers. Do not give me cause to be disappointed in you." He stalked off, once again radiating forbidding severity.

Cam buttoned his waistcoat, honestly baffled. St. Didier had been enjoying the morning's exertion, as Cam had. Yes, the correspondence was piling up, but correspondence could wait a few hours for once. The staff at Lorne Hall had a hale and healthy baron on their hands now, and Cam had wanted to…

He ran his hands through his hair, wishing he'd brought a pocket comb. Why had he abandoned his work to come out here, much less dragged St. Didier along?

"Best get your nooning, milord," Parkin said, materializing from nowhere. "A haying crew makes locusts look like slackers, according to Cook."

"I'll do that." Cam picked up his scythe, which was overdue for peening and whetting, and took the place at the end of the line behind the gig.

No order of precedence here, no standing on ceremony, and what a relief that was. "Any left for me?" Cam asked when he was the sole unfed member of the crew.

Alice passed him a meat pasty. She, too, seemed to be assailed by a serious mood. "One, my lord, which I doubt will be enough, so we'll let you have first crack at the fruit tarts." She opened a second hamper. "Cherry on the right, lemon on the left. Bilberry in the middle."

"Which is your favorite?"

"Pear, and do not ask me to share your nooning, because I cannot, and you know it. Why is Mr. St. Didier looking so thunderous?"

"Because I dragged him out to play farmer with me this morning, and he will be sore for days." A good kind of sore, one Cam relished.

"Should you be doing this so soon after injuring your hand?" The question bore a hint of relenting.

"My hand is fine, and yes, I should be doing this. I enjoy it. I'm good at it." Two facts that had been obscured by time and temper. "I would have made a good steward." A good, happy steward.

"A post as steward would have wasted your talents." Alice passed him three lemon tarts. "Cook makes them with cinnamon. I'll see you at Sunday supper."

Thus dismissed, Cam took what passed for his meal and sat in the shade of an obliging maple with his head gardener, a merry old rascal who, when sober, answered to the name Oscar Cooper.

"Best not look at the lady like that in the churchyard, lad," Cooper said. "The old witch will take it amiss."

Cooper was outside staff, venerable, and from a long line of Lorne Hall gardeners. His place was secure, and he'd not married.

"You speak honestly of Lady Josephine."

"We all do, when private. Vicar is right enough. A bit serious, never mean. That mother o' his. She's hardest on the women, but we all give her as wide a berth as we can. Best not forget that, lad."

The joy Cam felt working Lorne Hall land—his land, his to look after at least—enjoying the gorgeous Yorkshire day, simply beholding

Alice faded. St. Didier was not one to overreact. Cooper was as honest as the harvest workday was long.

Alice had fended off anything approaching flirtation, a very different reception than Cam had had from her in the herb garden.

Lorne Hall was harboring a puzzle, and Cam had the distinct sense that unless he sorted that puzzle, he and Alice would not be sharing the happy future he was increasingly inclined to dream about.

He passed his last lemon tart to Cooper. "I've had enough haying for the nonce, but I'll be back tomorrow."

Cooper bit into the tart. "Unless it rains, lad."

Cam handed in his scythe, commended the crew chief on a good morning's work, and left by way of the footpath that wound along the home wood.

As a boy, he'd hiked the lanes and paths doing sums in his head. Now, his thoughts circled the morning's events. Had Alice been cool, civil, guarded, or merely polite? Had the silly business with slowly putting on his shirt been truly offensive, or had St. Didier become a prude in his dotage? Was turning an unused pasture into hay a genuine mistake, or was Singleton disdaining the idea to ensure Cam made a project out of it? Had Alice been reminding him—

"My lord, good day."

Bernard occupied a bench at the edge of the glebe land, his gaze on the church spire a few hundred yards off.

"Cousin." Cam sat, uninvited. "I made a fool of myself swinging a scythe all morning. I will regret this on the morrow."

"The old yearling pasture?"

"The very one. Tons of fodder going to waste, unless there's a new fashion for allowing pasture to fallow for an entire year."

"If there is, Thaddeus Singleton would know of it and have every pamphlet on the topic read and filed. He will be difficult to replace."

"Particularly if he doesn't want to leave his post."

Bernard sat back and crossed his feet at the ankles. "He doesn't want to lose his wages. For himself, he likely would not care, but he must think of Alice."

Did Bernard think of Alice as a handsome bachelor thought of a prospective wife? "Why have you always had the gift of casual elegance, Bernard? I resented you for it, but now you've landed in the vicarage, and one isn't permitted to resent you for anything."

Bernard passed a brief glance in Cam's direction. "Perhaps, if you hadn't clover in your hair, dust on your boots, and half your shirt buttons undone, you might make a better impression, hmm?"

"You are poking fun at me," Cam said, mostly to test an unlikely theory. "This is how you enjoy a bit of humor at my expense." He dusted his fingers through his hair and did up one more button.

"My lord, I depend upon you for the very bread on my table, and yet, *you* speak of resenting *me*. For that matter, I depend upon you to keep my mother's carriage in good trim, her wardrobe up to the mark, and her tea drawer full of the finest China black, which she takes with cream and sugar when nobody is watching. Ponder that for a moment."

Was everybody in a contrary mood today? "I thought Lady Josephine was quite well fixed."

Bernard shook his head. "Do you imagine she would rusticate with me if she could instead swan about York, calling on the archbishop's wife or holding fashionable at homes?"

An old memory swam up from the recesses of Cam's tired mind. His mother, who had been gathered to her reward before his eighth birthday, once made a disparaging remark about Lady Josephine being no better than she should be. Mama had been taking tea in the garden with her visiting sister while Cam had played with his soldiers.

He'd not understood the comment at the time, and it still made no sense. He was surely misremembering her words, because the implication was plain enough and utterly incongruous with the pillar of piety Cam knew as his aunt.

"I am under the impression," Cam said, "that Lady Josephine

enjoys being at the top of the social heap out here in the shires. In London, or even York or Edinburgh, a widowed earl's daughter of mature years would not have that much standing." Particularly if, as Bernard implied, she lacked significant means.

One could not pity Lady Josephine, but one could admit that, from her perspective, she was entitled to a measure of disappointment with her station. A small measure.

"Your impression is correct. Mama delights in managing the neighborhood, and I am sorry to say, she has every intention of managing you."

"My marital prospects, you mean? She has been far from subtle." Was Bernard speaking from the perspective of a cousin, a vicar, something in between?

"She will start there, then she will progress to managing the Hall. Before you know it, you will have spent five straight years anywhere but Yorkshire lest she drive you to Bedlam. By then, she will be hosting company at the Hall as if she owns it in fee simple absolute. And by the way, I myself am pursuing opportunities anywhere but Yorkshire."

"You'd take your mother with you?" Cam struggled to keep relief from his tone. Bernard might be a bit High Church in a lowly pulpit, but he was family and not a bad sort overall.

"If I can secure a post elsewhere, Mama will have little choice but to go with me, or at least absent herself from the shire."

Bernard's plan had a flaw. Cam knew that the way he knew when a negotiating opponent was bluffing.

"She hasn't the means to buy her own property?"

"She does not, unless it's a very humble property indeed. When Papa died, my mother got her hands on a tidy sum, and she promptly spent it on that enormous carriage, on fitting out every room in the vicarage, on fashion and whatnot. She spent mourning acquiring the trappings of a wealthy widow. How depleted her finances are, I do not know for certain, but she will manage best if she remains under my roof, wherever that roof might be."

"I don't want you to go." Cam made the admission with some surprise. Bernard was urbane, pleasant, well read, golden-blond, and a bit sanctimonious without being condescending. He was the pattern card of the perfect vicar, and Cam's resentment of him was—had been—real. "You are my only surviving blood relation."

"Don't be too sure of that. Alex was no saint. Neither were our fathers. Will you thwart my plan to leave?" No inflection illuminated the question whatsoever. "Alice claims that Mama will sabotage any offers to come my way, and Alice is generally right. Her surmise has been troubling me exceedingly, but I thought you'd be pleased to be rid of me. I am overpaid, lazy, and my mother can only wreak her genteel brand of havoc because I hold the living at St. Wilfrid's."

"You are not overpaid. I investigated discreetly what stipend a rural Yorkshire living brings in the general case. We are a prosperous parish, most years, and you are compensated accordingly. You have no curate, which allows more funds to be put in your pocket, though that also means you do more of the work."

Bernard looked faintly puzzled. "You make business out of even church affairs. Will you allow me to go?"

"Bernard, you are an adult male of sound mind. I could not stop you from leaving. I *of all people* understand that the power to depart is sometimes the only power left to us." Though how ironic that Bernard should now resort to the same tactic Cam had used as a younger man.

"You must do as you see fit, Bernard, and I will support whatever choices you make. Please consider, though, that Alexander has been gone only three months, and that's caused some upheaval for your congregation. I'm underfoot for the nonce, which is more upheaval. St. Didier is insisting that I must pension Mrs. Shorer, Beaglemore, and Singleton, and that will effectively upend the neighborhood."

Bernard uncrossed his legs and sat forward. "You have been paying attention."

One did not ignore St. Didier. "Good decisions are made based on good information, and for that, one must pay attention and mind the details." One also did not ignore the nagging sense that his correspondence was calling to him, and he'd been truant enough for one day.

"Please don't accept another post without giving me some notice, Bernard. If nothing else, I must find a replacement for you, and I will want your thoughts on who should fill your shoes."

"They're good people hereabouts," he said, rising. "Hardworking, tolerant, kind. They have their petty conceits and squabbles, but if nothing else, Mama has united them against a common foe, and they set aside differences because of her. Anybody you choose should prosper here and be happy."

Cam rose as well, his hips and back already protesting the morning's exertions. "Bernard, is there something you aren't telling me?" A pointless question, most times, but not always. Whatever the local puzzle was, Bernard was part of it.

"Much," he said, smiling faintly. "Much, of course, and much you won't tell me, but Alexander said you'd make a good baron. I enjoyed besting him or proving him wrong, though in this, he was correct."

Bernard bowed slightly and strode off. No handshake, no cousinly punch on the shoulder.

"Leave the man his dignity," Cam muttered, taking the path to the Hall. He moved mental chess pieces, considered options, and gave some thought to Sunday's menu and soon found himself once again at his desk, albeit in clean clothing and with a plate of sandwiches at his elbow.

The correspondence towered over the tray on which Beaglemore had delivered it.

Cam nonetheless began not by sorting and stacking, but by penning a short epistle to the family solicitors and setting it aside to be sent by express. Then he wrote an even shorter missive to Worth Kettering and set that aside to be sent by express as well.

If anybody knew the scandals, rumors, and on-dits polite society circulated behind fans and late at night in the clubs, Kettering would.

His sources were excellent, some of them quite venerable, some of them in the lowest of obscure places.

Having stolen a clerk, Kettering needed to make reparations, and Cam wasn't really asking much. Just following a hunch as sound businessmen were wont to do. Lady Josephine immuring herself in the shires out of maternal devotion was only semi-plausible. She was wellborn and greedy for power. That kind of person, regardless of gender, gravitated to Mayfair and Paris to play their nasty games, and yet, here she was, blighting the shire year after year.

One wanted more information.

Cam put the expresses out of his mind, rolled up his cuffs, and set about once again spinning epistolary straw into mercantile gold.

CHAPTER THIRTEEN

"I must have a word with Mrs. Shorer," Thaddeus Singleton said, rising. "You young people stroll about the terrace and talk philosophy or whatever the fashionable affectation is these days. My lord, thank you for a fine meal. Alice, don't lecture the man in my absence. He will have his blasted mill wheel, and there's an end to it. I'm sure the baron will be happy to see you home on such a fine evening if Mrs. Shorer takes me captive in her herbal."

Grandpapa stalked from the dining room, leaving the baron on his feet and Alice beyond mortified.

"He's matchmaking again," she said, whisking her napkin from her lap and slapping it down beside her plate. "That stubborn, ridiculous, bald-faced..." *Dear, dear old man.*

"At least somebody besides me favors the notion of you becoming the Hall's baroness," Cam said. "Shall we enjoy the evening air despite the implications?"

The meal had been scrumptious. A spicy gazpacho followed by grilled trout, then a roast of beef done to a turn, the kitchen's signature sour cream mashed potatoes, and all manner of garden bounty, followed by raspberry fool.

"Grandpapa still has a good appetite," Alice said, allowing the baron to assist her to her feet. "When he goes off his feed, I truly worry."

"You didn't eat much." The baron offered his arm and moved with Alice toward the door.

"I ate plenty." As much as her tentative stomach would allow. The meal had been served early—six p.m.—and two hours later, the sky was still full of light. "Where has Mr. St. Didier got off to?"

"York. I've asked him to look into a few matters for me."

Alice stopped as she and her escort gained the soaring main foyer. "You wanted him out from underfoot so you could woo me in peace. Does he think I'm not good enough for you?" Pointless question. In the eyes of Society, she was far from fit to become Cam's baroness.

"Boot's on the other foot," Cam said. "He warns me on pain of ruination that I must not trifle with you, to the point that I wonder if he's not a bit smitten himself."

"He isn't. We've barely exchanged two words." What did St. Didier know and to whom would he disclose it? How could he know anything?

"You're quiet, Alice. What troubles you?" His lordship had waited to pose his question until they were on the terrace, alone but for the evening sky and the sun turning the western horizon golden. An avian chorus drifted from the direction of the home wood, and a sliver of moon had already risen to the east.

A lovely night, and the automatic rejoinder—*I'm fine, thank you* —simply would not do. Alice was not fine. She was angry and hopeful and all in a muddle, and she was exceedingly unfond of muddles. The last time she'd felt this way had ended very, very badly, though she would never regret being Gabriella's mother.

The baron would see through any attempt at dissembling, unlike most of the local swains. Alice decided upon a course of half truths, though even that undertaking daunted her.

"Have you ever been taken advantage of in business?" she asked.

"A few times. The experience makes an impression. Shortly after

I mustered out, a former fellow officer suggested we partner on a shipment of rifle barrels. I wasn't keen on dealing in arms, but in the tropics, those barrels rust to uselessness in little over a year. He had secured the inventory at a bargain price. I paid the supplier, with the understanding that my partner's half of the payment would come out of our vast profits."

"There were no profits?"

"The inventory had been allowed to sit on the docks for months. The barrels were already rusted, and my erstwhile partner had been handsomely paid to swindle me out of my coin. I could prove nothing. I had the agreed upon rifle barrels delivered at the agreed upon date and time. I could do nothing at the time."

"You didn't inspect the inventory before purchasing it?"

"I looked over the few cases that weren't nailed shut. More fool, I. I haven't made the same mistake again."

"I have felt like that too," Alice said. "A complete, hopeless fool. I don't care for it."

They strolled along the balustrade, the walled garden in deepening shadows at the bottom of the terrace steps. Crickets sang slowly, a sign of summer's passing, and an owl hooted mournfully.

"Alice, I would like to marry you. I mean that sincerely. I will return to London fairly soon, but I won't disappear from your life. You need not fear that I will play you false."

"Said every handsome bounder to his gullible sweetheart." Alice took the steps, though she ought by rights to have called for her bonnet and shawl and marched off across the park in the direction of home. The baron was in the mood for plain speaking, though—something she usually admired about him—and Alice was resolved to oblige him.

"May I tell you a story?" she asked. She'd paused halfway down the steps, her escort remaining at the top. The waning light weathered his features and cast shadows around his eyes, giving her a glimpse of the older man he'd become. More formidable, more imposing, more... attractive, which ought not to be possible.

He came down the steps and gestured along the crushed-shell walkway. "I gather this story does not end happily."

"The story could have ended disastrously." But it hadn't. Not yet. "Let's sit." Alice chose a bench on the western side of the garden, one already in shadow. "Once upon time..." Alice had not meant to make these disclosures, but neither could she keep them hidden. Significant decisions could be like this, taking up every available iota of the imagination, and then, without warning, a fait accompli.

"Once upon a time," the baron said, "there dwelled in the bucolic purlieus of Yorkshire a young lady. We will call her—"

"We won't give her a name. She was lonely, this young lady." But the loneliness had followed so closely on a load of grief, she hadn't known it by name. "She was also quite honestly bored, keeping house for one distracted and somewhat crochety old relation."

Cam took Alice's hand, and she allowed it.

"A grandfather," Cam said.

"An uncle. In this story, he's an uncle." Alice focused on the shadow slipping up the opposite wall. "She was bored and lonely, and one summer, along came a winsome fellow. He was a friend of one of the local young men, a bit older than our protagonist, and a lot more worldly."

"The winsome cad ruined her." Cam loaded that short statement with loathing.

"He... Well, he broke her heart and went upon his way. She learned that her judgment regarding men is not to be trusted and that moments of pleasure can have unimaginable consequences."

"Who was he, Alice? You cannot inflict this tale upon me without realizing that I'll pummel him flat, at least financially, if I ever get the chance."

"You are angry with him?"

"As I hope you are, or were. He disgraced himself in his treatment of you."

The words were simple enough, but the *direction* of them— disgrace aimed at the marquess's darling boy, not at the foolish rusticating girl who'd allowed him liberties—left Alice feeling somehow more tense, more at sea.

Lady Josephine had taken a very different view of matters, and after years of pondering, Alice had reasoned that Lady Josephine was judgmental, manipulative, and untrustworthy, but she hadn't been wrong: Alice, despite her complete lack of experience, truly should have known better.

A marquess's worldly spare did not plight his troth with a steward's granddaughter.

I'll write. I'll write soon, darling Alice, and let you know when I'll return.

"A French cannonball pummeled him into the hereafter," she said. "I did not know what to feel about that either."

Candles were being lit in the windows of the Hall's lower floors. Time to finish this discussion and quite possibly bid his lordship farewell.

"You don't have to feel anything," Cam said, curling his free hand around Alice's fingers. "He abused your trust and left without a fare-thee-well, proving not that you lack judgment, but that he was a very good liar who lacked honor. Fortunately, his fate did not affect you."

Oh, but it had.

"I have forgiven myself," Alice said, which was true in part. "I've seen how hopelessly young I was at going-on-seventeen, how little I knew, how much I still missed my parents and a life I'd loved. Keeping house for Grandpapa was not how the headmaster's daughter saw her future turning out. I thought myself very much put upon because the closest thing to literature in Grandpapa's library was a pamphlet extolling the virtues of various types of manure."

Cam snorted, and even Alice had to smile. She'd read that pamphlet, the better to discuss the topic when Grandpapa had next grown testy.

"You were hardly as put upon as I was," Cam said. "I could not leave this place soon enough nor make a fortune fast enough.

Alexander lent me fifty pounds to get started. I paid him back with interest in less than a year."

The last of the sunbeams slipped over the opposite wall. "I should be getting home."

"You say that a lot." Cam rose and offered Alice his hand. "If you think that a bounder dallying with you years ago makes you any less attractive to me, you're daft. Are you less attracted to me because I bought rusty gun barrels?"

Alice rose and kept hold of his hand. "Not the same thing at all, my lord."

"Of course not. I lost a substantial sum because I trusted the wrong party while making a foray into a market I prefer to avoid. A minor sort of betrayal. You got your bereaved heart broken, and you are now entitled to hold at least one late aristocrat in abiding contempt. We are both older and wiser, and we do not give our hearts away easily."

Tell him the rest. Tell him about Gabriella and be done with this.

"I am used goods," Alice said as they started up the terrace steps. "A fallen woman."

"You are far too intelligent to accept either of those ridiculous labels. Try 'dear' and 'wonderful,' if you want accurate descriptors. I am in trade, and I plan to stay there. *Horrors abounding.* I can assure you, Alice, that because I am in trade and know how to manage coin and make more of same, this estate will be prospering long after the neighbors have gone bankrupt."

"An illicit dalliance is a different sort of shame than burying oneself in commercial undertakings." Why would he not listen?

"Alice, scandal is scandal. Hard lessons are hard lessons. We are not children, and I want to marry you. Give me leave to court you, please."

"You were supposed to grow all chilly and distant." Thoughtful at least. She'd expected him to allude to travel arrangements. *I'll write soon.* That sort of thing. She was older and wiser now, as he'd said.

Cam stopped at the top of the steps and smiled. "You were supposed to marry a noted amateur scholar of noble brow and independent means and preside over his household. You would raise learned brats with a genius for languages and carry on lofty correspondence with lady philosophers on the Continent."

How could she not love him? How could she not long to share the rest of her life with him?

"I would wear my hair down," Alice said, moving off across the terrace. She was near tears for no earthly reason. "At least during the day, and nobody would decry the color."

"The color of your hair is glorious. We'd best go in lest we be accused of trysting in the dark." He opened the door, and Alice stepped into the gloom of the back atrium.

Tell him. Tell him now. "I wanted children," Alice said, her heart thumping so hard Cam would surely hear it.

"I know something of children," he replied, possessing himself of both of her hands. "They are noisy, expensive, and take ten eternities to grow up, unless they belong to somebody else. I do believe it's my turn."

Alice had enough wits left to pose the only relevant question. "You don't care for children?"

"Children are a plague. Demons come to earth." His tone was jocular, but not humorous enough to empty the words of their plain meaning. "Kiss me, Alice."

She slipped her arms around his waist and leaned into him, her forehead braced against his shoulder. After saying so many right, kind, wonderful if slightly daft things, he'd said the wrong thing.

Alice hated feeling muddled, but about one thing she was very clear. She could not kiss him. Not now. The discussion had traveled in a completely unplanned direction and then gone worse than imagined. Alice distrusted her own assessments, and she still wanted to cry.

Children are a plague. "Take me home, please. I have much to think about."

"I am still asking to court you. Think about that."

She let him have the last word, because what was the point of further discussion?

Cam escorted her home in the last of the light, and even when they'd reached the cottage front door in nigh pitch darkness, she did not kiss him.

～

"Nothing," St. Didier said, eyeing the afternoon sky beyond the library windows. "Nothing recent, nothing for the past ten years. Lady Josephine is barely noticed in York's higher social circles. She has called on the wife or widow of a bishop or two. She corresponds with a few more. She patronizes the best shops, though far less extravagantly than in times past. I found nothing remotely scandalous from any quarter."

Cam closed the household ledger, which was a more complicated tale than he'd expected. Pensions, charities, tithes, wages, linen, wine, window glass... The list of expenses was enormous, the sources of revenue limited to rent, livestock, and crops.

"Perhaps you weren't asking the right parties," Cam said, setting the ledger at arm's length and rising. "Remind me never to lift a scythe again."

"Still sore?"

"Twinges. The ravages of aging, I suppose." Plus sleepless nights followed by too many hours sitting at a damned desk. "How did you conduct your interviews?"

"You will laugh."

"I will not." He hadn't been in the mood to laugh since leaving Alice on her grandpapa's doorstep two nights ago. Cam still hadn't figured out what the hell had gone so far amiss in their last conversation.

Alice had finally been forthcoming about her wicked past—her foolish past, at worst—and Cam had tried to be dismissive and sympathetic.

To no avail.

"I applied a judicious bit of rice powder to my hair," St. Didier said. "I also sported a slight paunch, altered my attire, and claimed to be considering Lady Josephine from a matrimonial perspective. I might even have acquired a hint of a Lowland burr and the privileges of a specious Lord of Parliament."

"Shameless." Also brilliant. One sympathized instinctively with an aging bachelor finally contemplating matrimony. He'd be dignified, hesitant, determined, and a little vulnerable.

Much like a younger bachelor.

St. Didier opened the French doors, letting in a gust of fresh afternoon air. "Her ladyship might simply be a higher order of meddler than one finds in the usual rural parish. She is basically a busybody. Obscure vicarages boast plenty of those."

As did clerks' offices. Cam could identify a garden-variety busybody easily enough.

"She's far worse than a village gossip with airs above her station. She plays God, all the while pretending to piety. She has a devoted son to dote on, a commodious dwelling, regular-ish income, excellent health, and plenty of social standing, and yet, she must hurt people who have done her no harm."

St. Didier turned from the French doors. "*Hurt* people?"

What had Lady Josephine made of Alice's little foray into wanton romance? No sixteen-year-old who fancied herself in the throes of true love could have been discreet enough to escape Lady Josephine's eye.

"Hurt people. Ruin their happiness. Force them to spend time in drudgery at her whim. Silence them when they would speak out. She thrives in the role of arbitrary oppressor of all that is joyful, pleasurable, and spontaneous, all in the name of propriety and piety."

St. Didier took the window seat. "She was nasty to you when you were a little boy. She's not the Corsican's diabolical familiar."

Cam took up St. Didier's post along the windows, which admitted abundant sunlight. To the east, clouds were building up, great towering billows of white that showed pewter across the bottom.

"Bernard is looking for another post," Cam said. "He expects to take his mama with him when he goes. I suspect he knows more than he's saying, and that Lady Josephine might well find a way to remain here. Alice claims Lady Josephine will thwart Bernard's schemes, that he has no prayer of ever escaping St. Wilfrid's."

"You've been conversing with *Miss Singleton?*"

"Not on that topic and not since she and Thaddeus came to supper on Sunday. She and Bernard apparently discussed his plans to depart." When and where? Alice would avoid the vicarage unless summoned by its resident gorgon.

"You are looking for a puzzle to solve," St. Didier said, getting to his feet. "Some way to control Lady Josephine with the sort of little secrets she uses to control everybody from the butcher's wife to the maids you depend on here at the Hall. She might well not have any, and you are building dungeons for her in Spain."

"I would not mind seeing her ladyship occupy a social dungeon." How to achieve that outcome, though, when Cam wasn't willing to bargain with the serpent in St. Wilfrid's garden? "Alice told me about her little misstep all those years ago. I can only imagine what hay Lady Josephine has made out of an orphaned sixteen-year-old being led astray."

Even if Lady Josephine hadn't divined the extent of the intimacies Alice had granted her false suitor, her ladyship would have smelled a source of leverage over a friendless and befuddled young girl.

"Miss Singleton has confided the details of her past to you?" The question was posed too casually, given how protective St. Didier was generally toward the woman Cam adored.

"Not the details, but enough of the general outlines. A tale as sad as it is common. What piques my curiosity is how Lady Josephine allowed matters to progress between the steward's granddaughter and some swell in the area visiting Alexander. Why wasn't St. Wilfrid's ever-vigilant crusader against moral lapses keeping a closer eye on matters?"

"That," St. Didier said, "is a valid and vexing riddle, but with a whole shire for Lady Josephine to mind and a bit of sneaking about on the part of the couple involved, Alice and her admirer might have escaped detection."

They hadn't. Cam could think of no other explanation for the great deference Alice showed to her ladyship. The year or two Alice had spent at finishing school took on a new light—an exile, perhaps. A punishment, to be parted from what family Alice had left and what friendships she might have formed, also a way to put Alice forever in her ladyship's debt.

"Don't you have correspondence to see to?" St. Didier asked, nudging a sketch that had hung perfectly straight, then nudging it back where he'd found it.

"Always."

"You aren't seeing to it."

"No one will steal my mail from my very own desk." And the entire stack held no replies from the family solicitors or from Worth Kettering. "I have asked Alice's permission to pay her my addresses."

Another sketch merited a nudge and un-nudge. "Fast work."

"That's all you have to say? Fast work?"

He swung around to face Cam. "What I have to say, were I not bound by discretion, would elaborate on the themes of fools rushing in, pride presaging disasters, and love being blind. You would not listen. I would regret the waste of breath and time. The only opinion that matters is Miss Singleton's, and you will abide by her decisions, as honor requires. If you'll excuse me, I have some correspondence of my own to see to."

Bother the damned correspondence. "Alice Singleton is not acting like a woman being courted by a peer, and she won't allow me to act like a man in love. What would you have me do?"

St. Didier seemed to take the question seriously. "The sortie into York yielded little information, and you are a great one for peering under every rock and sending your myrmidons to lurk in every doorway. Perhaps you should haul your scamps and pickpockets north and have them spy on your neighbors."

He decamped at his usual diffident pace, leaving Cam to wonder if that peroration had been a scold, a lament, or an honest suggestion. Cam considered possibilities while leaning on the jamb of the French doors and watching the trees of the home wood dance under a lively breeze.

The boys would hate to leave London, of that Cam was certain. They'd miss Cook's scolds and her puddings and... Cook would not hate to leave London. She was forever longing for her homeland north of the Tweed and likening London to Hades.

The lad Parkin went skipping across the back terrace, literally skipping.

"Parkin!"

He turned as if guilty of some misdemeanor. "Dint mean to make no noise, milord. Beg pardon. It's my half day."

The correspondence was piling up nearly as high as the damned clouds on the eastern horizon, St. Didier was in a snit, and Alice was being contrary. Cam granted himself the right to a single hour's truancy.

"Where can I find the sort of flowers that might please a young lady?"

Parkin rubbed his wrist against his nose. "In the conservatory?"

"I'm not looking for the sort of flowers the gardeners select and carefully arrange in the perfect vase, but real flowers. Yorkshire flowers any lad can pick for his mama."

"Cook likes flowers. Come along, I'll show you. We have a patch of daisies by the river and hollyhocks along the wood. I know where all the best flowers are, but you mustn't tell anybody. Potboys aren't supposed to know about flowers."

All boys—all children—should know about flowers, but it

occurred to Cam that in London, his boys hadn't much opportunity to learn about them. Twenty minutes later, he had a sizable if somewhat lopsided bouquet. He wrapped the stems in a few wheat stalks and left the lot where only his lady was likely to find them.

Alice was not acting like a woman being courted by a peer, but Cam would conduct himself like a man in love, because that's exactly what he was.

CHAPTER FOURTEEN

Lady Josephine had neglected her social correspondence, and thus Alice had been condemned to her ladyship's sitting room for the entire morning.

"Sooner begun is sooner done," Lady Josephine said, selecting another *macaron de Nancy* from the tray. "And now you will be home in time to share your nooning with your grandpapa, provided you don't dawdle."

Alice had not had the luxury of dawdling since she'd come to live with Grandpapa. "You're sure we've answered them all?" A pile of gossip, good wishes, and scriptural quotes penned in an epistolary game of battledore apparently enjoyed by ladies with churchly connections.

"We're caught up, I am pleased to say. If you'd return the lap desk to Bernard's study, I'll thank you for spending a pleasant morning on a pleasant task."

Alice had known pleasanter mornings pegging out the wash. As Lady Josephine munched her macaron, Alice mentally lectured herself about the virtue of patience while she organized the lap desk contents. Quill pens in this compartment. Ink bottles tucked in another. Wax and seals in yet another. The desk was a marvel of design, ornately inlaid, and quite heavy.

When all had been neatly stowed, Alice secured the latch and rose, taking the desk by its handle.

"Good day, my lady." *And blast you for wasting another beautiful summer morning. Blast me for allowing it.* "My regards to Vicar."

"That man... He has been particularly vexatious lately, though I'm sure you would never imagine him causing anybody annoyance, much less his doting mama. I cannot say I'm pleased with my nephew either."

If Alice had had hackles, they would have risen. "I doubt his lordship will be in the area much longer. He won't bother you at all from London."

Her ladyship put the last of the macaron back on the tea tray and gazed up at Alice. "Do you even know, Alice, are you aware that it was he and not Blessington Peabody who put those flowers at your back door yesterday afternoon?"

Alice affected a puzzled expression while her insides began to roil. "Flowers? You mean the bouquet Grandpapa brought in at supper? Blossoms common to any hedge? Your ladyship must be mistaken."

Her ladyship was not mistaken. Flowers gathered by the baron himself, stems cut on a slant as Alice had seen him cut the roses in the conservatory a lifetime ago. The whole wrapped with wheat stalks... Alice had nearly cried to see the profusion of posies sitting by the boot scrape. She'd already chosen a perfect primrose to press between the pages of last year's almanac.

"Come now, Alice. Thaddeus Singleton is the last man who'd bother to gather flowers for the kitchen table. Camden is behaving foolishly, trying to catch your notice with mawkish gestures. You must discourage him, Alice. He means your ruin, though he wouldn't call it that."

He means to do me great honor. "Ma'am, you must be mistaken. On the two occasions Grandpapa and I have dined at the Hall, his lordship has barely spoken to me."

"On Sunday, you walked with him in the garden after supper, Alice. That was noted."

The lap desk was growing heavier in Alice's hand, almost begging to be heaved through the sitting room window.

"The baron was merely being polite while Grandpapa went off to be harangued by Mrs. Shorer over some ache or pain. I assure you, his lordship doesn't view me in the light you suggest." To lie about something so precious, so unexpected and private…

Alice wanted to heave the lap desk at Lady Josephine's head. *Hard.*

Her ladyship poured herself another cup of tea. "Alice, you are too trusting of men. We know this. I hesitate to bring up your sordid past—I always hesitate, as I know the memories must mortify you— but you have learned little from your mistakes. The baron left those flowers for you, and I would not mind seeing him make a fool of himself, but he has no call to disrespect you. I won't have it."

Alice set the lap desk down. "Ma'am, his lordship is planning to return to Town soon. Mrs. Shorer has assured me of that."

"Eunice Shorer is frequently in error and seldom in doubt. Alexander's passing has set the whole Hall on its ear, and its housekeeper is more uppish than ever. Languishing in her bed for three days. Next, she'll be riding in the baron's coach to services. Even Bernard has grown contrary. Did you know he's seeking to leave St. Wilfrid's?"

The question was clearly a test. Lady Josephine collected gossip. She seldom dispensed it, unless to upset somebody. She was gauging Alice's reaction, assessing what Alice knew.

"We'll miss him," Alice said evenly. "Vicar is much respected, and I've always found him to be the voice of reason and probity. If he seeks a more prestigious post, nobody would blame him."

"The reasonableness and probity you note is my influence on an otherwise brooding and self-centered fellow. Bernard is not a bad man, but neither is he the exemplar his father was. Alice, might I—out of both kindness and duty—be blunt?"

"Of course." Though Alice well knew neither kindness nor duty would figure into whatever topic came next. If anybody was frequently in error and seldom in doubt, that person was Lady Josephine.

"Let us say, Alice, for the sake of argument, that the baron is truly courting you. An outlandish notion, I know, but stranger matches have been made."

Love matches, which were not strange at all. "He is not—"

Her ladyship held up a hand. "He's certainly not courting anybody else, and my sources are reliable, Alice."

Her sources were cowed and bullied and threatened into tattling.

"Camden has twice had you and Thaddeus to dine at the Hall, albeit once in company. On both occasions, he conversed with you privately. Now he's leaving flowers at your back door, and there was that business with you spending hours in his company, ostensibly to tend to his mail. The appearances speak for themselves."

Alice could guess where this sermon was heading, but to hear Lady Josephine say the words was somehow necessary.

"What would you advise, ma'am?"

"I advise that you consider carefully the decision before you. If you encourage Camden in any regard, he will ruin you. Your years of good behavior, your grandfather's standing, your admirable attempts to distance yourself from past mistakes will mean nothing. But say the baron is intent on matrimony."

"For the sake of argument."

"For the sake of argument and for your sake, Alice. Again, you'd face choices. You truly ought to consider marrying him if you can bring him up to scratch. He's titled, not bad-looking, albeit unfashionably largish. He won't expect you to cosset or dote upon him. Being lady of the manor would make you the envy of the female half of the shire."

His lordship is also kind, funny, patient, hardworking, generous, and honest. To say nothing of his kisses.

"Do go on, ma'am." This volte-face on the subject of the baron's ideal bride was tactical, and Alice should have foreseen it. Lady Josephine could intimidate Davina Halbertson and bully Dorothea Considine. She could *control* Alice. Of course, that made installing Alice as the next baroness her ladyship's preferred choice.

Why am I never ahead of her schemes? Why haven't I learned from those mistakes?

"Marry him," Lady Josephine said, "and we would certainly have to send the girl very far away. To have evidence of your folly—I do not call it sin; I know how young men are—on Lorne Hall's very doorstep would be utterly untenable. You certainly cannot disclose her existence to the baron and expect him to offer you marriage, though I suppose you could speak your vows and then explain. No man likes to be made a fool of, especially not by his wife. Camden has always claimed more than his share of pride too."

Her ladyship ate the last bite of her sweet, just a helpful adviser trying to present facts and possibilities in their most relevant light.

Alice picked up the lap desk. "You're suggesting I should send Gabriella away and encourage the baron?"

"Not suggesting, but asking you to consider that if the baron's intentions are honorable—which I beg leave to doubt—then you must cease meddling in your daughter's life. She's lucky, Alice, to have had the comfort and security of the orphanage as long as she has. A truly devoted mother would allow me to place the child in a situation where her path in life lay plainly before her. The child could then reconcile herself to her fate without distractions."

One story a week is not a distraction, and I am not the meddler here. "You advise sending Gabriella away?"

"The farther the better. I have always said that a clean break would be best."

Said it over and over, until Alice had nearly snatched Gabriella up and stolen off into the night with her. Then Alice had met the prospective adoptive parents, and they'd been so eager to love a squalling little bundle of noise and need.

So understanding of Alice's predicament and her broken heart.

"We have ranged far afield of present realities," Alice said. "While I always appreciate your ladyship's insights, in this instance, I hope you are in error. His lordship will return to London, he will not court me, and no drastic measures need be taken where Gabriella is concerned."

Her ladyship sighed gustily. "Sooner or later, Alice, you must make that break. For the girl's sake. You cannot acknowledge her, you cannot support her, you can only do her harm by hovering. If she costs you the baron's addresses, she is doing harm to you as well."

"You have given me much to think about."

"Good. Think long and hard if you must, Alice, but see that you reach the same simple, commonsense conclusions I do. I would not want to intervene unnecessarily, but I will if I must."

She sipped her tea, made a face, and put the cup down. "Do ring for a fresh tray while you're on your feet. I vow tea cools faster in summer than winter."

Thus dismissed, Alice descended to the vicarage's ground floor in a state between a waking nightmare and catatonic rage. She tapped on the study door, heard no reply, and entered. The room smelled faintly of lavender and books—Mrs. Shorer's sachets for keeping the bugs and mice from eating the paper—and could have been any vicarage study in any corner of the realm.

Where was Bernard? Out sending off another hopeless inquiry, perhaps.

The window looked over the rolling acreage of the glebe land, the home wood forming its distant boundary. A landscape of Lorne Hall held pride of place over the mantel. Sketches of St. Wilfrid's and the previous vicar were the sole art on the opposite wall.

The desk was serviceable rather than elegant, and the blotter sported a Bible, some commentaries, and a neat stack of foolscap covered in Vicar's exquisite hand. Several other letters had been opened and sat beside the wax jack, and on those Alice spotted Lady Josephine's looping scrawl.

They would require responses, but Alice was not in the mood—not at all in the mood—to tend to the task. Lady Josephine had casually threatened to rip out Alice's heart without even saying Gabriella's name.

And if Alice did marry Cam? Lady Josephine would always have Gabriella to hold over Alice's head, and thus Cam would have a traitor for a wife.

"Damn, drat, and perdition." Worse profanity was called for, but Alice didn't know any.

She set the lap desk on the blotter, opened it, and gathered up the additional mail. The lap desk had a small drawer available for the purpose, so Alice...

Some piece of paper was already caught in the drawer, or caught between the back of the drawer and the top of its compartment. Alice worked the jammed paper loose and found a note from a Mrs. MacDougal of St. Wulfstan's by the Forest.

Alice read the final paragraph while struggling to breathe.

The unfortunate girl will be sure to find her salvation in hard work and prayer. The Irish are nothing if not devout, and they are even afflicted with a disproportionate occurrence of red hair, so she'll be among those similarly burdened. Send her to me, and I will make all the arrangements. A reasonable sum for travel expense and so forth is all I ask...

Yours in prayer...

Alice knew not how long she stood in the study, staring at the little piece of paper, raging, despairing, and wishing.

But when she finished tidying up the lap desk and had stowed it on its assigned shelf, she had to admit that Lady Josephine was right in at least one regard: A clean break was best for all concerned.

The sooner the better.

"You need a new name," Cam said, patting the gelding's neck. "Gooseberry will no longer do." How much had the name—a cognomen for Old Scratch—influenced the horse's lot in life?

Since being exercised regularly, fed treats only from a bucket, and being verbally reprimanded for the near occasion of almost-naughty behavior, the beast had stopped nipping.

"A quick learner," Cam said, letting the gelding pick his way up the track. "Maybe you had to be, and won't they all be surprised when you take a first among the foxhunters?"

Farnes Crossing in all its modest splendor wrapped the foot of the hill. The village was not out on the Dales proper, but lay at the foot of a sizable ridge of green that anticipated the contours of the land farther west.

"If anybody asks, I came on inspection." Partly true. Cam had simply been unwilling to face another mountain of reports, complaints, requests, and invoices. The creditors were growing strident, the debtors increasingly apologetic, and none of that seemed to matter as long as the situation with Alice remained unsettled.

"I should be robbing Peter to pay Paul." Instead, Cam was taking in a view so purely Yorkshire and lovely and worth missing that he'd been unable to remain at his desk. "I have been knocked off my commercial horse, and I am disinclined to get back in the saddle."

He brought Gooseberry to a halt and surveyed the village below. On market days, the place would be thronged.

Farnes Crossing enjoyed coaching traffic along both north-south and east-west routes—it truly was a crossing, had been for eons—and yet, for those seeking metropolitan conveniences, York lay just a few stops on. Farnes Crossing was still a village, with a market green, a single house of worship, and one coaching inn, though town-hood wasn't far off.

Cam's excuse for making this trek had been duty. The barony

supported several local charities, and one of them, a home for orphans, lay just outside the perimeter of Farnes Crossing proper.

"Best get on with it." He nudged Gooseberry in a half circle and headed down the hill toward a manor house fallen on utilitarian times. He did not want to swill tea with Mrs. Dumfries, the headmistress, did not want to face the correspondence he'd once regarded as so much plum pudding.

"I want Alice."

The horse flicked an ear.

"Not in that sense... Well, yes, in that sense too, rather desperately, but also..." Cam fell silent, lest he sound like Armendink, who'd written to thank Cam for such a gracious attitude toward parting. "I miss her, when she's only five miles away. I want to talk with her almost as much as I want to kiss her. I worry about her and wonder if she worries about me."

That last was a reckless admission, even to a horse. Nobody worried about Camden Huxley. Not his family, not his clerks. Not... well, Mrs. Shorer probably kept him in her prayers, and St. Didier fretted in his quiet, sniffy way.

A burst of children emerged from the aging manor house, the little ones in their short dresses and pinafores, the older girls in longer dresses. They made noise to go with the energy they displayed, though they were apparently not bent on play.

A sturdy pair of females in mobcaps and aprons followed, and a pair of tall girls dragging a laundry cart brought up the rear. A well-rehearsed drill followed, with the laundry maids lowering the wash lines, the children affixing wet laundry to the lines, and the maids raising the lines when full by means of a pulley rope.

The drill would play out in reverse probably just before supper, when the brisk Yorkshire breeze would have thoroughly dried all those sheets, pillowcases, aprons, shirts, and whatnot. The whatnot—small articles of underlinen—went up last on the central of three wash lines.

With the outer lines hoisted, the undergarments were not in plain view, a tradition Cam had thought unique to the laundresses at the Hall.

"And the laundry will come in clean," he told the horse. In London, nobody hung laundry out of doors, lest it come in dirtier than it went out. The kitchen sufficed as a drying space for many households, or they sent their washing to the country.

"I am not precisely missing London." How much of Cam's perpetual exhaustion there had simply been bad air? "I am missing the boys." They would have liked hanging out the wash. Within five minutes, they'd have formed teams and started a race, or been wearing Cook's unmentionables on their heads.

The task complete, the children were herded back indoors. A little sprite with red hair won the honor of dragging the empty laundry cart, which meant she went indoors last. She spotted Cam riding down the hill and waved.

He waved back, and then she disappeared.

Inspection nominally completed. The children were energetic, clean, and... not loud enough. Not nearly.

"Suppose I should have a look."

Gooseberry completed the descent, and Cam turned him toward the posting inn. Wouldn't hurt to enjoy summer ale and a meat pie before calling on the headmistress. Mrs. Dumfries was probably a tartar who approved of snoods and knitting sessions.

"Nobody will steal my mail." And tending to that towering stack of responsibilities would not make Cam miss Alice any less. "I should have brought her roses."

He instead left Gooseberry munching hay at the livery and was halfway to the coaching inn when a lady marching along the opposite side of the street caught his eye. Something about the militant kick of the ruffle at her hem...

Cam crossed the high street, nimbly dodging a dog cart and an antique gig.

"Alice Singleton, good day."

She halted, skirts swishing about her boots. "My lord." A crisp, correct curtsey. "Greetings."

I've missed you did not strike Cam as a place to start the conversation, not when Alice was in high dudgeon over something.

"What brings you to Farnes Crossing?" Alice asked.

"Business, more or less. You?" He did not even offer her his arm, so self-contained did she seem. Not angry, but sharply focused on some serious end.

"An errand."

"A very weighty errand, if your mood is any indication."

Alice glanced around at the few pedestrians going about their day. "Important to me, but completed now. I suppose I'll see you at services on Sunday."

Not so fast. "Alice, might we talk?"

She shook her head. "We've talked enough, and that Lady Josephine hasn't yet acquired a written transcript of our very words is surely an oversight on her part."

Well, of course. If Alice was vexed, Lady Josephine was somehow the cause. "I offer a suggestion, then. We will proceed back to the Hall and stop at the lake to enjoy the view. We will be in public the entire way, but should have the privacy to discuss her ladyship's latest affront to common decency."

The glint in Alice's eyes became diamond bright. "She all but reads Bernard's correspondence. She and the postmistress at the inn are apparently quite in each other's confidence. He's trying to find another pulpit, and she has, with her usual efficiency, found the means to thwart him."

How had Alice uncovered the postmistress's collusion with her ladyship? "Bernard hopes to take his mama with him."

Alice finally looked at Cam as if seeing the man before her eyes. "Bernard told you that?"

"And I've sent out some inquiries of my own, including a few regarding church posts. Bernard is going to waste at St. Wilfrid's. He's well educated, shrewd, capable of hard work, and frustrated for lack of challenge." Also bored and lonely. Had the telltale ink stain on his cuff to prove it.

"Proximity to her ladyship seems to result in frustration," Alice said. "We mustn't tarry long at the lake, but you are right that we need to discuss some delicate matters. I owe you that."

"I won't hear a you-do-me-great-honor speech, Alice. Not from you. We'd suit, and you know it."

She started off in the direction of the livery. "We do, and I do, and yet, there is more that must be said."

Then Cam did not want to hear her announcements at the location traditionally frequented by Farnes Crossing's courting couples.

"Come to the Hall. Gather up more medicinals for Thaddeus, discuss his situation with Mrs. Shorer. Harvest has at least another week to go, and your grandpapa is looking distracted and tired to me."

"He might say the same about you, my lord. When we meet at the Hall, we are more or less under surveillance. Surely you know that." Alice offered that reminder tiredly and stopped at the edge of the livery yard. "We are likely being watched now, by some groom or chambermaid at the inn. That we met on the street will be reported to Lady Josephine, who has suggested that you mean to ruin me, by the way."

Cam realized then what affected Alice. She was in the same state he'd been in by the time he'd come of age. Perpetually angry, so angry that the litany of affronts ran like an off-key hymn in his head he could not escape, one that had to be ignored while making the great effort to appear calm and even good-humored over and over and over again.

People in that state made rash, brave, often irreversible decisions.

"If you will not meet me at the Hall, Alice, I will come to your grandpapa's cottage, and if you refuse me entry, I will sing beneath your window, or climb through your window, and Lady Josephine can make of my ardor whatever she pleases. She is not God, Alice, and we are not powerless."

"She might well be the devil, though, and in all of eternity, the celestial powers have not seen fit to excise Lucifer from existence, have they?"

The very last thing Cam was capable of discussing in that moment was theology. "Where, Alice? If we are to clear the air, you choose the location, and it must be soon."

"Because you are returning to London?"

"Because I am losing my mind, and I have already lost my heart."

She winced. "My wits went begging nearly a decade ago. I will see you tomorrow morning in the herb garden."

"When the dew has risen." Yorkshire fashion.

Alice nodded once, then swished away into the stable yard. Cam let her go, and when her gig tooled past, he merely tipped his hat.

As negotiations went, he hadn't distinguished himself. Alice was planning to cry off on an engagement that had never started, and all Cam had done was give her more time to prepare the little speech that would wreck him from the heart out.

She had made up her mind. Cam knew the look and knew how once a decision was made, dissuading a woman of Alice's formidable determination would be nigh impossible.

He made himself down a pint of ale and eat half a meat pie and considered that was head start enough for Alice—he'd interview the headmistress later. When he retrieved his horse, the groom kept a careful hand on the reins.

"This would be the famous Gooseberry?"

"You know this horse?"

"Oh, aye. The Goose will fly over anything. Hedges, stiles, the moon, but he'll as soon have you for breakfast as look at you. The squires all around thought it a great joke when he was sold to the lord of Lorne Hall. Goose seems a bit subdued today, or I'd be missing me ear."

The horse sent Cam a you-see-what-I-have-to-put-up-with look, or so it seemed to Cam.

"His name is Galahad, and he's only nippy when people are foolish enough to tempt and tease him, or inflict boredom upon him. I don't know this other horse you refer to, but if the beast is so talented, somebody ought to take the time to put a few manners on him lest a valuable animal end up in the knacker's yard."

Cam checked the stirrups and girth, led *Galahad* to a mounting block, and swung aboard. He left a slightly puzzled groom in the stable yard and set off at a brisk trot for the Hall.

CHAPTER FIFTEEN

The dew had risen. Alice's anxiety had risen with it, which ought not to have been possible when she was already as tense as a fiddle string, but still, the baron made no appearance in the herb garden. He was not rude by nature. Blunt sometimes, or direct, but he would never keep her waiting where half the staff could see.

Alice gathered up her courage and entered the Hall through the conservatory door. She put her bouquet of lavender into a crock of water, pinched a blooming purple stalk, and fortified herself with the aroma.

At this hour, his lordship would be in the library, muttering over his letters and ledgers.

Except that he wasn't. The library was not only devoid of handsome barons, no correspondence sat stacked on the desk. The blotter was bare, and neither wax jack, nor pen tray, nor ink was in view. Even the abacus on the windowsill had been removed.

He would not do this. Would not leave without a word, would not abandon Alice without a farewell.

"Miss Singleton." Mr. St. Didier had entered the library without making a sound. "Might I be of assistance?"

"I was to meet... That is... I have an appointment with his lordship."

Something annoyed flickered in St. Didier's eyes. "You'll find him in the baron's suite. Shall I escort you up?"

"I know the way, thank you."

If Mr. St. Didier thought it scandalous that Alice would seek his lordship out in his private apartment, he kept that to himself. He remained by the door, looking severe and unreadable.

"Miss Singleton, are you sure I cannot be of assistance?"

Whatever could that possibly mean? "I will keep my appointment with his lordship, thank you."

St. Didier gestured toward the door and made no move to follow Alice up the steps. She ascended, pausing on the landing to settle her nerves, or try to. The baron had not left. Had not fled in the night. Had not waved wistfully and promised to write.

Not yet.

And neither had Alice, though she intended to be on the afternoon express to York.

She rapped on the baron's sitting room door in the same rhythm as the tattoo of her heartbeat.

"Enter."

A singularly cheerless command. Alice lifted the latch and walked in on a scene of brewing chaos. Through the bedroom door, she spied the first footman packing a sizable trunk. In the sitting room, stacks of letters were arranged on the sofa and chairs. The escritoire by the window held more documents and an open lap desk even larger than the one at the vicarage.

Cam occupied the chair at the desk and paused halfway through sorting a stack of papers. "What time...? Damn. Excuse my language." He rose. "Chapman, go pester Cook for a cup of tea, please. I'll ring when you can resume packing."

Chapman, who'd known Alice since she'd joined Grandpapa's household, bowed to the baron, nodded to her, and exited through the sitting room door.

He'd report the morning's developments belowstairs, and somebody would carry the tale straight to the vicarage.

For once, Alice did not care who told Lady Josephine what.

"I'm sorry," Cam said. "I lost track of the time, which is no excuse. Please have a..." He moved several piles of paper to the windowsill. "A seat. Might I close the door?"

What did yet another breach of propriety matter? He was leaving, just as Alice had assured Lady Josephine he would.

"You may close the door," Alice said.

"This isn't... Well, it is what you think it is. I must return to London posthaste. I've had disturbing news from the solicitors."

Alice took a seat on the sofa. She had spent many an hour in this room reading, playing chess, and otherwise entertaining the late baron. The décor hadn't changed to speak of—more correspondence, some hydrangeas on the sideboard instead of roses, no pipe trays or pipe smoke—but the feel of the room was awake and lively rather than moribund.

"Disturbing news about your business?" What else would inspire him to a hasty departure?

"Indirectly. Alice, I am sorry, but it's a situation only I can address. I would have informed you in person of my plans before I absented myself from the Hall."

He took the place beside her without asking permission, which Alice assumed was evidence of genuine upset. Ironic, that he should be leaving now when Alice had been sure he'd linger at the Hall.

"Is the business in difficulties?"

He ran a hand through his hair. "The business is always in difficulties. I seem to prefer it that way, or I did. Now..." He glanced at the clock. "I'm sorry you had to come looking for me. Badly done."

"You are upset." Not in the same way Alice was, but his disquiet was palpable. In the normal course, the new Lord Lorne did not forget assignations in the garden any more than he forgot the price he'd offered for weaving services.

"I am upset, for all manner of reasons. Trouble in London is part of it, but also... I have created a business that only I can run, and that's not prudent. It's not smart. Why do that?"

"Because then you are always needed. Nobody can throw you off the property or force you to join the military against your better judgment. You were right to leave Lorne Hall all those years ago, but I doubt the army was a good fit for you."

He stared at the carpet, a fading Axminster chosen by his grandmother and woven to depict a profusion of summer flowers bordering a green wood.

"Leaving was the only thing I could think to do. To remain was... I would have lost my wits or run afoul of the law sooner rather than later."

Alice wanted to take his hand, to anchor him to her somehow. She smoothed her skirts. "I have run afoul of Lady Josephine, and I must leave here." For the space of two ticks of the mantel clock, Alice wished the words back.

"Explain. Rather, might you please explain?"

"You are right that Lady Josephine has become more troublesome of late. I cannot marry you, because she will use me to invade the Hall in the very fashion you've described. She will make us both miserable."

"We'll live in Town."

"She is free to travel to London. She is an earl's daughter and has connections everywhere."

"Not in York, none to speak of. I asked St. Didier to nose around, and except for a few church acquaintances and some of the better shops, her ladyship avoids York."

He ran his hand through his hair again, and Alice realized that for all his apparent calm, the baron was truly distraught.

"Her ladyship is too busy wrecking lives here in the shires, I suppose, and she is set upon wrecking mine—and, by extension, yours—so I am determined to leave. I should have left years ago."

Alice braced herself for rage, derision, a coldly polite dismissal... or worse, a pointless negotiation intent on ripping apart her logic. Her reasoning was sound, but based on evidence the baron hadn't seen and hopefully never would.

"I know that feeling, Alice, the compulsion to go, to be anywhere but where one is expected to dwell. To choose homelessness over bodily safety. I wouldn't wish it on you."

He was thinking, moving chess pieces in his head. Alice could hear the slight distracted note in his tone that suggested strategies in development. She did not want him embarking on any sort of bargaining. That time had long since passed.

"I have created a problem," Alice said slowly, "and I must solve it. I've let every other problem in my life be solved by others. What to do when my parents died, how to keep a roof over my head, how to go on here... I respect my elders and my betters and my neighbors, but I have forgotten to respect myself."

His lordship frowned at the carpet. "Lack of respect figured in my own departure from Lorne Hall, but I hadn't the words for it then. I respect you, Alice Singleton."

How much easier if he'd said she meant nothing to him. "I know, and that has been wonderful and exhilarating, and now I cannot accept anything less from myself."

He aimed that frown at her. "So wonderful that I am about to lose you?"

Logic. Blast him for the logic. "I've said enough. I should have told you earlier that I have long been considering a remove from my grandfather's house. You distracted me."

"You knocked me witless, and you are a bad liar, Alice."

If he knew all the lies she'd told. *I'm fine, Grandpapa. No trouble at all, your ladyship. A lovely sermon, Vicar. Your advice is always appreciated, Lady Josephine.*

"I'm telling you the truth when I say I must go."

The frown had turned into a perplexed scowl. "And you won't come back?"

"Not if I can help it."

He rose and prowled to the desk. To the casual eye, he might have looked annoyed or preoccupied. To Alice, he seemed intently focused on thoughts she could not divine.

"Will you at least let me provide you some funds, Alice?"

She rose as well, wanting both to flee and to wrap her arms around him and never let him go. "You are supposed to berate me for waving false colors, to be wroth and dismissive."

"I spent most of my minority angry because others were dismissive toward me. My ire solved nothing, but I suspect you have yielded to the sin of wrath too. It's a good sin, very passionate. What puzzles me is, why is Lady Josephine so angry?"

Alice wanted to ignore the question, but couldn't. "She *is* angry. She can go on tirades with the vicarage staff that would shock you. She is certainly mean."

He sat at the escritoire and opened a drawer.

"My lord, you cannot give me money." Too late, Alice recalled that telling this man what to do generally resulted in the opposite outcome. He was as contrary as she was submissive—as she *had been* submissive.

"I will be most unhappy with you, Alice, once I locate my missing wits. I will be furious, though, if you expect me to send you out into the world, I know not where, with just the pin money you've saved while drudging for your grandpapa. The very thought..."

He withdrew some papers from a drawer, uncapped the ink, and scrawled a few lines. "I have a supply of coin in the safe in the library. You will accept some ready cash too, Alice."

"I cannot take your charity. Not when I'm..."

"Lying to me?" He sanded the little document. "Lying to yourself? Breaking my heart? I suppose I had that coming. I've been disdainful of those struck by Cupid's arrow. I never expected the dart to be aimed my way. Never had the courage to be that hopeful."

Drat him forever. "I would stay if I could."

"I would go with you if I could."

Alice sank back down onto the sofa. She hadn't foreseen... hadn't in her wildest imaginings... "You mustn't say such things. You employ many people, and Peruvian bark alleviates terrible suffering. Your business matters."

He blew the sand into the dustbin. "Oddly enough, it's not the business that's inspiring my departure." He took a single sheet of paper from the top of the stack on the corner of the escritoire. "The family solicitors are being discreet."

He passed Alice the note.

Your lordship's return to London is most urgently advised. Discretion forbids details, but all haste is recommended. Junior staff has become entangled in a personal matter requiring your lordship's presence at the soonest possible moment.

Respectfully Yours,
Isaac T. Claplady

"Cryptic," Alice said, choosing the word carefully. *Cryptic* rather than *discreet*. "Nearly hysterical with urgency."

"The business solicitors would simply state the problem. That the family solicitors are communicating regarding my junior staff suggests one of my boys has imperiled his health or lost his liberty to Bow Street's vigilance."

Alice stared at the note, an instinctive distaste coloring her regard. The words were manipulative, guaranteed to send his lordship south without revealing the true nature of the problem.

She set the epistle on the arm of the sofa. "What boys?"

"I collect clerks, very junior clerks whose previous professions tended to be illegal or dangerous. I have two former climbing boys on my payroll, several failed pickpockets, and one who escaped from the mines. Another went to sea at age eight and has a ferocious head for rum. He has a prodigious memory, though, and keeps order in the ranks."

"Boys? I thought you didn't care for children."

"I care for my own pack of demons, and they can eat their weight in bread and cheese every day. They know they're valued, though. They know if they don't come home, somebody will notice and go looking for them." Cam picked up the document he'd written and passed it to Alice. "If you don't want my heart, at least take some blunt. I would like your trust in return, but if you can't give me that, then know that wherever you go, my love goes with you."

He was returning to London with all possible haste because he feared for some child he'd plucked off the street. Alice absorbed that fact, absorbed that Cam Huxley more or less ran his own personal orphanage, because he well knew how it felt when nobody came looking for a missing boy.

She stared at the piece of paper in her hand. Cam's tidy penmanship and... he'd written her a bearer note for *five hundred pounds*. "You cannot afford this."

"I can. My business would be a trifle pressed to cover it, but that's drawn on a personal account. You are leaving your home, your aging grandpapa, the people who care about you, and the people you care for. That's a desperate measure, Alice. I know. I also know that you can't simply show up at a regimental office and be guaranteed housing, food, and respectable work."

Five hundred pounds. "Why? Why do this when I'm refusing your addresses?"

He sat beside her. "Because you *see* me, see why I indulge in all the busyness, and see why the busyness has been so alluring and meaningful. I tell you I employ budding thieves, and you have no lectures for me about encouraging sin or giving the lower orders airs. You put your reputation at risk to help with my stupid letters. You look after my old guard so they can look after the Hall."

"The letters aren't stupid." And yet, the solicitor's note was disrespectful in a way.

"You manage Lady Josephine," Cam went on. "As long as she can bully you, summon you, make you work for no pay, and treat you as the homeliest spinster in the parish, she has less time and attention to spend on other victims. Between you and Bernard, she's placated. If you leave, she'll find new victims. I feel compelled to make that point."

But Gabriella would not be one of them. "I must leave nonetheless. I have a year of finishing school, I am passably musical. My French is adequate, my needlework superb, and my penmanship exemplary. I can find work." And with five hundred pounds for Gabriella, Alice might also find peace.

But she would never, ever find a man to love who was even one-quarter as decent as the one sitting beside her.

She pushed forward and Cam was instantly on his feet, his hand extended. "I will kiss you good-bye, Alice, and bedamned to whose turn it is."

"We will kiss each other good-bye."

They went about it slowly, a farewell kiss, but also, for Alice, a celebration. She *loved* Camden Huxley, and he loved her enough to respect and support her decisions, even her decision to leave. A bittersweet irony, that she wished he'd instead demand that she marry him, come what may, while some convenient magic spell sent Lady Josephine to the ends of the earth.

Cam did not rush, but when Alice broke the kiss, he allowed it. "I can only ask that you let me know you are safe. That you don't need anything."

"I can't write to you here." She ought not to write to him at all, in fairness to him.

"Write to me on Backneedle Street in Town. As attentive as I am to my correspondence, I will positively dwell at the posting inn until I know you are safe."

Alice bussed his cheek rather than make promises she wasn't certain she could keep.

"I'm not sorry you came to the Hall," she said. "I'm not sorry for loving you."

"But we are both sorry you must leave and that, now of all times, so must I. Alice, what aren't you telling me?"

That Alice had reduced him nearly to begging shamed her. The temptation to confide, to burden him with the whole tale had her taking a turn staring at the carpet.

The note from the family solicitors had been carried to the floor by some wayward breeze. Alice knelt to retrieve it, scanning the words a final time.

"Alice, you regard that note as if it were a lewd verse."

"I don't care for the tone, and something..." A realization emerged from the miasma of Alice's emotions like the physical and aural blast of a harbor cannon firing through fog.

"Alice?"

"The J," Alice said, shaking the note at him. "That is Lady Josephine's J, and your solicitors did not write this note."

∽

"Loitering in the herb garden." Lady Josephine's tone suggested this offense eclipsed all seven deadly sins put together, which, given the potential consequences, it well might. "Loitering, like a goosegirl hoping to catch sight of the pantry boy."

She ceased muttering long enough to tie her bonnet ribbons in a tidy bow three inches to the right of her chin. The mirror over the sideboard in the vicarage foyer suggested that chin was sagging a bit, but only a bit.

"I vow Alice Singleton is simple." Her ladyship retrieved her reticule from its designated drawer in the sideboard. A cursory inspection revealed a half-dozen pennies in a side pocket—alms to be given to urchins and beggars in public locations—as well as a small bound version of the Gospels, also for brandishing in public. A pocket comb, bulging coin purse, folding mirror, and a vial of smelling salts completed the list.

"If Alice sought to give the baron the set-down he deserves, she should have known better than to dawdle about where the entire staff could see her."

Of course, Alice might not be planning any sort of set-down for the baron. She might—the girl was lamentably fanciful—be planning to become his baroness.

"And I have strategies in place for all eventualities, because somebody must." Her ladyship folded her lips together, then pushed them out. A modest touch of color about the lips was becoming at any age.

"Then too, Camden isn't exactly a temple of brilliance either." Her ladyship inspected herself in three-quarter profile from both sides. Bernard had the same nose, positively patrician.

"Did I or did I not send dear Camden instructions to get back to London more than twenty-four hours ago? And he has yet to summon his traveling coach. That St. Didier fellow has been a bad influence indeed, or perhaps my wretched nephew is hoping to entice Alice into leaving with him."

The situation wanted a firm hand. Alice knew better than to elope with the baron. She would know better still when Lady Josephine controlled all information regarding the whereabouts and welfare of Alice's bastard daughter. Such a harsh word, but the truth must be faced, and a clean break was—had always been—the wisest course.

Her ladyship withdrew a pair of black gloves from another drawer in the sideboard.

The note to his lordship had been a bit of inspiration. Alice tried hard, and she meant well, but she was utterly lackwitted when it came to men and their designs. Then too, tell Camden Huxley that a lady wasn't interested, and he might well be buying a special license in the next instant.

"He has always been hopelessly contrary. Too convinced of his own conclusions to listen to the voice of reason." The situation wanted simplifying if all was to be properly managed. "And as usual, I must do everything myself if I want it done at all."

Her ladyship tucked a missive into her reticule, a little message addressed to Mrs. MacDougal at St. Wulfstan's by the Forest. A five-pound note had been sealed within, which ought to be sufficient to buy both silence and services promised.

"Mama, are you going out?" Bernard, looking too dapper and handsome for St. Wilfrid's, had emerged from his study.

"I must tend to some errands in Farnes Crossing." Mendacity was a sin, and her ladyship avoided sin at all costs. Putting that infernal little girl on the stage coach qualified as an errand. "Duty calls, and I am a good and faithful servant, if I do humbly say so myself."

"I plan to go into Farnes Crossing later today. Might I spare you the journey?"

Doubtless to send off more inquiries regarding a new position, the ungrateful boy. "Unless you've taken up knitting, Bernard, I must refuse your kind offer. I can have the coach back by noon or shortly thereafter if you'd like to go by carriage."

"No need. It's a pleasant hack over and back. You must not wait your nooning on me."

"If you don't need the coach, then I will make some calls while I'm out and about. Thaddeus Singleton has looked unwell to me lately. The harvest is too much for him, and why a man his age thinks he's equal to such a challenge defies common sense and the plain evidence of one's eyes."

"And yet," Bernard replied, "harvest progresses well, as it tends to do under his guidance, and the talk is we're to have a fine crop this year. I'll see you at supper."

As last words went, that was a poor effort, and Bernard must have known it, because he disappeared back into his study.

Her ladyship collected a plain parasol from the stand in the corner and inspected her lip color one more time—subtly done, if she did say so herself. She waited by the foyer window until the coach had halted at the foot of the steps and then descended at the brisk pace of a woman with much to accomplish and not nearly enough time to accomplish it.

∼

Cam took the piece of paper from Alice's hand. "You're sure?"

Alice paced off across the sitting room carpet. "I manage her ladyship's correspondence, just as I do Grandpapa's. I know her hand, my lord, and it is atrocious. A fidgety schoolgirl writes more legibly. Her ladyship is particularly vain about her majuscule J's. The double loop with the bar across the top is part of her signature. She has no doubt tried to copy the solicitor's penmanship, but the J gives her away. The L in London is hers too. Nearly unrecognizable for all the curling flourishes."

"She would have seen plenty of reports and epistles from that office," Cam said, though a pair of messy capital letters was hardly enough evidence to convict her ladyship of a bad forgery. "Would she really do this?"

Even for Josephine... but then, Cam knew her ladyship only as the nasty-polite aunt of his youth, the busybody trying to matchmake in recent days. Alice knew her far better.

Alice knew her as an enemy.

"She would," Alice said, going to the window. "She would, and you must believe me. If you have pigeons, send one to Town. If they are as fast as Grandpapa claims, the bird will be there before you've finished your noon meal."

The best pigeons could fly from John O'Groats to Dover in a day. "A reply will take some time."

"Squire Huffnagel has pigeons in Town. His daughters married Londoners, and Mrs. Huffnagel insisted they both have pigeons. I can give you the direction."

Cam examined the note more closely. "I don't need more proof, Alice. You are right that no law clerk wrote this note, at least not when sober, and neither did Isaac Claplady. His closing is always 'Your Obed Serv,' and this isn't quite his signature."

Alice turned, the window at her back. "But to Lady Josephine, he'd sign a letter 'Respectfully Yours.'"

Cam was honestly taken aback by Lady Josephine's audacity, while Alice appeared unsurprised. No wonder Bernard wanted to relocate his mother to parts distant. Tampering with the king's mail was a felony, and if her ladyship persisted, she would sooner or later meddle herself right onto a convict transport ship.

"What will you do?" Alice asked, resuming her pacing. "You

cannot allow Lady Josephine's mischief to pass unremarked. The whole shire pretends she's not that bad, that she means well, that she knows not what she does, but she knows very well the consequences of her schemes."

Alice knew the consequences, too, if Cam was to believe her, and the only recourse she could think of was to flee. Why? What would make a woman of Alice's fortitude and integrity turn her back on an aging Grandpapa, on a chance at marital happiness, on…

On the terrace below, Parkin was again skipping off on some errand known only to him and Cook. Berry picking, gathering flowers, taking a note to the home farm on another beautiful Yorkshire morning.

He might not be the best potboy in Yorkshire, but he was certainly among the most indulged. Clearly, the whole kitchen doted on the boy.

As Parkin tried with limited success to slide down the stone banister into the garden, a theory popped into Cam's head. Lady Josephine had accurately predicted that when faced with the prospect of a child in difficulties, Cam would make all haste to safeguard the child. He'd set aside business, pleasure, courting, *everything* for the sake of a child for whom he felt responsible.

In that moment, Cam hated his aunt. Hated her as he'd never hated anybody and hoped never to hate again.

"Tell me about your experiences at finishing school, Alice. Your grandpapa thinks Lady Josephine sponsored you for two years, but you have alluded to only a single year of studies. Thaddeus enjoys excellent recollection, in the general case."

Alice ceased pacing at the window and stood up quite tall. "My past is not your concern."

Everything about you is my concern. "Forgive me. I should have phrased the request more respectfully. Forewarned is forearmed, and good decisions are made based on good information. You apparently have some information that I need, and I ask you, for my sake and for the sake of others who cannot defend themselves from her ladyship's deviltry, to trust me with the truth of your past."

Alice remained by the window, the brilliant blue of the Yorkshire morning sky behind her as the clock ticked and Cam waited.

"You ask me..." she said at length. "You ask me for everything." A single tear slipped down her cheek.

Cam had made her cry, and yet, if he offered comfort, she would storm off, never to return. The decision to share the truth with him was Alice's and Alice's alone.

"Know, Alice, that I pledge everything in return."

Another tear followed the first. Cam dared to offer his handkerchief, a plain white square of unstarched linen. "Alice, I cannot bear that you are—"

She snatched the handkerchief and pitched herself against him, silent sobs racking her. Heat rolled off her and the occasional muffled moan that tore Cam's heart to shreds. This outpouring was not sadness or frustration or the weight of a hard day. This was the burden of an impossible life, a heart that had given up on comfort, a body possessed by despair for too long.

"Mrs. Shorer has considered poison," Alice said when the storm had passed. "So have I." Her voice was low and bitter, far from her usual lilting contralto.

Cam stroked Alice's hair and plotted vengeance. "Mrs. Shorer considered poison for Lady Josephine. You thought to take your own life."

Alice pushed away, dabbing at a pink nose with Cam's handkerchief. "Not recently. I haven't the right. We should sit."

Cam let Alice choose an end of the sofa and then came down right beside her and took her hand. "Where is the child?"

"You are so quick. No wonder Alexander was jealous of you."

"He wasn't."

A watery smile. "Was too. Told me so himself. Wished you the best, though. Admired you."

"I appreciate the news and will consider it later, but you are stalling, Alice." And Cam had never loved her more.

"Gathering my courage."

"You have been gathering your courage since your parents died. Just tell me."

She nodded. "The child is a girl, Gabriella. I named her for the angel, and the adoptive parents respected my wishes. They were good people, the best, extraordinarily kind. Gabriella had a wonderful and loving start in life."

Were good people. "What happened?"

"The wife died of influenza when Gabriella was about four. The husband decided he had a missionary calling. He placed Gabriella at the orphans' home in Farnes Crossing and ensured that I would have regular access to her, then went off and expired of a tropical fever. Gabriella is an orphan as far as anybody knows, and Lady Josephine is the patroness of the orphanage."

And thus Lady Josephine could bind Alice with the heaviest chains known to a loving heart. "You meant to take Gabriella and flee."

"I *mean* to. Lady Josephine has arranged for Gabriella to be put in service in some Irish household. I saw the letter myself. If Gabriella is sent to Ireland, her ladyship would hold Gabriella's location and welfare over my head for all the rest of my days. I would never know where my daughter was or how she fared, though I'd be given the occasional well-timed and certainly fictitious hint."

Cam kissed Alice's knuckles, locked a good quantity of rage in his mental safe, and considered what Lady Josephine's tactics said about her mettle as an opponent.

"She's consistent, or lacks imagination. Her ladyship tried to use the boys to manipulate me. Probably learned of the composition of my household through the family solicitors. She then gambled that alluding to a junior member of the staff would pluck my heartstrings past all bearing."

"She nearly won that bet."

At some point in this exchange, Cam had put an arm around Alice's shoulders, and she had let her weight fall against his side. She drew her knees up, positively cuddling against him.

"I am so afraid," she said, "and I have been afraid until I'm sick with it. I would like to see my daughter. I would, in fact, like to provide my daughter a home, to raise her, and to blazes with what polite society or the church or Lady Rubbishing Josephine has to say on the matter. I want to be a mother to my child, if she'll have me, and if that means I cannot be your baroness, I am sorry. I am truly sorry, but my decision is firm."

The rest of Alice was all soft curves and sweetness. Cam kissed her on the lips simply because he could and because those lips said such wonderful things.

"There is room for Gabriella right here at the Hall and certainly room for her in my heart. What do you think of adding some noisy, rambunctious boys to the household too?"

Alice murmured something about "all the children" and "kiss me again," and while Cam wasn't quite certain what the first phrase was in reference to—though he had a good idea—he knew exactly what to do about the second.

CHAPTER SIXTEEN

There is room for Gabriella right here at the Hall and certainly room for her in my heart.

Alice had never heard such blessed, beautiful, luminous words. Better still, she could rely on them wholeheartedly because they came from Cam. She kissed him back, for relief, for joy, for hope, and then for sheer animal pleasure.

He knew what he was about, did the baron, and Alice knew what she wanted.

"The bedroom," she said when fifteen stone of amorous peer had somehow arranged himself atop her on the sofa. To be fair, Alice might have wrestled him to that location, and he might well have gone all unresisting. "We should remove to the bedroom."

Cam levered up, looking disheveled and determined. "You will marry me, won't you, Alice? I will happily live with you in an irregular union if that's what you prefer, but I would much rather be your husband."

He was learning to ask, and Alice was learning to adore being asked. "We will marry each other, and by special license if you like. Kiss me some more."

He got up, scooped Alice into his arms, and carried her to the bed, whereupon he deposited her. While Alice struggled to her elbows, Cam locked the bedroom door.

He stood at the foot of the bed, hands on hips. "Now then."

So fierce, and all hers. "Now suits wonderfully. You might want to remove your boots. I could certainly do without mine."

His expression suggested boots were a complicated concept not relevant to anything of interest, but he sat on the side of the bed and slid Alice's skirts up to her knees.

"Lacy garters. Miss Singleton, you shock me."

"See if you might return the favor, hmm?"

He laughed and made short work of her boots and stockings. To Alice's chagrin, he *could* shock her, simply by stroking her knees, and then higher, and ever so impossibly more delicately, and higher still.

"If you do not remove your own boots," she panted, "I will fling you out the window." He'd brought her to a state of urgency that justified giving orders *and* making threats.

Cam rose and dispensed with his boots, then kept going. While Alice watched, one article of clothing after another was draped over the vanity stool. He unwrapped himself like a holiday gift all done up in bright paper and colored string, slowly revealing an article of beautifully worked oak. A treasure box, a puzzle of a healthy, aroused, male treasure box.

"Madam is overdressed," he said, all naked nonchalance. "Might I be of assistance?"

Alice struggled briefly in search of a witty retort and found only more urgency. He was magnificent, and they were to be married, and they would have years...

"Please." She lifted her wrist for him to undo the cuff. "And be quick."

He was the opposite of quick, bless his contrary nature. Camden Huxley was capable of making a lady's wrist the site of raptures, of tickling her ribs and collarbone and nape with his nose, and what he could do with his hands...

Alice was floating on a sea of pleasure when it occurred to her that the negotiation had so far gone all Cam's way. She bestirred herself to try an experimental caress over his bum, and the whole, entire fifteen stone of him went still.

"Shall I do that again? I daresay I shall." What glorious fun to learn him as he'd been learning her, to indulge and explore, to taste and tickle. Alice was not nearly through with her investigations when she again found herself on her back and her favorite blanket in the whole world draped over her on all fours.

"My baroness is imaginative."

"She's half mad with desire," Alice said, circling his wrists with her fingers and undulating luxuriously. "Completely mad."

Two people could travel to a place beyond madness, where all was light, pleasure, oneness, and joy, and that was precisely where Alice and Cam took each other.

Though the second time, Cam might have led the way. Alice was too overwhelmed, too replete with emotions as varied as they were enormous. She dozed off in a fog of peace, Cam spooned around her and all right with the world, or soon to be made right.

"What the blooming...?" Cam's arms withdrew, and Alice became aware of a soft tapping.

"Somebody is knocking on the sitting room door."

"Somebody with a pressing need to be heaved over the Dales." Cam nonetheless rose from the bed and retrieved a dressing gown from a hook on the bedpost. "Stay right where you are, please. I have plans for you."

Alice sat up, unease threading through her languor. What could be so urgent that it warranted disturbing the lord of the manor as he ostensibly packed for a hasty departure?

"Bernard is paying a call," Cam said, returning a moment later. "Beaglemore says the vicar looks intent on seeing me sooner rather than later. I'm sorry."

Alice slogged to the side of the bed, feeling more comfortable in her own skin than she'd ever thought possible. Cam had done that. Being with him had done that, rather.

"Might we see him together? If we're engaged, he's probably the first person we should inform."

Cam's brows rose. "I envy your ability to think. I want to toss dear Cousin into the North Sea and resume anticipation of our vows."

Alice indulged in a yawn and a stretch. "We can anticipate them again soon. And often. I seem to have misplaced my lady's maid, and you lack for a valet. Let's contrive as best we can, shall we?"

Despite a few kisses and caresses, dressing each other proceeded efficiently. Whatever business Bernard sought to discuss could not be good news. The urgency Alice had felt earlier in bed had been quite thoroughly satisfied.

But a new urgency, an anxiety, had taken its place. When Cam would have lingered to make up the bed, Alice instead led him out the door and down to the family parlor. They found Bernard pacing and muttering and in a very unvicarish frame of mind.

*

"Humble apologies, Lady Josephine, but the stage is delayed." The innkeeper's wife positively smirked that announcement from behind her standing desk in the inn's capacious foyer.

Such disrespect was what came of fraternizing with the lower orders. Had Mrs. Chudlow not also been the postmistress in Farnes Crossing, Lady Josephine would have fashioned a scathing reply.

Instead, she sighed patiently. "I suppose it cannot be helped. Perhaps if the coachman wasn't so fond of his flask, the schedule and these good people might not suffer so."

The *good people* looked to be middling sorts. A yeoman and his wife and small son. A pair of dowagers in outdated carriage dresses. A bankerish sort of fellow whose jacket was shiny at the elbows and whose boots needed new heels.

"This lot's on the next Flyer into York. You asked after the

Crossbow to Leeds, Manchester, and Liverpool. We have one inside fare and one outside fare left, but horses will go lame, and accidents can happen. Won't see the Crossbow for an hour, maybe two."

Two hours to idle about Farnes Crossing... a penance. A sheer, undeserved penance, though at least it was market day.

"The traveler will be a child." The weather was fine, and many a child rode safely on the roof of a stagecoach. Outside fares were usually half the cost of an inside seat, and the open air up top was healthier too.

Lady Josephine caught Mrs. Chudlow exchanging a glance with the older ladies. They would all remark the parsimony of begrudging a child—a girl child, at that—an inside seat.

"The inside fare will do."

"Luggage?"

"One satchel." Why any small girl needed three dresses, spare boots, a night dress, three pinafores, a shawl, and a coat, in addition to stockings, underlinen, and handkerchiefs, Lady Josephine did not know, but such was the wardrobe of every girl at the home. Mrs. Dumfries would not be reasoned with.

Surely hoarding clothing like that qualified as a sort of gluttony or greed.

"With the satchel, inside, one unaccompanied minor..." Mrs. Chudlow named a fare that Lady Josephine was certain included vales for the coachman, guard, horses, and grooms.

Her ladyship nonetheless passed over the coins. "A window seat, please. It's not every day a child gets to see the marvelous breadth of her homeland." Probably for the first and last time.

Mrs. Chudlow wrote something on a printed slip of paper and passed it over. "You should be here at the stated hour for departure, even if the stage is delayed. The coachies do their best to make up lost time, and the roads are quite passable at present. Provide the child some tucker. The fare at a few of the inns west of here isn't fit for dogs, and a body hasn't time to both use the jakes and eat the slops."

A glint in Mrs. Chudlow's eyes suggested she positively delighted in inflicting vulgarities on her betters and in telling them what to do.

No matter. Let her have her little stratagems. For a sum certain, Mrs. Chudlow tampered with the king's mail, which was malfeasance sufficient to put the inn out of business, if handled adroitly.

"Thank you ever so kindly," Lady Josephine said, smiling. "One appreciates the generous advice of an expert. I do wish I could send the child in a private conveyance, but those are in short supply at the vicarage."

"I'm sure they are, your ladyship." Some of Mrs. Chudlow's smirk faded. "I'm sure they are."

"Until later, then." Lady Josephine beamed at the assemblage and left.

Disrespectful fools, the lot of them.

∼

"Miss Singleton, my lord." Bernard offered two bows. "My apologies for intruding at an unfashionable hour."

Cam did not know his cousin all that well. Bernard, in addition to being several years older, had always held himself somewhat aloof. Bernard and Alexander had been friendly, but Cam had never known whether that was simply Alexander's general good-heartedness extended to a family member or a true bond.

Even Cam could tell that Bernard was agitated. His attire was faultless as usual, but the pin holding his cravat in gently cascading folds was a half inch off-center. The toes of Bernard's boots were dusty, and the loop of his watch chain wasn't threaded through a buttonhole.

"We are in rural Yorkshire," Cam replied. "The hour is fashionable enough." The scores of workers bringing in the harvest would be looking forward to their nooning, and the sun would soon be at its zenith.

"Shall I ring for a tray?" Alice asked.

"Not on my account," Bernard replied. "The reason for my call is brief, and now that I'm here..."

"Bernard, have a seat," Cam said. "Anything you have to convey to me can be shared with Alice."

Bernard's expression progressed from distracted, to puzzled, to—for him—pleased. "I see. Quite so. Congratulations and best wishes, though in the circumstances, my mother will attempt to meddle. If she supports the union, she will meddle. If she is against it, she will meddle, and it's about my mother that we must speak."

Alice took a wing chair by the empty hearth, and to Cam, she looked perfectly, wonderfully at home. Even the ruffle about her hem had earned a certain tolerance.

"Your mother has been meddling for ages," Cam said. "She will not come between me and Alice." No more than she'd already tried to.

"You say that, but she excels at thwarting other people's reasonable desires. She comes between me and my parishioners, me and my bishop, and she has tried to come between me and you. You thwart her at peril to your peace."

Cam waited for his guest to sink onto the sofa and then took the second wing chair. "She can't fight the whole shire, and as far as I know, she has no true allies here."

Lady Josephine had at least one enemy, though, in the person of her own nephew.

"Mama might not have allies, but she has minions. She has been reading my mail. Reading my outbound letters and their replies. I've taken the trouble to conduct certain correspondence from Farnes Crossing. As you both know, I'm seeking another post."

Cam had another post in mind for Bernard. The notion had popped into his head between passing Alice her jumps and rolling up her stockings.

"We don't blame you in the least for seeking a change," Alice said. "Though please no far-flung missionary ventures."

"I haven't the vocation. I haven't much vocation at all, truth be told, but I do a passable job, and to learn that Mama is reading my mail... How can she do that?"

"She bribes the postmaster," Cam said, "or the postmistress, or the boy who catches the incoming mailbag and tosses up the outgoing sack."

"Bribery is a crime, correct?"

Good heavens. The last two inches of a fuse two miles long were finally burning up. "Yes," Cam said. "Bribery and tampering with the mail are crimes. Also some sort of sin, I'm sure."

"Mama is a sin on two dainty feet, and I came to tell you that she's up to something."

"Bernard," Alice said, "she's always up to something. What has you so alarmed?"

"She took the hampers. When she went to Farnes Crossing this morning, she took the hampers. She mentioned something about knitting, would not let me run her errands for her, and she took the hampers. They were on the boot at the back of the coach. Both of them."

"What have hampers to do with criminal activity?" Cam asked.

"She takes the hampers to the orphanage," Alice said. "Two large wicker hampers, and she could have put them inside the coach, but she wants them to be seen. We never bring enough to fill even one of them, but the contents are distributed between the two. Her ladyship says a balanced load is easier on the horses, but the point is the display."

How petty, but also... calculating. An eye for the telling detail, for the convincing subtlety.

"So she's ostentatious about her generosity," Cam said. "We expect that from her, along with frequent allusions to her own humility and selflessness. She's bold."

"She's bold," Alice said, "and she has already made her royal progress to the orphanage this week. Why go twice, and why on market day, when the roads are busier and the journey will take more time? Why not drag me along?"

"She's bent on some scheme," Bernard said, rising. "I know not what, but I've come to ask for immediate permission to take a leave of absence from my post. I must also suggest, given Mama's penchant for breaking the law, that as a family we consider having her committed to an institution catering to parties suffering from nervous exhaustion."

"She is scheming," Alice said quietly, "to kidnap my daughter."

For once, Bernard's visage was completely, genuinely blank. Not carefully composed, not arranged to convey detachment, *blank*.

While Cam's heart welled with pride and relief. Alice would acknowledge her daughter, no subterfuges needed and no air of secrecy to be further exploited by a conscienceless monster. The truth kept Alice and Gabriella, and by extension Cam himself, safer than commending Lady Josephine to any walled estate ever could.

"A child," Bernard said, "explains a lot. I take it this child resides at the orphanage?"

Alice nodded. "She does. Has for the past several years. Gabriella is eight, and I have reason to know that Lady Josephine is making arrangements for my daughter to be sent into service somewhere in Ireland. The offices of a Mrs. Kendra MacDougal, St. Wulfstan's by the Forest, will facilitate the mischief, though I can't imagine in the short time..."

Cam stood and extended a hand to Alice. "Imagine it. Imagine your most dreaded nightmare. Then imagine something even worse for Lady Josephine when we catch up with her."

Alice rose and kept hold of his hand. "I thought we had time. A few days, at least. I'm abruptly nigh incoherent with anxiety for my daughter."

Alice was fearless about the words *my daughter*, and her worry was palpable.

"I came on foot," Bernard said. "Mama has the coach, but I could hack over to Farnes Crossing..."

Cam shook his head. "I'll take Galahad by the bridle paths and pastures."

"Bernard and I can go by coach." Alice squeezed Cam's hand and let go. "Should we collect Mr. St. Didier?"

"Good thought. He knows the law like I know shipping routes. He has the most enviable cold temper, and we might need that if her ladyship thinks to steal Gabriella away today."

"She could not possibly," Bernard began, then started for the door. "Well, yes, she could. She lies, she extorts, she mispresents, she causes suffering on the blameless... The seven deadly sins are mere shortcomings in comparison. My father used to say that Mama is a woman scorned, but in the name of all that is reasonable, what scorn could justify behavior such as this?"

He sailed out the door, leaving Cam alone with his intended.

"We will stop her," he said, gathering Alice in his arms. "We will stop the harm she intends to Gabriella, and we will stop her entire campaign of intimidation and misery. Bernard's idea has merit."

"Committing her to a walled estate?"

"Containing her," Cam said. "We can discuss details later. I'm off, and I will make straight for the orphanage. Don't let Bernard do anything stupid, and if St. Didier gets officious, please humor him. He has a cool head, and he will do his utmost to keep all parties safe."

Alice squeezed Cam about the middle and stepped back. "Who will keep you safe?"

"You have my back. I have your love. I will be careful. Don't spare the horses." He kissed her soundly and, as soon as they were in the corridor, bellowed for St. Didier.

CHAPTER SEVENTEEN

"Why does throwing some clothes into a satchel require more than a few minutes?" Lady Josephine infused her question with just a touch of impatience. Mrs. Dumfries took her position as headmistress seriously, which was all well and good, but a headmistress owed a patroness more deference than Mrs. Dumfries usually exhibited toward Lady Josephine.

Today was not the day to make that point.

Mrs. Dumfries was a substantial creature, tall and mannish, though one could not in fairness call her stout. She ran the organization efficiently and with a minimum of apparent sentiment. Lady Josephine had nonetheless concluded that Mrs. Dumfries was that most vexatious of entities, an honest woman. She did not slack. She maintained order while eschewing harsh punishments for the children. She wasn't prone to tippling, kept accurate books, and had no sons incarcerated for debt.

Mrs. Dumfries held her post because she regarded caring for orphans as a moral obligation, and Lady Josephine had yet to find the threat or innuendo that might encourage the headmistress to reevaluate her loyalties.

Her loyalty, blast the woman, was to the children.

"A quarter hour to collect one's worldly goods and say farewell to friends is far from excessive," Mrs. Dumfries said. "And your ladyship must admit that for Gabriella to leave us with no notice is an extraordinary, nigh miraculous, turn of events. You know we are pleased for her—these girls all dream of having a family of their own—but we are also fond of Gabriella and will miss her. Our Gabby has a quick mind and a pleasant temperament, and she doesn't balk at hard work."

The quick mind would be of no use to her in service, but of hard work, she'd know an abundance.

"Then you must admonish your charges regarding the sin of envy, Mrs. Dumfries. True, Gabriella will be going to a loving home, but we all must be prepared to make sacrifices for the sake of those we care about. If the girls intend to pout and sulk, then I will cease my efforts to locate families for the rest of them."

Not, of course, that Lady Josephine had made any such efforts, but one might speak prospectively without actually dissembling.

With Gabriella gone, the orphanage would have one less mouth to feed. The resulting economy should surely redound to the credit of the patroness who'd achieved it. The actual handling of the coin would take some delicacy, but Lady Josephine excelled at finessing sensitive matters.

"Your ladyship is doubtless correct," Mrs. Dumfries said. "Jeanine, you may speak."

Jeanine, a little sly boots who was destined for no good end, hovered in the doorway to Mrs. Dumfries's sitting room. The child was all big eyes and trembling smiles around her betters, but she was lazy at heart—never a perfect verse from her—and expected that charm would see her through life.

"Beg pardon, Lady Josephine, Mrs. Dumfries, but Gabriella cannot find her locket. We're searching for it everywhere, even Mary is helping us, but Gabriella must have her locket."

Oh, for pity's sake. "We can send the locket to her later, assuming it hasn't been stolen."

Mrs. Dumfries sat very tall. "My lady, I do apologize. That locket is Gabriella's only connection to her mother. We will turn the orphanage upside down to find it for her. Coaches come and go every day, but Gabriella has only that locket as her birthright."

The girl's birthright was a locket, a load of scandal, and hideous red hair. "The children may have a quarter hour," Lady Josephine said. "The stage is delayed, but the fare has already been purchased, and I do not intend to see that precious coin go to waste over a cheap trinket."

"Jeanine," Mrs. Dumfries said, "tell the girls to keep looking and to search the classroom and the library if they must but to be quick about it."

Jeanine stood with her head bowed and her hands behind her back. A proper little actress already and precociously sporting the dearth of morals common to any thespian. Ireland might be just the place for her too.

"You indulge them," Lady Josephine said when Jeanine had curtseyed and backed out the door. "I applaud your generous spirit, but given their circumstances, you must resist the temptation to coddle them. The kinder course would be plenty of discipline, the occasional deprivation, and a good deal of prayer."

Mrs. Dumfries rose from her wing chair and opened the drapes.

At midday, the manor's yard was flooded with sunshine, though who would want to gaze out over a lot of perpetually grazing sheep?

"Your ladyship is absolutely right. Fortunately, the girls have a surfeit of discipline here, in the schedules we keep, the chores they must complete, the curriculum and skills they must master. They have been deprived of families and, in many cases, respectability through no fault of their own. And believe me, your ladyship, this is a prayerful house. Tell me again where Gabriella will bide?"

"With a wonderful family near Liverpool." Not a lie, though Liverpool was merely a stopping point on the way to Ireland or somewhere equally obscure. "The lady of the house wrote to me because she knows through church connections of my devotion to this fine establishment. She and her husband—he's a vicar—have not been blessed with children. A girl who is past infancy and still in the schoolroom would suit them wonderfully. If Gabriella does well with them, they might even take a second child."

A bit of embellishment for the sake of credibility never hurt.

"What a fortunate turn of events for Gabriella, and all thanks to your ladyship. But where is this vicar's pulpit? I will, of course, write to Gabriella from time to time, to ask after her studies, to let her know how her friends go on. This will be quite a change for her, and—"

Lady Josephine held up a hand and shook her head. "A clean break, Mrs. Dumfries, is always best. You must trust me on this. No letters. Look at all the fuss we're enduring over one silly locket not worth tuppence. A clean break, I must insist."

Mrs. Dumfries remained by the window, arms crossed, expression polite. "Your ladyship, would a discussion of this matter with the baron be in order? Surely he should know of the extraordinary measures you've taken to improve the prospects of one small child, but that you had to go as far afield as Liverpool to place her... Mightn't that reflect poorly on the peer purporting to sponsor this institution?"

Of all the times to sprout a sensitivity to appearances. "That will not be necessary. I am his lordship's supernumerary in all matters relating to this house. Two previous barons were content to operate in that fashion, and this one is too. I know my nephew, Mrs. Dumfries. He will not look with favor on a dithering headmistress. Because I *am* devoted to this institution and the good work you do here, I grasp that you are concerned for Gabriella."

Lady Josephine aimed a telling look at the mantel clock and rose. "Lord Lorne, however, will regard your attitude as disrespect for my judgment. He is a notably proud man and will not tolerate you questioning my decisions."

"My lady, you are all that is patient," Mrs. Dumfries said. "I mean no disrespect to anybody, but Liverpool is so far away, and in my position, one hears heinous tales of children, girls especially, being sold."

"Mrs. Dumfries! How on earth...? Of all the...? Madam, the question is intolerable." *Sold.* Of all the filthy, unimaginable... The child would be earning a wage, for the love of winged cherubs. The very opposite of sold. She'd have a post and belong to a household and enjoy the comfort of good, honest work.

"I confide my fears to you in Gabriella's best interests," Mrs. Dumfries rejoined. "Too much of society dwells in unfortunate darkness, as your ladyship has often remarked. Questions will haunt me: How well do you know these people who simply wrote to ask that you send them a sweet little girl? Did they offer references? Did a bishop vouch for this vicar? Gabriella is a dear, precious, blameless child, and she will think we've flung her onto a coach without a second thought. Surely the new baron doesn't expect that of us?"

Much more of this moralizing, and Gabriella would not be on the coach. The situation wanted both subtlety and a quick resolution.

"Mrs. Dumfries, as insulted as I might be by the questions you raise, I must commend your caution instead. Gabriella has been entrusted to your care, and you are protective of her in a world that can be uncaring. I forgive you for your outburst and, in strictest confidence, will explain to you the urgency of the situation."

Seven of the children's allotted fifteen minutes remained.

"I love my nephew," Lady Josephine went on, "but I must admit, again, *in strictest personal confidence*, ma'am, that his is a mercantile nature. He deals in pounds and pence. This is unbecoming in a man of his station, and in time his focus might shift, but for now, he is a highly pragmatic, financially motivated man. His support for this orphanage... Well..." Her ladyship hoped the baron remained ignorant of his own generosity. "One mustn't rely on it."

"He'd abandon us?"

"I did not say that, but there he is, a newly fledged peer, and he's ridden his acres, attended services, entertained the neighbors... Doing the pretty in every direction despite his brother's recent demise, though his lordship has yet to look in on these poor children. That speaks volumes, Mrs. Dumfries. Sad, sad volumes."

"He's a busy man."

That reply had the gratifying ring of ineffective self-comfort. "In all modesty, I must remind you that I am a busy woman. If you will inspire the girls to make their final farewells to Gabriella, I will see her personally onto the westbound stage."

The moment became gratifying. Mrs. Dumfries had no personal shortcomings or missteps that could be exploited, but she was genuinely devoted to her charges. Simple enough to threaten the whole institution, such that allowing one little lamb into the worldly wilderness took on the patina of a sensible solution. A necessary compromise offered by an ally.

"You vouch for these people?"

"I have known the vicar's wife for ages. Our husbands were well acquainted earlier in life." True in a sense. They'd both attended Oxford and had some acquaintances in common.

"The girls still have five minutes," Mrs. Dumfries said, shifting to peer out the window. "Let's keep our word to them in that regard, shall we? As your ladyship knows, they turn into little barristers when adults break promises. Some fellow is going to get himself killed galloping down that track."

Lady Josephine joined her at the window. "Late to market, perhaps, though putting a valuable animal at risk like that is most irresponsible..."

A frisson of unease crept down Lady Josephine's spine and curled into a cold knot in her belly. She knew that horseman, or had known his earlier incarnation. As a youth, Cam had ridden like a demon, pushed himself to enormous feats of equestrian skill, and won any number of horseback races. Surely a sober and mature Camden would not...

The horse galloped on, gradually descending the hill as the track wound lower.

"Let's see what's keeping the girls, shall we?" Lady Josephine said, moving briskly toward the door. "One little locket is not worth throwing away the chance of a lifetime, and you can send it on later if it should turn up. I will happily post the package myself."

⁓

What saved Cam at least three times was Galahad's lack of condition. The horse was fit in a general sense, but not in peak form. He lacked that little extra edge of energy necessary to bolt, to take the dangerous long spot over a stile, to ignore a check on the reins when the track changed pitch.

Cam clung on, barely, his biceps and thighs burning as Farnes Crossing came into view at the foot of the ridge.

"Another half mile," he muttered as Galahad plunged along the glorified goat track that passed as a bridle path. "That's her ladyship's coach, and by God, she means evil this day."

Galahad was tiring, but game. He'd taken every fence, ditch, and hedge Cam had put him to. The horse had forgiven clumsy steering, his rider's occasionally unsteady balance, and an undignified clutch on his mane all without slowing.

"Galahad," Cam said, giving the reins enough of a tug to slow the horse to a canter. Would not do to come a cropper a quarter mile from the finish.

Lady Josephine emerged from the orphanage, half dragging a small, red-haired child by the hand. The girl was putting up a fight, and all the other denizens of the institution were filing out onto the front steps to watch the drama. An old fellow pushing a wheelbarrow across the yard stopped his progress, and a dozen sheep went on the alert.

"One last leap," Cam said, sinking his weight into his heels and getting a firm hold of Galahad's mane. "Get me over that fence, horse, and we'll forget you ever bit anybody."

The beast knew his job. He increased his speed slightly, aimed squarely for the stone wall encircling the orphanage's yard, cleared the obstacle with a mighty leap, and pounded on past clothes lines full of flapping laundry.

Cam hauled hard on the reins and got some curvetting and prancing as the horse deigned to trot, then walk.

"Well done." He thumped Galahad on the neck as the gelding stood, head down, sides heaving. "You earned your oats this day and then some."

The old fellow had abandoned his barrow and was advancing on Cam in a purposeful, uneven stride.

"I'll be walking yon horse, young fool. That is no example to set for t' children. Shame upon ye, and them poor dears already beyond upset." He ran up stirrup irons and loosened the girth, muttering in broad Yorkshire accents all the while.

"Thank you," Cam said. "His name is Galahad. I'm Lorne, and I'm upset too." He marched off to the present scene of the drama.

Beside Lady Josephine's coach, an embarrassed footman seemed to be puzzling over how to pick up a child who could bite, scratch, kick, and keen more fiercely than a robust barn cat. Lady Josephine grasped the girl by the wrist, and her grip had to hurt.

"Do not," Cam said, "touch that child. Lady Josephine, step away from her."

"My lord." Her ladyship made an attempt at a curtsey while the girl yanked hard against her captor. "How fortunate that you're here. Please explain to this *creature*"—she gave Gabriella's arm a jerk—"that if she's to have a smoother path in life, she must leave this charitable institution and accept the opportunity for gainful employment I've been able to locate for her."

"Josephine Huxley, get your hands off that child, *now*."

Either Cam's tone or the absence of an honorific must have made an impression. Her ladyship turned loose of Gabriella, who immediately darted back three steps.

Cam hunkered down. "Gabriella."

A terse nod. The girl never took her eyes off Lady Josephine.

"I'm Lord Lorne. You don't want to leave, do you?"

A vigorous shake of her head. "She was stealing me. Mary said to pretend I could not find my locket and to use the time to run away, but I don't want to run away. I *live* here."

Lady Josephine let out a huffy sigh. "My lord, I must explain the appearances. The child has an unfortunate obstinate streak, and of course, I take responsibility for that, as the orphanage has been one of my causes for ever so long. Mrs. Dumfries and I have had many a discussion regarding the consequences of excessive coddling where the girls are concerned."

Cam rose and spotted a tall, pretty blonde on the front terrace with the other children. "Mrs. Dumfries is too softhearted?"

Gabriella sidled closer to him.

"My lord, I would never speak ill of one whose motivations are above reproach—far, far above reproach—but in this case, to be painfully blunt—"

"She's about to lie," Gabriella said. "The more Lady Josephine apologizes and explains and pretends to be sorry, the more she's lying."

Lady Josephine's hand drew back, and Gabriella huddled against Cam's waist.

"Try it," Cam growled. "Please. Strike an honest child when I'm available to hold you accountable for your ungovernable temper."

Lady Josephine's hand returned to her side, and for once, she kept her mouth shut.

Cam possessed himself of Gabriella's hand. "I do believe her ladyship just revealed the truth, Gabriella. An honest child enrages her. This is surely not acceptable in one who calls herself the patroness of this orphanage."

"Camden, I know not what—"

"I have not given you leave to address me familiarly, madam, and I am out of patience. You have comported yourself disgracefully. You shall not further traumatize these children with needless histrionics. Wait in the coach."

The footman assumed an eyes-front at-attention stance by the coach door.

Cam addressed the coachman. "She can pound on the roof until it's in splinters, and your team is not to move. Understand?"

"Aye, milord. We'll bide until Domesday, if that's your lordship's pleasure."

Lady Josephine turned a glittering, frankly hateful gaze on her only extant nephew. "You forget yourself, young man. Dignity forbids me from explaining the egregious error you are making, but you will regret this."

Gabriella took a tighter hold on Cam's hand.

"Get into the coach, your ladyship, and prepare to be held accountable for years of inexcusable behavior."

"Cam—my lord, the child is *illegitimate*, and if you knew her provenance, you would understand that the difficult decisions I have made were made for *your* sake."

"You're lying again. Into the coach, now."

She climbed in, and the footman tipped up the steps and closed the door.

"Do not let her out. No matter what she threatens or promises, do not allow her out of this coach."

"Aye, milord."

Cam had been too busy trying to stay in the saddle to think through the next part, but he knew that further dealings with Lady Josephine at that moment would try his temper past all bearing.

He hoisted Gabriella to his hip and strode across the yard, the sheep trotting off at his approach. Galahad, his coat damp with sweat, was toddling laps around the manor house, the old fellow muttering to him as they went.

On the terrace, a knot of girls of varying heights and in uniformly gray dresses crowded around the sole adult in their company.

"Lord Lorne." The lady curtseyed, and like a breeze riffling across a wheat field, the girls did likewise. "How very lovely to make your acquaintance."

"You are Mrs. Dumfries?" Cam had seen the name in the ledgers under wages.

"I have that honor. I apologize for the drama."

"May I get down?" Gabriella asked. "I want my locket."

"I put it in the dictionary," one of the taller girls said. "Look in the G's."

Gabriella sent a questioning look at the headmistress, who nodded. "And tell Cook we need a pitcher of cider and some biscuits out back. Time to practice our cricket."

The children disappeared like so many seeds of thistle on the wind.

"What will you do with her ladyship?" Mrs. Dumfries said. "She claimed you wanted to close the orphanage, and Gabriella's only chance for a better life was placement with a family near Liverpool."

What Cam wanted was to lay eyes on his intended and assure her that Gabriella was safe. Then he wanted to consign Lady Josephine to a solitary eternity scrubbing steps in the pit.

"The orphanage is safe," Cam said. "Lady Josephine had arranged for Gabriella to be put in service somewhere in Ireland. I am ashamed to say that she used church connections to plan that horror."

"A post *in service*? As a scullery maid or turnspit?" Mrs. Dumfries's gaze narrowed on the elegant coach at the foot of the drive. "Her ladyship assured me that Gabriella was to be taken in by a vicar and his wife. That she'd have a family of her own..."

Mrs. Dumfries paced off across the terrace, skirts swishing. "Miss Singleton once told me that I must never take what her ladyship says as the truth. Gabriella is right. Lady Josephine lies."

"What else did Miss Singleton say?"

"That one does not win a confrontation with Lady Josephine." Mrs. Dumfries marched back to the center of the terrace. "One asks her ladyship questions, seeks her opinion. 'My lady, does it strike you as odd that...' Or, 'Does your ladyship have any concern about...' Never disagree with Lady Josephine and constantly offer her subtle flattery. Had it not been for that guidance… My nature is to confront. Had I confronted Lady Josephine today, you would have arrived too late. You've met Miss Singleton? The children adore her."

As do I. "I am engaged to marry her, and if I am not mistaken, that is Miss Singleton in my traveling coach. I am certain that she will want to spend some time with Gabriella."

"Gabriella holds Miss Singleton in particular esteem, as do I. You are a very fortunate man, my lord. Very fortunate."

Considering that Mrs. Dumfries was delivering felicitations, her tone was quite stern. Cam smiled at her anyway.

"I know. I am the luckiest of men, and my task and delight shall be to see that my baroness considers herself the most fortunate of women." He bowed to Mrs. Dumfries and went to greet his bride.

CHAPTER EIGHTEEN

"That's her ladyship's coach," Mr. St. Didier said. "Lorne arrived in time to prevent unnecessary upheaval."

St. Didier would not lie. Alice took a peek through the coach window for herself. There, indeed, sat her ladyship's stately vehicle, the coachman on the bench, the footman and a groom loitering by the door.

Thank heavens, and thank Camden Huxley, disaster had been averted. "You had doubts, Mr. St. Didier?"

"Concerns. His lordship isn't much of one for the saddle."

Alice pulled on her gloves. "He has you fooled, then, or perhaps he's been fooling himself. Camden Huxley was so skilled on horseback that the local boys stopped racing him. He never rode the made mounts his brother was given, so Cam had to learn to actually ride. One doesn't forget that skill."

One would also never forget the sight of the vicarage coach sitting at the foot of the drive, hampers on display. Empty hampers, in all probability.

"I had concerns too," Alice said as the Lorne Hall coach drew to a halt. "The best jockeys fall. The fleetest mounts can trip or land in bad footing." And Cam was no longer that brooding young fellow trying to gallop his way to paternal approval.

St. Didier climbed out and offered Alice his hand. Bernard descended from the box and treated his mother's vehicle to baleful scrutiny.

"I wanted to be wrong," he said. "I wanted to be guilty of a complete, foolish overreaction that misread evidence and jumped to erroneous conclusions. She meant to steal that child."

"Of course she did," St. Didier retorted. "And she would not trouble herself in the least if great harm befell the girl, provided no taint of scandal resulted for her ladyship. Truly, Huxley, I pity you your mother."

What would Gabriella think of her own mother, assuming Alice found the courage to broach that topic?

"You gentlemen can debate the details of Lady Josephine's venery all day. I would like to consult the baron." Alice strode forth before they could stop her, escort her, admonish her to exercise caution, or remind her of the need for discretion.

She was done with all that.

By the time she reached the terrace steps, she was nearly jogging. Cam met her on the stairs and wrapped his arms around her.

"Gabriella is safe, Alice. She's safe, she gave a very good account of herself, and she has many allies in this house."

Alice allowed herself one moment to cling, to rejoice, to acknowledge the battle nerves, and to let the what-might-have-beens terrify her anew.

"Thank you. Thank you from the bottom of my much-shaken heart. Lady Josephine was ready to cast my daughter out into the world, friendless, prey to any who'd take advantage of a helpless child."

"And all the while," Cam replied, "she'd be congratulating herself on having done an orphan *and you* a good turn. She even informed me that her actions were for my benefit as well. I am angry enough to set the magistrate on her."

"Not the magistrate." Her ladyship would weep and sniffle and plead good intentions, all the while pretending ignorance of the terrors a lone little girl in service faced, assuming Gabriella had ever made it to Ireland. "We can discuss Lady Josephine's fate later. Right now, I want to see Gabriella."

"I believe the household is preparing for a game of cricket on the back lawn. Cider and biscuits were mentioned."

Cam offered his arm. Alice took him by the hand instead and led him across the terrace. "We are engaged to be married, and the day has been trying. Modest displays of affection are permissible." Also necessary, given the state of her nerves.

"Set a reasonable pace, please. I am not the equestrian I used to be and will have the sore muscles to prove it. Galahad is quite a horse."

Galahad. Oh, of course. "He simply wanted for some proper attention, and there are remedies for sore muscles, my lord."

What could remedy the breach between Alice and her daughter? Years of deception, distance, and worry, and Alice's defense would also be that she had meant well.

"What do I say to her? I have longed for and dreamed of this day, but now... Cam, what do I say to my only child when I have been such a shamefully inadequate parent?"

Entering the orphanage had abruptly become daunting.

"You will know what to say, Alice. She's a very astute little girl—gets that from her mother—and she knows firsthand what a besom Lady Josephine has been. Would you like me to join you?"

"Yes." Alice answered instinctively. "Please."

"Then lead on, and let's hear the tale of Gabriella's adventure from the child herself."

As it happened, the retelling of the day's developments involved all of the girls. When Alice emerged onto the back porch, the girls swarmed her, and Cam at some point let go of her hand.

He remained near, a quiet, smiling presence, while Alice enjoyed a barrage of hugs and greetings. Mrs. Dumfries smiled a welcome while arranging cups on a long wooden table in the shade.

"Miss Alice, Miss Alice. Lady Josephine tried to steal Gabby," Jeanine bellowed.

"We didn't let her," Lizzy shouted. "Mary made a plan, and we all pretended to look for the locket, and Jeanine was the lookout, and Gabriella wouldn't run away."

Penelope tugged on Alice's skirts. "Will you read us a story, Miss Alice?"

"She can't read us a story," Jeanine retorted. "We're to play cricket, and I am on Miss Alice's team."

A riot of *pick me* and *me too* and *that's not fair* ensued, and all the while, Gabriella stood quietly, her gaze moving between Alice and Cam.

"But who will be on my team?" Cam asked at a moment when the pandemonium ebbed slightly.

The uproar crested again, and Alice used the moment to bend low and whisper in Gabriella's ear. "Let's introduce ourselves to his lordship's horse, shall we?"

Gabriella nodded.

While Cam distracted the horde, Alice sauntered off with Gabriella. The moment should have been prosaic. Mother and child going to pass the time with a horse, but for Alice...

All the gratitude, hope, and joy she was capable of filled her heart and gave her courage. "Gabriella, what did you make of Lady Josephine's actions today?"

"Lady Josephine is mean, and she lies," Gabriella said, pausing a good dozen yards from where Galahad cropped grass.

Archibald had removed the horse's gear and found a halter somewhere, then gone back to his weeding near a corner of the back wall.

"Her ladyship isn't very nice," Alice said. "You don't have to pretend otherwise now."

"But we did pretend, didn't we? Mrs. Dumfries was always making excuses for the mostly empty hampers and for how Lady

Josephine didn't even know her Proverbs. Mrs. Dumfries didn't like making excuses, but she always made them."

"Let's sit on the swing, shall we?" Alice had never sat beside her daughter on a swing before, never had a private conversation with Gabriella before. "Galahad looks to be having a fine snack. We might as well leave him to it."

"He's very grand."

"I think so too. Did Lady Josephine upset you?"

"Nah." Gabriella hopped onto the swing, but her legs were too short to reach the ground.

Alice sat to one side of her and gave the swing a push. "She upset me. She's been upsetting me for years, but I was also afraid of her."

"Did she threaten to put you on bread and water?"

"In a manner of speaking."

"Or make you copy out a whole Gospel with perfect penmanship?"

How to make children resent their Bibles. "She threatened to harm somebody I care about very much. To toss them onto a coach, never to be seen again."

Cam was in the middle of a knot of little girls, each one trying to instruct him on the niceties of cricket. Even Mary was smiling at his exaggerated stance with the bat.

He's here. I am fortified by the mere sight of him pretending to negotiate the rules of cricket with a lot of juvenile experts.

"She said I was going to a loving family," Gabriella muttered. "Mary said that was a lie. Mary is a grouch but she doesn't lie. I was scared, and I was mad. I haven't been bad, and I did not deserve to be kidnapped."

Alice slipped an arm around Gabriella's shoulders. "His lordship said you were very brave."

"I wasn't brave. I was scared. I live *here*. These are my friends. They tried to help. Lady Josephine is bad, and nobody puts her on any coaches."

Gabriella's composure was slipping, and so was Alice's. "When we are scared, when we are terrified, it's hard to be brave, but you were."

And so was I. The thought bloomed like the first rose in spring, too bold for the winter-dull garden, too much, too bright and undeniable. *So was I. For years, I was brave, and I kept trying, and I did my best.*

"I can run fast," Gabriella said. "Mary told me that if Lady Josephine took me to the inn, I should ask to use the jakes and run like hell. 'Hell' is a bad word."

"Mary was being emphatic. We cannot fault her for that in the circumstances." And sometimes, even the most demure lady needed a bit of colorful emphasis in her words. "Lady Josephine would never, ever have been able to catch you. She does not run, she never plays cricket, and she thinks fresh air is bad for the complexion."

"She's bigger than me."

Than I. "But she's slow and nowhere near as nimble as you are, and nobody likes her. If she'd shouted, 'Stop, thief!' nobody would have stopped you. She would have looked very foolish, and somebody might even have tried to trip her if she gave chase."

Gabriella peeped up at Alice in a manner reminiscent of Jeanine. "And I would have got away."

"Of course, but fortunately, your friends came to your aid, and the baron dealt with Lady Josephine. I wish I could have seen that."

Gabriella wiggled a little closer. "He was mad. Not mean-mad, but actions-have-consequences mad." She'd raised her voice to imitate Mrs. Dumfries. "I hate Lady Josephine. I'm glad the baron stopped her."

So am I. "She is very hard to like, but I doubt you will ever see her again."

"Good. Somebody should put her on a coach to darkest Peru."

Not a bad thought. Alice brushed a hand down Gabriella's braid and searched for a way to embark on the next part of the discussion.

Gabriella, have you ever wondered about your mother?

Gabriella, have you thought it odd that we have the exact same color of hair?

Gabriella, could you find it in your heart not to detest a mother who gave you away?

How on earth did one cross this bridge?

Cam somehow extricated himself from his team members, who were herded by Mrs. Dumfries to the wooden table. He approached the swing, a cup of cider in each hand.

"Is there room here for one more?"

"On the other side of Miss Alice," Gabriella said, sitting up. "Did you bring cider?"

Cam passed her a cup and sat. "I did. Miss Alice and I will share. Now, what have you two been whispering about while I received the most expert coaching on my cricket form?"

He gave Alice the second cup and toed the swing a little higher.

Alice sipped and passed the cup back to him. How to be honest and apologetic without putting the weight of any expectations on the child? She had never truly thought this through because that would have been hoping for the impossible in a very painful level of detail.

"We weren't whispering," Gabriella said, taking a drink. "I love cider. Our cider is the best because it comes from our trees. I had a question for Miss Alice."

"Ask me anything, Gabriella. Today is not a day to stand on ceremony."

"Why do we have the same color hair? Nobody else has hair like ours. Lady Josephine said it was unfortunate hair, but hair is just hair, and I like our hair. Do you think your hair is unfortunate?"

This child. This wonderful, magnificent, unspeakably dear child...

"That is an interesting question," Alice said, "and as it happens, I love that we have the same color hair, and there's a reason why we do. A reason you should know."

Cam settled an arm around Alice's shoulders, and Alice prepared to be very brave and very honest.

An odd realization emerged from the welter of emotions swirling inside Cam. Between the pride he took in Alice, Gabriella, the children, and even the horse, beside the rage he harbored for Lady Josephine, the relief, the gratitude, and the joy for how the day had unfolded, was the knowledge that he need not negotiate anything.

Sitting on that swing with two ladies for whom he already cared a great deal, he need not strike a clever bargain.

He wasn't obligated to be a wily bargaining opponent.

He had no cause to worry that the whole discussion would result in hurt feelings, sore tempers, and unworkable agreements.

All Alice and Gabriella needed from him—and they did need it—was his presence and his care for them. He was not called upon to *do* anything. He contributed simply by being with them on whatever terms they required.

Very... strange to have nothing to prove or win. Very... different, and important.

"The baron doesn't have hair like us," Gabriella said. "His is darker."

"I like my hair," Cam said. "Many fellows go bald, and I hope to never be among them." Though it would not matter to Alice if he were. The day was full of revelations.

"Why is my hair the same as yours, Miss Alice? I told Mary it was because you are my mama, but Mary said it might be a co-indigent and not mean anything. Jeanine said we could be sisters or cousins, but Jeanine will say anything just to talk."

"That we have the same hair is not a coincidence," Alice said, enunciating carefully. "May I tell you a story, Gabriella?"

"Will the story explain our same hair?"

A tenacious child. That quality would serve her well in life.

"It will," Alice replied.

"Is there a moral, like with Aesop?"

"Yes," Cam said. "The moral is, children who keep asking questions never get to hear the story, and I'm sure it's quite an adventure."

Alice sent him a *do hush* look. Engaged couples exchanged such glances. Cam returned fire with his best *I adore you* expression.

"Once upon a time," Alice said, "there was a lonely young lady. She lived with her grandpapa, who was honestly a bit of a grouch."

"Like Mary or Archibald?"

"Yes, like that. A good fellow, but testy and always busy. He had no time for his granddaughter, though in truth, he simply did not know what to do with her. He'd only raised a son, and there was no grandmama to smooth things over."

Alice apparently found telling this story easier for having rehearsed it with Cam.

"I'm not lonely," Gabriella said firmly. "I have my friends."

"Good," Alice said. "Friends are a very great blessing in life. Anyhow, this young lady met a young man. He was charming and sweet, and she was much taken with him."

"Was he a knight?"

"He was the son of a marquess, and he became a soldier, so yes. He was a variety of knight."

"Did they kiss?"

"I'm afraid they did. The young lady was smitten, and she thought the young man was too. Maybe she was just glad to have a friend, but when the young man had to go away to join the fighting, he said he would come back. He promised he would write and promised they would be together again soon."

"This is not an adventure, Miss Alice. This story needs a dragon."

The child was brilliant. Cam gave the swing a gentle push.

"The young man went away. He did not come back. He did not even write. In fact, he went off to fight Old Boney and died defending his country."

"Boney was a dragon, but Wellington beat him to smithereens. Sometimes we play Waterloo, and the French army has to speak in French." Gabriella passed Alice her cider, popped off the swing, and brandished an imaginary sword. "'*Chiens anglais, préparez-vous à mourir!*' English dogs, prepare to die! We *vous* because that's easier."

She hopped back onto the swing, wiggled close to Alice, and reappropriated her cider. "Do we get to the dragon part soon?"

"I like some dragons," Cam said. "They breathe fire and guard their treasures, and some of them can fly."

Both of Cam's swing companions gave him the *do hush* look.

"The young lady," Alice resumed, "found she was to have a child. She had not married the young man, and when she tried to inform him of the situation by letter, she received no reply, even though he had yet to die in battle. Society prefers that young ladies have husbands before any babies come along."

"Mary is a bastard." Gabriella offered that comment in the same tone she might have observed that autumn would soon arrive. "Polly is, too, and Jeanine is a just-plain orphan. Lizzy's papa got transported, and her mama died, so we aren't sure about her. She might be half an orphan."

Cam gave Alice's shoulder a gentle squeeze.

"Right," Alice said. "Well, the young lady's baby was both illegitimate—that's when your parents aren't married—and an orphan of sorts, like Lizzy, because the young lady could not bring the baby home to live with her grandpapa."

"Was the grandpapa mean? Is he the dragon?"

"The grandpapa is, at heart, very kind. He's simply gruff. The young lady let herself be convinced that nobody would like her or help her if she tried to raise the baby herself."

"I would like her. Mrs. Dumfries raises us, and the baron helps her with his money, and you come and help us with our verses and read us stories."

"You are smarter than the young lady. She let her baby be raised by strangers—kind strangers—but the strangers died, and so the baby, who grew to be a very fine little girl, was placed in a rural orphanage. She had friends, but she didn't know that her own mother still cared very much for her."

Gabriella took a drink of her cider. "Why didn't her mother tell her that? Friends are friends, but a mama is your mama, just for you."

"The young lady, who is the mama in our story, became afraid. She was afraid the person saying nobody would help her was right. The same person said the mama and daughter would starve in the street if they tried to make a life together. That the grandpapa would be so ashamed he'd die of mortification. All kinds of terrible, awful, dire things would happen if the mama tried to raise her daughter, and the mama knew that some of those things could truly happen."

"Mary had a sister," Gabriella said. "She died in the poorhouse. Lots of people die in the poorhouse, but Mrs. Dumfries says we are not to dwell on that, and we must remember the baron in our prayers. Does this story have a happy ending, and when do we get to the part about the hair?"

"This story has a happy ending. Somebody was lying to the mama, Gabriella. The somebody who never ceased nattering about doom and despair, who always seemed to be bringing up all the terrible things that can happen to children when their mamas are poor."

"That's the dragon," Gabriella said, grinning. "That's the serpent in the garden. Mrs. Dumfries talks a lot about the serpent in the garden. Maybe serpents are dragons that got their legs cut off, and that's why they are so awful."

"They can't breathe fire either," Cam said.

"And they don't have wings," Gabriella added. "What happened to the dragon?"

"The dragon said over and over again to the mama: 'Nobody will help you. Nobody will care if you and your daughter suffer or die. If you love your daughter, you will never tell her that she has a mother, because she will hate you for not taking care of her. Society will hate you if you even try. You will both be miserable.'"

Cam felt an urge to leave the swing, haul Lady Josephine out of her coach, and plant the old besom a facer.

Gabriella sat up. "That's *awful*. That is mean. I'd be their friend.

Mary and Jeanine and Lizzy and Penelope would too. Mrs. Dumfries says, 'Judge not,' and that's from the *Bible*."

"Matthew, chapter seven, verses one through three," Cam murmured.

"Well, the dragon was wrong, and you are right," Alice said. "The mama and daughter have friends. Very, very good friends who love them and care about them and who say it truly doesn't matter very much if the mama and papa ever married."

"Doesn't matter *at all*," Cam said, because the story should have accuracy in important particulars.

"*I* don't care," Gabriella rejoined stoutly. "The dragon person lied. They told mean lies. Lady Josephine lies like that."

Cam felt the bolt of anxiety go through Alice. The bolt of hope wrapped in dread. He could speak up, take over the narrative, but the story wasn't his to tell.

"Lady Josephine has been very naughty," Alice said. "The only part of the story I haven't yet shared is that the mama and daughter had the very same unusual color of hair, darker than rubies, but equally red."

Gabriella pulled a braid forward and narrowed her gaze on Alice's tidy bun.

No snood.

"Oh." She snuggled back against Alice's side. "You are the mama, and I am the daughter, right?"

"Yes. I am the mama, and you are my daughter."

"Lady Josephine was the mean liar. The baron put her in her coach when she tried to steal me."

"That is all true, and the story is also true, Gabriella. Our friends don't care that I never married your father. They love us just the same."

"Lady Josephine is mean. Nobody likes her. She said nobody would like *us* if you were my mama. Are you truly my mother?"

"I am absolutely and truly your mother."

And I will soon be your step-papa. Time for the step-papa story later, and what did the *step* part matter, anyway?

"Our hair is not a co-ind... co... That word you said?"

"Not a coincidence. My own mama had hair the same color, and so did her mama. The name for it is Titian, after a painter who liked models with hair this color."

"I like my hair. My hair is Titian, and so is yours." Gabriella lapsed into silence, and Cam again stifled the urge to sum up, to recount agreements reached, to reiterate understandings.

"Will you be my mama now?" Gabriella asked. "My real mama?"

"Will you be my daughter?" Alice asked. "You have many friends here, and they are very dear to you, Gabriella. I would not ask you to leave them. They have protected you and supported you when I could not. They will miss you terribly if you leave."

Cam cleared his throat and earned no reproving looks. "Your mama will live with me at Lorne Hall soon, which is just a few miles away. I have asked her to marry me. I was hoping you and your friends might come for a visit later this week. The place is very large, and I live there without much company."

Though in London, Cam had had no company at all, other than the boys, of course.

Gabriella drew the end of her braid across her mouth. "Mrs. Dumfries says Lorne Hall is enormous. We could play cricket in the ballroom."

Interesting notion. "We could also play cricket in the park," Cam said, "or go fishing on the lake, or fly kites, or—"

"Who is he?" Gabriella asked, gaze narrowing on a figure on the terrace steps. "He looks serious."

"That," Cam said, "is one of the good dragons. His name is Leopold St. Didier, and you are right that his is a sober demeanor. I suppose he's looking for me." Cam rose. "Ladies, are we sufficiently sorted that I might excuse myself?"

Gabriella looked puzzled.

"We are wonderfully sorted for now," Alice said. "Delightfully sorted. Time enough later to deal with next steps. For today, we are... marvelously sorted." She glowed and beamed and twinkled at him, once again the Alice who as a girl had turned every head, who had seized life with both hands and hugged the stuffing out of it.

"I thought so. Then excuse me for the nonce."

Cam wanted to write down every word of the story he'd just heard, the story he'd just been invited to join going forward, the story with the happiest of all possible endings. Instead, he blew the ladies a kiss and bowed and strolled off in no particular hurry.

"What was my father's name?" Gabriella asked, curling into her mother's side as Cam sauntered away. "Did you know his name?"

"I know his name and a great deal about him," Alice said.

Cam slowed his steps.

"He was Throckmorton Gabriel Lucius Wendover DeSales, Lord Throckmorton," Alice said. "Fourth son of the Marquess of Hampton. He was merry and sweet and very handsome too."

Lord Throckmorton. Lord Throck-rubbishing-morton. Well, of course. Truly, a certain dragon had much to answer for.

Cam continued his progress toward St. Didier, who stood on the steps, looking impatient and unhappy.

"What are we to do with the kidnapper?" St. Didier asked. "The coachy will sit at the foot of the drive until Michaelmas, but we must determine what's to be done with her ladyship. Huxley is quoting the Old Testament and looking choleric. He doesn't seem to have much of a vocation, if you ask me."

"Lady Josephine's fate should be decided by the person upon whom she wrought the most evil, and that would be Alice Singleton."

St. Didier's brows drew down in a manner that suggested even his vast knowledge of Society, life, and learned subjects was confounded.

"What have you learned, Lorne? You know something, something important."

"You and Huxley can convey her ladyship to the Hall and see her confined under guard to a third-floor guest room. She is to be given food and water if she requests same. She will otherwise await sentencing at the whim and pleasure of my prospective baroness. If you have suggestions, please direct them to Alice, assuming Gabriella ever turns loose of her mother."

On the swing, Gabriella and Alice were cuddled up, whispering and smiling, and Cam did not have the heart to interrupt them. Captain Lord Throckmorton DeSales, of all the handsome, charming... The story was not quite over and the ending not quite as happy as Cam would have preferred.

Yet.

"I'll deal with the baroness," St. Didier said. "I hazard you have not once, this entire day, spared a thought for your correspondence, and I must say, Lorne, I finally have occasion to be proud of you."

He marched off and did not see Cam smile at his retreating form.

CHAPTER NINETEEN

"My feelings are hard to describe," Alice said, sitting back against the squabs of the Lorne traveling coach. "Not giddy, though I am full of elated disbelief and relief and sheer joy, but more... I feel more like myself. Like the Alice I am meant to be. Whole and at peace and looking forward with only the normal anxieties of a mama and prospective bride and... I am babbling."

She was also holding Cam's hand, which a prospective bride was allowed to do, and traveling alone with him in a closed carriage, which was on the scandalous side.

And—Alice noted with significant relish—that mattered *not at all*. Lady Josephine had been caught in time and would be prohibited from poisoning all the wells of goodwill and good cheer for miles in every direction. She would never again set neighbor against neighbor, mamas against daughters, or swains against damsels.

"You are quiet," Alice said, snuggling up. "You were wonderful, on the swing. Gabriella likes you very much."

"I like her too. She's brilliant and sweet and fierce and has the very best hair. Did you ladies make any plans for the future?"

"Yes and no." Cam had been fairly quiet on the swing, too, but his mood was different now. More brooding. "We agreed that we are mother and daughter. We agreed that you are a fine fellow. We agreed that a visit to Lorne Hall for all the girls will be an enjoyable day out. We agreed that people who think less of us because I did not marry my handsome, fickle cavalier cannot be allowed to decide our lives for us. Gabriella might regret that last part, and I will try to explain it to her, but we decided what mattered most for today."

Cam kissed her knuckles, and though the gesture was affectionate, Alice sensed reserve even in his kiss. Distraction, perhaps. Preoccupation.

"You are pondering what we should do with her ladyship," Alice said. "I don't want to think about it. Bernard votes for a walled estate, and he is her son."

"Your vote is the one that will decide the matter, Alice, and before you cast that vote, I would like to tell you a story."

Oh dear. "Two stories in one day. This one has a dragon in it, too, I take it?"

"Of a sort." Cam looped his free arm around Alice's shoulders. "More of a demon, in my estimation. The tale is short. Once upon a time, there was a young fellow. He was sweet, kind, charming, and—being a younger son—a soldier. He went off to Portugal—the war was just getting started—and fought nobly and well, but whenever he'd gather around the fire with his fellow officers, he was always pining for some female he'd left behind in the wilds of Yorkshire."

"Cam, no."

"Yes. He wrote to her endlessly, though she never wrote back. He'd wanted to marry her before leaving England, but she was so young, and a soldier's lot is uncertain, and one did not ask for a commitment when that might result in the lady of one's dreams being yoked to an invalid, and so forth."

"I do not care for this story." All the joy in Alice sank into a small determined flame, one that would not be extinguished because of ancient history, however sad or difficult.

"I don't care for it either, and the tale grows darker. The young man hadn't been in uniform very long before he was called to his eternal home, courtesy of the French army, and no letter from any young lady in York ever arrived for him. He was brave, he was honorable, and, Alice, *he was loyal to you.* I had the pleasure of serving with him, and I am not telling you a story so much as I am reciting facts you have a right to know."

The coach rumbled along, Cam's arm was snug around Alice's shoulders, and his hand wrapped about hers, and yet... Alice could not make sense of what Cam had just told her. Could not bear to see where the story led.

"Once," Alice said, "when I was a girl, we had one of those winter storms that comes out of nowhere. The day was almost mild. The sunshine brilliant, everybody thinking thoughts of spring, and then... in minutes, I swear it was in minutes, Cam, the sky went dark, the temperature plummeted, and the snow came down at a blinding rate. The farmers lost livestock, and old Mr. Beckenbaugh would have died had he not been able to grab a cow by the tail and follow her into a byre."

"Today is still a happy day, Alice. You and Gabriella are family now."

And yet, Cam's tone was solemn.

"I am family with my daughter now, true, but her poor father. *I wrote to him over and over,* Cam. Alex told me his posting, and I felt I owed him cheerful letters even though it wasn't quite proper. I was no great fan of propriety at the time. I was in love. Then I *needed* to get in touch with him, but he never once wrote back."

The realization that two young people very much in love and trying to remain connected had been thwarted by Lady Josephine's evil...

"He wrote to you too, Alice. I assure you of that. I *saw* him writing to you by firelight. Without mentioning your name, he spoke rhapsodies about your smile, your laugh, your joie de vivre. The rest of us grew tired of his panegyrics, and we resented you mightily for never sending him a line."

The horses picked up speed, as did Alice's thoughts.

"It never occurred to me that he'd written and that Lady Josephine had stolen his letters. Our mail sits in our slot at the posting inn, and she doubtless sorted through it at her leisure. The outgoing pile sits in plain sight, but I never... She is shameless."

"She is dangerous," Cam said.

That was a more accurate word. "I agree. She has no sense of right and wrong outside of what is right and wrong for her. In that regard, she is like a hungry, slithering creature, meaning no insult to serpents."

Serpents at least had the decency to look like what they were. Lady Josephine, by contrast, was all gracious smiles, Scripture, and pleasantries, until she'd cozened from her victims a trust she would heartlessly betray.

"When you decide what's to be done with her, Alice, you must bear in mind that she is a menace to all in her ambit. Had Lord Throckmorton known your situation, he would have been back in Yorkshire on leave to marry you faster than a homing pigeon flies to his roost. Lady Josephine instead broke his heart, put you under her thumb, and saw Gabriella saddled with illegitimacy. Those are egregious wrongs against people who did nothing to hurt her."

The sheer cruelty... The meanness and cunning. "I have no interest in revenge, Cam. Revenge feels too much like what Lady Josephine has been about all these years, playing God, appointing herself the judge, jury, and executioner of other people's happiness."

And their legitimacy, blast and damn her. Of course, Lady Josephine had wanted Alice to make a clean break with Gabriella. All the better to establish a clean break from the truth of her ladyship's evil schemes.

"I agree," Cam said. "Lady Josephine is a monument to moral bankruptcy. She'd count it a victory to move you to vengeance. Perhaps what I'm asking you to consider is what justice requires. If her ladyship's scheme with Gabriella had succeeded, Mary or little

Jeanine would have been next. Mary would not have gone into service in a proper household, or not for long."

Grim thought. Mary would have no hesitation about putting her ladyship on a transport ship, or worse.

"While I consider her ladyship's fate, might we discuss another topic?" Alice was loath to consider anything about Lady Josephine, other than her permanent absence from the shire. The thought of her was a foul miasma on Alice's mental landscape. "I mentioned your boys to Mrs. Dumfries, and I believe the girls overheard me."

"My boys?"

"Your junior assistant clerks in training who lurk in doorways and patrol the parks and chat up your competitors' clerks. Those boys. You must miss them."

Something in Cam's posture subtly shifted, becoming a tad less loverlike. "I have written to them."

"Camden Huxley, you miss them. They are doubtless missing you."

Cam shifted on the bench. He adjusted the window shade. He kissed Alice's fingers again. "One does. They are absolute scamps, but one does miss them."

One fretted over them, worried for them, and tended to their every need as well. "They should pay a visit to the Hall. A boy whose entire childhood is spent in the confines of London will develop weak lungs."

"My boys do not have weak lungs."

Alice patted Cam's thigh. "Summon them for a visit, Camden, and perhaps to attend our wedding. They will have advice for you, and you must thank them and heed them as best you can."

"Gabriella had advice for you?"

The subject was changed, which had been Alice's objective. Cam was very protective of his collection of scamps, and they were doubtless protective of him, as family should be toward one another.

"Gabriella said I am to be kind but firm with you, as Mrs.

Dumfries is with her charges. When you are overly tired, you must be allowed to nap or to read to yourself, and when you are sad, I must take you out for some air."

"Will you nap with me?"

"Three times a day, my lord, for our entire honey-month and on every available occasion thereafter."

∼

Alice had taken the news of Lady Josephine's perfidy—her original perfidy—well, in Cam's opinion, while Cam had silently been howling, raging, and kicking mental tree stumps.

He paced the library, his temper only slightly abated.

To abuse trust like that, to condemn innocents to misery, to play skittles with other people's lives, and all the while demand the respect due a proper, selfless lady... The whole shire knew Lady Josephine to be otherwise, and yet, she'd played her games for years, no consequences, no comeuppance.

"She deserves the noose," Cam said. "And if the letters between Alice and DeSales are to be found at the vicarage, she might get it."

St. Didier manned the decanters. Alice had gone abovestairs to tidy up, and Bernard was stalking along the shelves like a cat who heard mice behind the walls.

"She'll have hidden them," Bernard said. "I know my mother, and any letters from Lord Throckmorton are likely in the false bottom of her jewelry box. They might have been useful for extorting favors from his family at some point. Who knows? Alice's letters might also still be extant. Mama keeps ten pounds there as well."

Cam sorted through the stack of mail on his desk out of habit, though he wasn't inclined to open what had arrived. A well-trained secretary could handle most of it.

"Huxley, you surprise me," St. Didier said, handing drinks all around. "Snooping?"

"I wasn't. I needed something sharp to get a splinter out and did not dare disturb the order of Mama's sewing basket. It occurred to me that a brooch or watch pin would have a sharp point on its fastener. The false bottom is obvious, and a corner of the ten-pound note was sticking out. I did not, in fact, snoop even when tempted to do so."

St. Didier served himself a modest portion. "Something has caught Lorne's attention. If you sit at the desk and start opening mail, your lordship, I will toss you out the window. Miss Singleton will expect you present and focused on the instant difficulties, not wooing your abacus with one hand while you admonish your factors with the other."

Cam brandished the note in his hand. "Worth Kettering has consulted with his dowagers, old soldiers, and beldames."

"Of which he has an enviable collection." St. Dider sipped delicately. "They invest with him, and they keep him apprised of every on-dit, courtship, and failing marriage in Mayfair. Their godchildren, nieces, nephews, grandchildren, cooks, lady's maids, and pensioned retainers add to their stores of intelligence, as do their old flames. I vow that's half the reason Kettering has succeeded."

"They dote on him?" Cam asked.

"And he dotes on them. Listens to the old dears reminisce and speculate and imply. Kettering is married now. The mind boggles at the stores of knowledge he and his lady will collect, and he is said to have the royal ear as well."

"Happily married," Cam said, scanning the single page written in a tidy, slashing script. "And his old dears, in this case, have come through for us. God bless dear Dinky for jumping ship."

St. Didier looked intrigued, and Bernard's pacing became more of a thoughtful saunter around the room. Cam finished reading the letter and passed it to Bernard.

"Well, well, well," Bernard said, looking, of all things, pleased. He, in turn, handed the letter to St. Didier.

Alice joined them and, before St. Didier could see to it, served herself a drink. "You lot look conspiratorial. If you're thinking to settle my delicate nerves with your gentlemanly discretion—which we call keeping secrets and sneaking about in small boys—spare me your consideration. I've decided that Lady Josephine deserves to see more of the world."

Bernard's scowl was ferocious. "You'd put her on remittance? She has terrorized my congregation, tried to terrorize me, and served you one bad turn after another, and you'd simply set her loose on some unsuspecting Welsh village?"

St. Didier passed Alice the letter from Kettering.

"Bernard," Cam said, "you don't snoop, you have an instinct for fairness, and when you aren't in a pulpit, you can be refreshingly blunt. When we have dealt with your mother, you and I need to have a long talk."

"You shall not force a bishop's miter on me. I have never sought to be a bishop, nor do I want any parts of any musty cathedrals. While we're on the subject, you may spare me the blandishments of an Oxford appointment."

St. Didier peered into his drink and might have muttered something about *no vocation whatsoever*.

"Oh my," Alice said, folding up Worth Kettering's epistle. "Lady Josephine was imprudent."

"She was played for a fool," Cam said. "Set her cap for a duke's son and allowed him liberties. When he was unforthcoming with a courtship, Josephine had to settle for the pity proposal offered by Uncle Ambrose."

"If I could choose a parent to disassociate myself from," Bernard said, "it wouldn't be Papa. He was always kind to me, and he referred to Mama as a woman scorned. Now I know why."

Alice brandished the folded letter. "Kettering's sources put it in a different light. Lady Josephine made a first-class fool of herself. She'd had three Seasons and no offers. She was desperate enough to openly pursue a younger ducal son known for indiscriminate raking. She neglected to consider the fellow's family resources and her own family's need for coin. One might feel sorry for her, were it not apparent that she was well past twenty at the time and brought her fate upon herself, aided and abetted by her own mercenary family."

"Hence," Cam said, "she avoids the higher reaches of polite society and contents herself with tunneling among the distaff side of churchly circles. Obscure, but not too obscure."

"What will you do with her?" St. Didier asked, directing the question to Alice.

"She is to be removed to the Antipodes. Whether she puts us to the bother of a trial or flees the threat of prosecution is up to her, but I will happily lay information regarding kidnapping, and I suspect Bernard has a few complaints regarding his mother's interference with his mail."

"We have better than that," Cam said. "Bernard is confident that Lord Throckmorton's letters to you are secreted among Lady Josephine's effects, and any Yorkshire jury will find something to convict her of when it becomes known she thwarted a deceased soldier's attempts to behave honorably toward his sweetheart."

And if the jury didn't convict her, public opinion, especially churchly public opinion, finally would.

"I want this dreadful business concluded," Alice said, taking a seat behind the desk. "Might we please get this over with? She all but thrust me into Lord Throckmorton's arms on at least three occasions, and my temper might soon get the best of me."

Alice's temper did not get the best of her. She stated plainly to Lady Josephine the options that remained: voluntary immediate emigration to the Antipodes, involuntary transportation, or an indefinite tenancy among the inmates of a walled estate.

Lady Josephine wheedled and wept, threatened and thundered, and snorted and sniffed—did she *ever* sniff—and in the end, she was made to appreciate the advantages of voluntary passage. Bernard nevertheless unearthed the letters as well as correspondence belonging to half the shire and passed them to Alice for safekeeping.

Having dispatched Lady Josephine to a less severe fate than she deserved, it was agreed that the evidence of her felonies would be preserved in perpetuity against any and all contingencies.

And when her ladyship was once again confined to a guest room, and St. Didier and Bernard were off to indulge in a game of billiards, Alice and Cam retired abovestairs for some private discussion that inevitably ended in a protracted, extremely enjoyable afternoon nap.

The first of many.

EPILOGUE

"I do believe the girls are noisier than the boys," Cam said, selecting a cinnamon biscuit from the tray on the low table. He and Alice had box seats on the terrace overlooking the pitch, though they were spoiling their nooning by snitching biscuits. "I would not have thought such a thing possible."

Mary's bat connected with the ball and sent it flying halfway across the park. Golden leaves littered the grass, and the sheep were sporting fluffier coats than they'd worn all summer. The day was mild, but Thaddeus Singleton predicted frost in the next fortnight. He was coming over for the picnic and would doubtless be inveigled into telling a story or two.

"The noise is happy," Alice replied, "regardless of its source. St. Didier makes a fine pitcher."

He challenged the older children while throwing easy hits to the younger. Mary's solid performance resulted in much cheering as she sprinted away from the wickets. St. Didier pretended to scowl, hands on hips, at his detractors.

"Has Gabriella made a decision yet?" Cam did not entirely

approve of leaving the choice of dwelling in Gabriella's hands, but most decisions could be revisited if need be.

"She is hesitant to say what she wants, but I'm almost certain she'd like everybody here, together at the Hall."

Cam studied his baroness, while trying to keep his own expression merely interested. "What do you want, Alice?" Cam knew precisely which outcome he favored, but he had forbidden himself from arguing for it.

Let the Hall, with its countless climbing trees, stables, vast library, and enormous park speak for him. Let Thaddeus, Mrs. Shorer, and Beaglemore, with their stories, humor, and endless patience, speak for him.

Let Alice, with her bottomless heart and great good sense, speak for him.

He could have no more devoted or articulate advocates than his home, his friends, or his beloved baroness.

"The boys have not once mentioned returning to Town," Cam said. "That nigh astonishes me." Of course, Cook had come along with the boys and had insisted on cooking for her wee lads. She was also happy to cook for the girls on their weekly visits to the Hall.

"You ask what I want, and part of me is delighted simply to be asked, Cam. Another part of me is new to this business of organizing my own affairs, much less those of anybody else."

Alice had no hesitation at all about stating her needs as they related to the more intimate blessings of matrimony, much to Cam's delight.

"Whatever you and Gabriella decide, the agreement will likely need refinements," Cam said. "If the children all come here, what's to be done with the orphanage? Do we make it available to former soldiers out of work? Do we make it over into a widow's retreat? Do we sell the place and good riddance? Do we keep it for a year to guard against second thoughts?"

Years in business had taught him to hold even signed and sealed deals loosely, to be on the alert for changes in circumstances that required changes in terms. Commerce had been an unlikely but useful preparation for the sort of marriage he hoped to have with Alice.

The sort of family he hoped they'd have.

"I want us to be happy," Alice said. "All of us, including you. You sent Bernard to London when I know you'd rather have gone yourself."

This clearly worried her. Remiss of Cam, not to see that sooner. "I do not, as it happens, want to be in London, Alice. If I went to Town, I could call on Kettering, I suppose, or drop around to look in on some of my competitors, but that never made London home. Bernard pens his dispatches, and from all indications, he's taking to the job like Mary has taken to playing cricket. He relishes the challenge."

"So do you."

"So *did* I, and that was fine when I had something to prove to the world, and especially to my father's ghost, and to myself. I am proud of those accomplishments, but the challenges I relish now are all right here at Lorne Hall."

Alice studied the tray of biscuits. Once the inning was over, that tray, and nearly every plate and bowl on the buffet the footmen were setting out, would be empty. Not a crumb for the sparrows, and Cook would be in alt.

"Grandpapa wants the children here," Alice said. "He claims it's a sin against nature for a dwelling this size to be all but empty of children. He, who had the one son."

"He wants the children here for Mrs. Shorer." Though at some point, Cam might get used to referring to his housekeeper as Mrs. Singleton.

Alice had quietly informed her grandpapa that he was a great-grandpapa, and this had inspired two days of Thaddeus stomping about the fields and lanes, forgetting to light his pipe, and glowering at Cam when their paths crossed.

Thaddeus had surprised Cam and Alice thoroughly by

announcing that Alice had a step-grandmama. Thaddeus and Eunice had quietly married some years past and said nothing about it, lest Eunice lose her post, or Thaddeus be forced into retirement, or a Certain Party undertook to use the news to otherwise bedevil a couple who had no need of bedevilment.

To say nothing of how upset Alice might have been at yet another upheaval in her life.

"And that child is my great-granddaughter," Thaddeus had said. "Try to pretend otherwise, and I will disown you, Alice. Same goes for you, my lord. Not a body in the shire will judge the child for the frolics of her parents. Not a body in the shire will dare judge you either, my girl."

The shire was speculating that Gabriella was actually Cam's daughter, which made for a fine Gothic novel, but was not, alas, true in the biological sense.

Which to Cam mattered little.

"What do you want for yourself, Alice?"

She set her biscuit back on the tray, uneaten. "I have everything I want and more. I want the people I love to be happy. I want all of creation to be as happy as I am, though, of course, that's not possible."

What she did not say, as Cam well knew, was that Lady Josephine might remain miserable with no objection from the present assemblage. Her ladyship was on her way to Rio de Janeiro, en route to the Antipodes.

The denizens of a penal colony would deal as well with her as anybody, and Cam wished them the joy of that challenge. At Alice's suggestion, he had sent a letter to the governor by a fast merchantman, as both a warning and an apology.

"Shall I tell you what I want, Alice?" Making that offer had been more difficult than Cam would have supposed. "What I really and truly want, even though, like you, I am abundantly happy with the present situation?" Unspeakably happy. Grin-for-no-reason happy.

"Tell me."

"I want them all, every one of those children, with Cook, Mrs.

Dumfries, Archibald, and the old guard. I want them here at the Hall, making noise, getting into spats and scrapes, getting stuck in trees, and sliding down the banister. I want them excelling at their studies to the best of their abilities—we'll need some tutors and assistants to aid Mrs. Dumfries—and I want us to help the children find the situations in the world that suit them best. Peruvian bark is a fine place to start, but to truly do the world a power of good, I want to raise these children with you."

"Mrs. Dumfries would approve of that plan. I cannot speak for Archibald."

Cam could speak for Archibald, because he'd had a few discussions with the old fellow. Winter at the Hall rather than in the drafty quarters over the orphanage stable loomed as a promised land for Archibald's chilblains.

"Speak for yourself, Alice."

St. Didier's next pitch sent the wickets crashing and ended the innings. A raucous cheer went up, and the stampede for the buffet took off.

"I want them too," Alice said. "I want them here, with us, with Grandpapa and the rest of our people. I cannot be certain, but I strongly, strongly suspect that Gabriella wants the same thing, though she is hesitant to ask for it."

"We can offer our preferred solution to her in the simplest terms and let her think it over."

"Let's do. Here they come." Alice rose hand in hand with Cam and, simply by her presence, brought the surge of sweaty, laughing, boisterous children to a halt on the steps.

"Basins and towels are by the door," Alice said, "and the child who pushes and shoves now that the stirring athletic display is over will go to the end of the buffet line."

A general groan sufficed to express the sentiments of the athletes, but they went to their ablutions in good spirits nonetheless. They also fell upon the buffet like the proverbial locusts and were soon busy consuming their tucker.

Cam bent near to Gabriella as she was finishing up her shortcake with peaches and cream. "Might you indulge your mother and me in a short constitutional around the garden?"

"Yes," Gabriella said, putting her spoon in her empty bowl. "Mrs. Dumfries says no seconds, and that means we aren't to wheedle or whine, or we will get extra verses."

Cam held out his hand, and Gabriella took him in a firm grip. "Mrs. Dumfries is very stern, isn't she?" he asked.

"Not really, but she doesn't make many exceptions. Did you ever wheedle and whine when you were a boy?"

"Of course, and I got extra verses most of the time too. I was so contrary at the time that I would memorize even more extra verses just to vex my tutors."

"I am not that contrary," Gabriella said. "Mary might be. Mrs. Dumfries says Mary is a natural-born teacher. She's good at cricket too."

Alice was particularly fond of Mary, while the girl's fierceness impressed Cam.

"I was a natural-born reader," Cam said. "I read everything and asked for more."

"I read too. Does my mama read everything?"

A large part of Cam's conversations with Gabriella consisted of this covert intelligence gathering. *Does my mama...? Did my mama ever...? What does my mama think about...?*

And his response was often the same. "You should ask her." In fact, Alice was eager to discuss any and all topics with her daughter, but they were so considerate of each other, so new to the joy of having each other, that all discussions proceeded by cautious, polite, tentative steps.

"My lady." Cam kissed Alice's cheek when they joined her in the sunken garden. "I can report that our Gabriella is fond of shortcake with peaches and cream."

"So am I." Alice held out a hand, and Gabriella took it, meaning she had an adult on each side.

Cam was ambushed, not for the first time, by a sense of sweetness. Of all coming right and patience rewarded. He would never have predicted that what he'd needed was to leave London, delegate the business workings to a relative tyro, fall in love, and fill his days with estate business and children, but the evidence of his own heart could not be denied.

"I like a quiet stroll through the garden," Cam said when they'd gone the length of the lavender border in silence, "but I suspect my favorite ladies in the whole world are too shy to mention what's on their minds."

"Camden. I am giving Gabriella a chance to digest... Oh feathers. I am not shy."

Gabriella peered up at her mother. "What aren't you mentioning?"

They were out of earshot of the terrace. Cam gestured to a shady bench bookended by yellow chrysanthemums. "Let's sit, shall we?"

They arranged themselves with Gabriella between the adults. She wiggled, she squirmed, and then she settled and sighed.

"I like the Hall," she said. "The other girls say I should come live here."

Alice rose to the occasion, as Cam had known she would. "What do *you* say?"

"Friends were all I had. I can't leave them now, but I only have one mama, and we've missed... a lot." Gabriella stared hard at the crushed-shell walk. "My friends like it here too."

"You want both, then?" Alice asked, tucking an arm around Gabriella's shoulders. "Your mama and friends, all together?"

Gabriella nodded. Cam discreetly fished for his handkerchief.

"B-but you are married to *him*, and he lives *here*, and he has *all those boys*. Mrs. Dumfries says it's complicated."

Alice hauled Gabriella onto her lap and wrapped her arms around her daughter. "It's not complicated. We love you, and your friends are welcome here, and we can all be together, even the boys. Not complicated *at all*."

By the time agreement to that proposition had been expressed all around, Cam's everyday handkerchief and his formal handkerchief had both been pressed into use. The ladies fell to making plans, while Cam mentally rehearsed a similar conversation he and Alice would have with the boys.

Ideally minus the handkerchiefs.

"I want to go tell Mrs. Dumfries," Gabriella said, scrambling off her mother's lap a quarter hour later. "She can come, too, right?"

"Of course," Alice said, "as can Archibald."

"And Jezebel?"

Alice's smile faltered. "Who is Jezebel?"

"His donkey. She can come too?"

"Of course, and the pantry mouser. The sheep won't want to leave their home pastures, though, so don't ask. Away with you, child, and mind you don't trip on the steps."

Gabriella was off like a March hare but did an about-face at the foot of the steps, pelted back to the bench, hugged Alice, hugged Cam, and then disappeared onto the terrace.

"Has a lot of energy," Cam remarked. "This won't be simple, you know. A dozen children, all of them rambunctious and loud, all of them in a new home."

Alice leaned against him. "I'm in a new home, too, don't forget."

He kissed her cheek. "Right. So am I. Very taxing. We will need a lot of naps. I prefer napping to reading to myself, for the record."

"We will need abundant stamina," Alice said, "and good help, and lots and lots of love."

"We have all three. I wasn't speaking entirely in jest about the nap, Alice."

"You weren't jesting about the stamina either. Lucky me."

They remained on the bench in a pleasant fog of affection until the bell sounded for a return to the field of play. The girls beat the boys, very probably on the strength of high spirits alone, because Jeanine had overheard Gabriella's conversation with Mrs. Dumfries, with inevitable results.

The boys were somewhat cast down at supper, until Cam and Alice explained to them that the Hall was also large enough to house the very best collection of junior clerks in the history of commerce, though some of the clerking tasks might have to go by the wayside for a few years.

The whole undertaking was in one regard complicated. A dozen children had that effect on even the best-run households. In the most pertinent particulars, however enlarging the family at Lorne Hall was very simple indeed.

All it took was lots and lots of love, and of that Cam, Alice, and their family had a vast, wonderful abundance!

Made in United States
North Haven, CT
08 October 2025